# THE Ghost AND THE Goth

## STACEY KADE

HYPERION

NEW YORK

Text copyright © 2010 by Stacey Kade

Printed in the United States of America
First Hyperion paperback edition, 2011
10 9 8 7 6 5 4 3 2 1
V567-9638-5-10105
ISBN: 978-1-4231-2487-0

Visit www.hyperionteens.com

To Linnea Sinclair,
my mentor and my friend.
This truly would not have been possible
without you.
Thank you for believing in me.

## ❧ PROLOGUE ❧

# Alona Dare

*I*t was easy enough to sneak out of school. I knew that from previous experience. This time, all I had to do was wait until Mrs. Higgins had led everyone onto the outdoor track and then slip behind the bleachers and walk down to the other opening in the chain-link fence.

Sneaking back in, though . . . that would be a bitch. But I'd just have to deal with that when I got back. Like always.

I shivered in the cool morning breeze. It was 7:00 a.m., or a little past, on the first day in May, and it wasn't nearly warm enough to be out walking around in the stupid thin T-shirt and short shorts they made us wear for gym. At least on the track, the bleachers blocked the wind and the black cinders held some of the heat from the day before. Out here,

I had nothing but anger to keep me toasty.

How could she do this to me again? Didn't she get it? It was never going to happen. There would be no fairy-tale ending for her, not this time. And I was sick of all the stupid phone calls from him asking about her, and the thinly veiled questions about him from her.

I picked up the pace, heading toward the tennis courts. After a quick glance over my shoulder to make sure I'd cleared enough distance between me and the track, I opened my cell phone, which I'd kept hidden in my closed hand to avoid Mrs. Higgins's wrath, and hit speed dial. Number one, of course.

The phone rang on the other end, and I pictured it flashing hopefully in the dark kitchen on the sticky granite counter. She wouldn't answer. That would defeat the purpose, but she'd know it was me calling. She'd be clutching the up-stairs cordless phone to her chest, checking the caller ID, hoping it was *him* and not me.

I hoped somebody would kill me before I ever became that desperate for someone's attention. Seriously, it was pathetic. And she was ruining lives. Specifically, MY life. Now, not only would I have to lie again to Mrs. Higgins about why I'd dipped out on class—something I'm not op-posed to in the right circumstance for the right reason, but this was neither—I'd also miss meeting up with Chris and Misty, my boyfriend and best friend, before classes officially started, which would require another lie. They only tolerated each other for my sake and would hate it if I wasn't there to referee. Worse yet, it was Senior Celebration Day, and now Chris's locker, unlike those of the rest of the senior athletes, would have to remain unadorned until lunch, when I'd have time again to decorate.

Not that *she* would care about any of that. She never cared about anyone but herself.

By the time the answering machine picked up, I was beyond pissed. I stomped past the tennis courts toward Henderson Street, waiting for the piercing beep. When it sounded, I shouted into the phone so she could hear me all the way upstairs in her nest of tangled bedsheets and crumpled-up tissues. "I know you can hear me, and I can't believe you're making me do this again. Don't you have any pride? He called me, *me*, not you. Are you sensing a pattern here yet? My God, just get over it already and—"

A blast of hot air pressed against my skin, startling me into shutting up for a millisecond, and I realized I'd crossed the curb into the street without even noticing. In that moment, I heard the blare of the horn, smelled the reek of exhaust and burning tires, and witnessed the flat, bright orangey-yellow nose of a school bus approaching my face at an unstoppable speed.

God, buses are so ugly when you see them that close up.

※ 1 ※

# *Alona*

*D*ying should have been the worst moment in my life. I mean, hello, getting run over by a school bus full of band geeks while wearing the regulation gym uniform of red polyester short shorts and a practically see-through white T-shirt? It doesn't get more tragic than that. Or, so I thought.

On Thursday, three days AD (after death . . . duh), I woke in the usual way—flat on my back and just to the left of the yellow lines on Henderson Street with the heat of a bus engine passing over my face.

It wasn't "the" bus, obviously. The one that killed me was probably still being repaired or maybe decommissioned or whatever they do with vehicles that now have bad juju.

I coughed and sat up, waving the hot plumes of bus

exhaust away. I know, weird, right? No lungs, no body, no breathing, but hey, whatever. I don't make the rules, I just live here . . . sort of.

I got to my feet just in time for Ben Rogers's Land Rover (his dad owns a dealership . . . lucky) to pass right through me. I flinched, but it didn't hurt. These days, nothing did, but it was taking a while to get used to that. Ben, of course, didn't notice a thing, just kept jabbering on the cell phone pressed to his ear. He couldn't see me. Nobody could.

If I seem pretty calm about this whole being-dead thing, it's only because I've had a few days to adjust. The first twenty-four hours? Definitely not among my best. Listen, if anyone ever tries to pull that whole "I had no idea I was dead until I turned around and saw my own gravestone" cliché on you, they're lying.

First of all, headstones, as they're properly called, take months. Especially special order Italian rose-marble ones with weeping angels on top. Second, if standing by your own crumpled and limp body on the street isn't enough of a clue, try following it to the hospital and watching a hassled and tired-looking emergency-room doctor pronounce "you" dead, even as you're shouting at him to listen to you, to please look at you. Then, how about when your dad finally arrives at that cold little room in the hospital basement, where the hospital people show him "you" on this grainy and horribly unflattering closed-circuit television?

I tried to talk to him. My dad, I mean. He couldn't hear me. Nothing altogether new about that. Russ Dare only hears what he wants to hear—or so he always says. That's what makes him such a good corporate negotiator . . . or a complete bastard if you listen to *some* people. But this time, he wasn't ignoring me. I could tell—his eyes weren't doing that squinchy annoyed thing at their corners. And then he started to cry.

My dad—the one who'd taught me that "show no emotion" is the first rule of getting what you want—stood in that tiny antiseptic-smelling room alone, his face gray under his golfing tan, and tears lighting up like silver streaks on his cheeks in the flickering fluorescent lights.

That's when I knew. Even before he said, "That's her," in this choked-up whisper that was nothing like his normal booming voice. I was dead. Maybe not all of me—after all, some part of me was still here and watching everything happen. But it was definitely my body on that television screen, covered by a crisp white sheet, looking smaller and frailer than I'd ever seen myself, and my hair all tangled and snarled around my too-still face.

That had been the breaking point for my dad. Even as the hospital people had shoved forms at him to sign, he'd asked over and over again, "Someone will fix her hair? She doesn't . . . it's not like her to look like that. She would hate it."

I drew in a deep breath (ironic, I know) and shook my head. None of that mattered now anyway. Sometime soon, very soon, a big bright light was going to shine in the distance and suck me in. Then I'd be living the life—or some imitation of it—of sunbathing on a white sand beach with NO sunscreen, nonvirgin mojitos, and an endless selection of shoe stores where everything was free. Hey, it was heaven, right? Before that happened, though, I wanted to see everything I could. A girl only dies once, you know?

I rounded the corner to the parking lot with a spring in my soundless step and realized that for the first time in my . . . well, for the first time ever, I couldn't wait to get to school.

People always assume that being popular and pretty makes high school some big playground. Shows how stupid people can be. When you're homecoming queen three years running, varsity cheerleader cocaptain, and first attendant on the prom court as a junior, there are certain responsibilities and expectations that must be met. The slightest variation—talking to the wrong person; wearing the same sweater that a geek, in a rare moment of fashion consciousness, wears as well; buying a burger instead of a salad—can tip you into obscurity or worse.

Case in point: Kimberly Shae. Kim had everything going for her—a rich family, flawless Asian features, and a metabolism that let her eat anything and still stay light enough to remain at the top of the cheerleading pyramid.

Like most of us in the inner circle, Kim got drunk, or pretended to, at all of Ben Rogers's weekend woods parties. Except, this one time, Kim drank too much, or at least enough to forget one of the major popular girl tenets: drink enough to be silly and flirty, not enough to be stupid and horny. Someone with a camera phone caught her in the act with her longtime crush and our host, Ben Rogers, behind the school-spirit tree.

Yeah. All the guys would have killed to be in Ben's place, and not a single girl at that party could honestly say that she hadn't fantasized about doing the same thing. (Ben's been considered the most eligible guy in our class since the third grade, and consequently, every girl dreamed of being the one to break him.) But getting caught? That's a whole 'nother story.

Pictures circulated within hours, and as of Monday morning, Kim knew better than to sit with us in the caf. She relegated herself to one of the second-tier tables. Our cafeteria doubles as an auditorium, with a big stage at the front of the room, so there are steps and levels built right in. The closer you are to the orchestra pit—the smallest, most exclusive level—the more popular you are.

I'd worked hard pretty much my whole life to maintain my status at the pit table (a disgusting name, but not my idea, so whatever). You can't just coast on your looks. My mother taught me that, in her own messed-up way. Maintaining the illusion of perfection, and being the envy of every other girl in school, took a lot of time and effort, but I gave it my all, and it was worth it.

I mean, take my funeral yesterday, for example. I'd never seen so many people from my school show up in one place. Outside of school, of course. (Thank God my mother had been too "distraught" to attend the graveside service.

Emotional outbursts would have been okay. Vomiting into the flower arrangements . . . not so much.) Anyway, someone had gotten organized and handed out black armbands with my name puffy-painted in pink on them. They brought flowers and candles and boxes of Kleenex. People I didn't even really know—like that one chunky girl in pre-calc who always wore these ugly baggy sweaters like they made her look thinner . . . yeah, right—came and cried over my casket. Well, near it anyway.

I'd even heard talk of a permanent photo memorial of yours truly in the main hall, right next to the glass case of baseball and soccer trophies. (As a varsity cheerleader, I can assure you we suck at football, and if the trophy cases were any indication, we had sucked at it since about 1933.)

It sounds bad, but to be perfectly honest, I felt a little relieved to be dead. Not at first, of course. After I'd gotten over the shock of it, I'd been well and truly pissed for a while. Then again, spending the night in the morgue with your body does tend to make you a bit grumpy. All I could think about were all the things I'd be missing. No more hot fudge sundaes on the sly? No more *kissing*? Or anything else? I'd died a freaking virgin—that was so not the plan.

But then, the next morning, when I'd found myself transported to the center line on Henderson Street, the sun warm on my face, the roar of the buses overhead, I'd realized something else. All the things I *wouldn't* miss. Among them, I'd been dreading the thought of college next year. Starting over, building up followers again, and competing with other girls like me from surrounding schools . . . ugh, totally exhausting. Now I didn't have to worry about it. My popularity was frozen forever at its peak. I felt like I'd crossed the finish line of a race that I hadn't even known I was running. I'd died before I could ruin my life, and while that sort of tanked, in a way it was kind of great, too.

Anyway, after yesterday's impressive display of mourning, I couldn't wait to see what my friends would come up with next. Had my fellow cheerleaders, Ashleigh Hicks and Jennifer Meyer, had time to work on the candle-wax sculpture of my face that they'd discussed yesterday between hiccups and sobs?

I picked up my pace, eager to get to the building and take a look at the main hall before the bell rang and everyone started milling around. All those bodies passing through me—they couldn't see me to avoid me, and I couldn't dodge all of them—made me feel queasy.

The first sign of something wrong, though, appeared before I got even close to the main hall. Halfway through the parking lot, I caught Katee Goode, a wannabe popular sophomore (third tier in terms of caf tables), glancing around covertly before pulling off the black band around her left arm and letting it drift to the ground.

The fabric caught the brisk breeze and scuttled across the gravel, finally catching on the rough edge of a rock near my feet so I could read the words: *Alona Dare, Rest In Peace.*

"Hey!" I called in outrage after Katee, but, of course, she didn't even twitch at the sound of my nonexistent voice.

I crossed my arms over my chest. Fine. Let her be the one weirdo without the black armband. She'd never make the pit table at that rate.

Except as I watched Katee join her group of stupid little sophomore friends, I realized that none of them were wearing armbands anymore either. The cluster of band geeks (fourth tier, better than math geeks but not as good as science geeks because the science geeks could always be counted on to blow something up), just behind Katee's group of friends, were also black armband–less.

My heart started pounding a little harder, and a cold film of sweat covered the back of my neck. For being dead, I certainly still "felt" a lot, and right now, that feeling was complete and utter horror.

I turned in a circle, just to be sure, the gravel strangely silent beneath my heels. But no . . . not a single person in view wore the symbol of mourning they'd all so proudly displayed yesterday. How could that be?

Ignoring the long-held instinct to remain calm and look bored, I bolted for the school entrance and the Circle.

Three wooden benches, donated by alumni, made a U shape around the flagpole out front, and this was the domain of my people. First tier, all the way. The popular crowd had lounged and lingered here for the better part of a decade, handing possession down to the next group of young hopefuls.

The benches were worn smooth by hundreds of perfect asses—like Ben Rogers's—and the flagpole had borne silent witness to, like, hundreds of pre-first-hour hookups. All of it took place right in front of the office, too, because we could do that. We were "the good kids." Let a burner try any of that, and you'd see detention slips flying. I'm not saying it's fair, just that that's the way it works. Everybody knows it.

I arrived at the Circle a little out of breath (yeah, I know, dead! Still . . .) and a lot closer to the bell ringing than I wanted to. It was harder than usual to get through the crowds of students ambling toward the building. I never realized how much I counted on people recognizing me and getting out of my way. Shame that was over.

As seniors, we finally rated seats on the benches, and my friends had taken their usual places. Ben Rogers was stretched out full-length on the bench closest to the parking lot, his group of would-be concubines encircling him. Seriously, all they were missing were the grapes to hand-feed him, and those big Egyptian fans.

No armband on Ben's Abercrombie-covered arm, but then again, he hadn't bothered to wear one yesterday either.

I wended my way through Ben's future conquests to find Ashleigh and Jennifer, along with Leanne Whitaker, another senior varsity cheerleader, huddled near the flagpole and texting fashion critiques of the unwashed masses in Target jeans and no-name T's to each other.

They were armband–less too.

Swallowing the urge to throw up, I turned in a quick circle, looking for the trademark glossy black hair that belonged to my BFF and cheerleading cocaptain, Misty Evans.

After an endless moment, when my heart would have stopped if, you know, it already hadn't, I found her on the bench farthest from me, half hidden by Leanne and the others.

I could only see Misty's left shoulder and the side of her head, her ponytail bobbing as she talked to whoever was next to her. That was enough, though, because at the top of her left arm, I caught a glimpse of familiar black fabric and pink lettering.

With a smile of relief, I started toward her, carefully avoiding Miles Stevens as he paced back and forth talking to Ben and Leanne (who refuse to speak to each other for reasons unknown to the rest of us), and then dodging Ashleigh and Jennifer, who decided to ditch Leanne and leap, giggling and squealing, on Jeff Parker's lap, nearly crushing his guitar in their hurry to pretend to be his groupies.

Ashleigh and Jennifer had been friends since kindergarten, and they did everything together, including buying matching—or at least color-coordinated—outfits for the entire year. It stopped being cute in about seventh grade, but they'd figured out their gimmick and they were sticking with it, no matter what. Just one of the many reasons Leanne called them the Idiot Twins. To their faces. Their response? "Duh. We don't look anything alike." Um, yeah. Leanne might be a bitch, but that didn't make her wrong.

As it turned out, Leanne wasn't wrong about much.

"God, Misty's such a whore. Alona's not even cold yet," Leanne said to Miles, just as I passed by.

I froze at the sound of my name. In that moment of distraction, Ashleigh—Jennifer right next to her—darted through me; they were trying to get Jeff to chase them. The sensation of her all-too-solid and warm body passing through me stole my breath and rocked my stomach. But even that was not enough to let me miss Miles's response.

He snorted. "Alona was cold even before she was dead."

"True dat." Leanne grinned at him, her freckled face crinkling by her eyes.

I stared at them, stunned. Neither of them had ever talked about me like that before . . . at least not to my face. I wouldn't put it past Leanne to talk trash when my back was turned, but Miles? I was the one who freaking brought him into the Circle when he was new here last year. He was the only black kid in our school who wasn't an athlete. He'd actually been a member of the chess club, for God's sake, before I saved him. Not that it was entirely selfless or anything. He'd helped me with trig, and in the process, I discovered his ability to run wicked commentary on just about everyone in school. Including me, it seemed. God, what else had he been saying about me?

"Ungrateful dork," I said in disbelief.

Years of habit had me striding toward Misty to tell her what I'd overheard, before two very obvious things clicked with me. First, Misty wouldn't be able to hear me. Second, the Leanne and Miles bitchfest about me had actually started as an insult about Misty. Leanne had called her a whore, something Misty would deny, despite her string of one- or two-week relationships with fraternity boys from Milliken, the college in town. High school boys weren't worth the effort, according to Misty.

I couldn't figure out what would have triggered Leanne's assault on her character. It wasn't like there were any college guys here or that I would have been interested in any of them, even if there were.

But then, when I finally ducked and dodged my way to Misty, everything became clear.

Misty's black armband with my name on it stood out crisply on the white long-sleeved T-shirt she wore under her cheerleading uniform top. Her black and glossy pony-tail ("Condition with mayonnaise and rinse with beer," she used to advise me) still bobbed with her movement. But she wasn't talking. She was kissing. My boyfriend.

"Misty!" I shrieked. Of course, she didn't react. She just kept kissing Chris in front of the whole school. ONE day after my funeral.

I didn't know if it made me feel better or worse, but he, too, was still wearing his armband. Misty looked exhausted with dark circles under her closed eyes, and her mascara had dried on her cheeks in long tear tracks. But they were *kissing*.

"Do you think Alona knew about them?" Leanne asked Miles, her words drifting back to me. "I mean, I heard that's why she threw herself in front of that bus. She found out and couldn't face them and everybody knowing."

"I did not throw myself in front of anything," I shouted

at Leanne, though I couldn't tear my gaze from Misty and Chris. "It was . . . an accident."

"I kept waiting for her to see them, and come here and throw some big screaming fit." Leanne paused. "Now, that would have been something, right?" Her voice held as much disappointment as evil glee.

"Please, Alona didn't see anything but Alona," Miles said.

Pushed to my breaking point, I turned away from Misty and Chris, feeling like I was going to throw up. It didn't seem likely considering I hadn't actually eaten anything in three days now, but I wasn't about to bet against it, given how things had been going. Cold sweat covered my skin, and my stomach lurched alarmingly. I swallowed hard.

"Why else would she be running away from school in the middle of zero hour?" Leanne continued.

"Shut up!" I bent in half, arms cradling my stomach, and realized I could see through my legs. As in, completely through them, like they weren't even there. From the knees down, I'd started to disappear.

"No!" I howled. This wasn't fair. I was being taken away now? Why not yesterday when I could have died, or passed on, or whatever, in happiness? And there wasn't even a white light . . . not anywhere!

"Maybe she forgot her backup mascara and had to run home for it," Miles offered, a sneer in his voice.

I jerked my head up to glare at him. I'd told him about my backup-makeup theory in confidence.

Leanne snickered.

I tried to run, to get out of there, but my legs, half gone as they were, wouldn't work. I collapsed on the grass, watching the line of invisibility climb to the bottom of my shorts. At this rate, I'd be gone in less than a minute.

Unable to help myself, I turned my head to see my former best friend tangling tongues with my former boyfriend, something that was not even a new development, apparently. How long had they been hooking up? How long had they been laughing at me? Misty knew almost everything about me, stuff I didn't want anyone else to EVER know. She was the only person I'd allowed to come over to my house for years. Had she told Chris all about it? Had Leanne been mocking me behind my back this whole time? Worse yet, what if people had felt sorry for me, Alona Dare?

Hot tears slipped down my cheeks, but when I reached up to wipe them away . . . no hand.

"No, no, no. This is not fair. This is such bullshit. I do not deserve this. I did everything right!" I sobbed, losing control completely. Crying ruins your makeup, not to mention the eventual cascade of snot you have to deal with, which was why I'd never allowed myself to shed a single tear in the company of these people. But none of them could see me now, and I'd never see any of them again, so who cared, right?

The bell rang, and everyone around me scrambled to gather up backpacks, purses, and guitar cases. Then they walked right through me on their way to the door. First, Jeff, who was quickly followed by Ashleigh and Jennifer (whose minuscule purses did not have any room to hold any kind of candle-wax sculpture, no matter how small). Then Ben sauntered through with an arm around his two chosen underclassmen virgin sacrifices. Leanne actually stood on me and checked her lipstick in her reflection on the shiny surface of her cell phone.

"Bitch," I spat.

Chris and Misty, holding hands, did not walk through me, but only because they were already close to the door. And besides, hadn't they walked *over* me enough?

With only my head left, I watched as the entire school paraded past me, laughing and joking and worrying about pop quizzes like I'd never even existed. Like I hadn't just tragically died only THREE days ago.

"This is hell. This must be hell," I said, my voice nasally and clotted with tears.

As if to confirm that fact, Will Killian, the biggest weirdo loser of all time, looked right at me and smirked as he ambled by, just ahead of his pot-smoking buddies.

"Hey," I shouted, furious. Like he had the right to laugh at me! Even dead, I was more popular than him. He was total loser material, skin so pale he practically glowed, and shaggy black hair that hung down in front of his creepy blue eyes. Seriously, they were so pale, they were almost white. And hello, he acted like such a freak, always wearing head-phones and pulling the hood of his sweatshirt up, even inside the building. Rumor had it he'd even spent a summer in some mental hospital somewhere. There wasn't a tier of popularity low enough to signal where he belonged. And he was laughing at me?

Killian looked away quickly, hunching his shoulders in his sweatshirt and staring at the ground, his usual antisocial, psycho-in-training behavior.

Wait . . . wait. Something about that . . .

I frowned, even though I was pretty sure my mouth was gone, and my thoughts were getting fuzzy. If he was laughing at me, that could only mean that he could see me. And that meant . . .

# ❧ 2 ❧

# Will Killian

Laughing at the dead is never a good idea. But I couldn't help it. The great Alona Dare, reduced to a crying, runny-nosed bobblehead? How often do you get to see stuff like that?

Not often. Unless, of course, you're me. Lucky, lucky me.

But it was also me who, above anyone else, should have understood that laughing at someone else's expense always comes with a karmic price.

"Mr. Killian." Principal Robert "Sonny" Brewster greeted me as soon as my foot crossed over the threshold into the school. "Glad you could join us today. Though you seem to be running late . . . again."

"I'm not—" I protested.

Brewster pointed at the ceiling, and, as if he'd willed it, the bell rang.

"Late," I muttered.

Behind me, Erickson and Joonie scrambled to get through the door and to class, leaving me to deal with Brewster again. Joonie gave me an apologetic look over her shoulder, but I didn't blame her or Erickson. They were just glad he'd decided to focus on me and leave them alone. After all, they were just as late as me, but apparently, they didn't set off Brewster's "freak-detector," as he called it, like I did. I found that a little hard to believe, considering the number of piercings Joonie wore in her face and how bloodshot Erickson's eyes were. But, for whatever reason, I was just Brewster's favorite.

Brewster smiled, an expression that did nothing to soften the hardness of his face and the brutal line of his buzz cut. Former military all the way, that was Brewster. Oh, and don't forget barely repressed homophobia, testosterone driven violence sprees, and a hard-on for following rules because they are RULES.

"I think it's time we have another conversation about your future, Mr. Killian." He caught his hands behind his back and rocked back on his heels.

"Again? People are starting to talk."

His hand snapped out, snatching the shoulder of my sweatshirt and crushing the cloth in his fist. I stumbled toward him under the force of his grab. His dark eyes gleamed with fury and eagerness.

"Go ahead," I said. If he hit me, he'd be fired. He knew it. Everyone knew it. There'd already been a couple of complaints against him for his temper. So what if I helped him along a little? My life would be so much easier with him gone.

He released me and wiped his hand down his suit coat, like touching me had covered him in slime. "My office, now."

He stalked across the main hall toward the administrative offices without even checking to see if I followed. It was tempting to ditch and leave him sitting there alone, but I only had a few weeks left. Just twenty-eight more days, and I'd be eighteen and a high school graduate, both conditions for accessing the little bit of money my father and grandmother left me. Once I had that, I'd be out of here, bound for someplace with only a few people and, therefore, even fewer ghosts. Like some deserted island . . . or Idaho.

If Brewster suspended me, that would be the end of that plan.

So, I followed him, as he'd instructed. I just took my own sweet time about it.

See, here's the bullshit about high school, and believe me, I've had plenty of time to think about this. Teachers, parents, guidance counselors . . . all of them are always pushing this crap about how it's okay to be different, just be yourself. Don't give in to peer pressure, blah, blah, blah. The truth is, it's really only okay to be yourself if that self is within an accepted range of "normal." You like soccer instead of basketball, Johnny? Well, okay, I guess, so long as you still like sports. What's that, Susie, you want to wear the blue sweater instead of the red? You know we're all about express-ing individuality here . . . so long as it's still a sweater.

How can you expect any of us to believe that it's okay to be different when even the adults don't believe it? Just because the popular, so-called first-tier kids look "normal" and say the "right" things, no one even looks twice at them. Ben Rogers supplies weed for most of the school, but has he ever been searched? This year alone, I've been called to Brewster's office twelve times and had my locker searched once a week.

Brewster was waiting at the door of his personal office when I finally made it to the secretary's desk. I could see his jaw muscle twitching from where I stood.

I nodded at Mrs. Piaget, the school secretary, who smiled in return but quickly looked away. She always had a soft spot for me, probably seeing all the notes over the years for various doctor appointments and illnesses, but even she knew better than to challenge Brewster.

Brewster slammed his office door shut as soon as I stepped inside, nearly clipping my shoulder in the process.

"Backpack," he demanded, his hand out.

Oh, please. I resisted the urge, barely, to laugh at him. I'd learned a long time ago that backpacks were, for all intents and purposes, seen as school property. You'd never find any-thing illegal in mine.

I slid the pack off my shoulders and handed it to him, and then I dropped into one of the blue plastic visitor chairs in front of his desk.

"Who said you could sit?" he demanded.

I shrugged and didn't move. He'd be far too interested in catching me with something in my backpack than to force the sitting issue right away. I'd been through this routine enough times to know that.

Brewster unzipped the bag and dumped its contents on the immaculate and polished surface of his wooden desk. From the shine on that sucker, Brewster had been working off some serious sexual frustration.

I leaned back in my chair, tilting it back up on two legs. "Do you polish it yourself? That must take a lot of wrist action."

His gaze jerked up from the now untidy pile of folders, papers, and books to gauge my expression.

I opened my eyes wide, the very picture of innocence. "What?" I'd long ago mastered the art of keeping my true feelings to myself. Trust me, you see the dead walking around, you learn not to scream, laugh, or piss yourself pretty quickly.

"You think you're clever, Mr. Killian?"

I shrugged. "Not particularly." I knew it irked him, though, because he'd seen my test scores. Thirty-two out of thirty-six on the ACT last year, and I'd totally blown the curve on all the standardized tests they could offer. I couldn't help it—just one of the few, very few, benefits of my gift. After all, it wasn't hard to remember history when I was surrounded by people who'd lived it, and the ghosts who hung around the school all the time were often bored enough to read over your shoulder and do the homework aloud with you, even if no one could hear them. No one, except me, of course.

"You've only got a month left here, and then you're out in the world, far beyond my reach." He began shuffling through my stuff, like he was looking for something. Dude, there's nothing to find, I could have told him. "And yet, Mr. Killian, I'll feel like a failure as an educator—"

"Hey, don't be so hard on yourself, Mr. B., everybody fails sometimes." I couldn't believe he was handing this to me. "Some people more than others, though, I guess."

He gritted his teeth, and the knuckles on the hand gripping my physics book turned white. "I'll feel like a failure if you don't leave here without at least one lesson learned." He dropped the book back on his desk and dug into my backpack again, this time the small pocket in the front. "Ah, here we are."

He dropped my iPod nano on the desk with a careless clatter, the tiny headphones trailing after it.

"Hey, watch it!" I set my chair on all four legs again with a thump. The nano (I'd nicknamed her Marcie after the logical and brainy chick in the Peanuts cartoons) was my lifeline these days.

"The lesson being," he continued as if I hadn't spoken, "that you can't always have your way." He scooped up Marcie, wrapped the earphones around her, and dumped her into his top desk drawer. "No music for a week."

"You can't do that," I said immediately. My palms began

sweating, itching for the cool comfort of Marcie in my hand. "I have a medical condition that—"

"Oh, yes, Mr. Killian, I know all about your 'illness.'" He smiled, all too pleased at having gotten a reaction from me. "Twice-a-week visits with your shrink, during school hours, no less. Permission to leave class as needed. Music allowed during your lessons so the 'voices'"—he waggled his hands near his head—"don't bother you.

"But do you know what I think?" He closed the drawer with a snap and pulled a key ring from his inside suit-coat pocket. "You're a bad seed. Somewhere along the line, you figured out how easy it was to fool everyone and coast through life with a 'disability.'" He separated a small silver key from the jumble on the key ring and locked the drawer. "But you don't fool me."

Without Marcie, I was toast. The dead talk all the time, even when they think no one is listening. The noise is overwhelming, not to mention the effort it takes not to respond.

Suddenly, I couldn't breathe. Going to class, walking the halls without my music . . . I'd be curled up in a corner somewhere before first hour was even finished. The week Marcie had been gone, getting her battery replaced, my mother had nearly signed the commitment papers then and there.

I couldn't let that happen again. I'd have to take the risk with Brewster.

Brewster shook his head, tsking. "Too much coddling at home and self-indulgence in these flights of fancy. If your mother had sent you to military school as I—"

"Like your grandfather sent your father to military school, hoping they'd beat the fairy out of him?" I asked, unable to believe that the words were slipping out despite everything I'd vowed. He really should have left Marcie out of this.

Brewster's face turned white and then red.

I tensed in my seat but kept my voice steady. "It worked for a while too," I continued. "Till your mom died and he retired to Florida where he met this nice neighbor guy, Charlie—"

Brewster didn't even bother to come around the desk. He shot out of his chair, his hand stretching out to close around my throat.

I shoved the chair back in the same instant, and his fingers caught nothing but air.

"You can hear me." Brewster's dead grandfather—young again and dressed in his World War II uniform—gaped at me from his seat on the highly polished wooden credenza next to the desk. His unfiltered cigarette, still burning, fell from his mouth to the floor and rolled to a stop next to my foot.

I ignored Grandpa Brewster and the cigarette with the practice of many visits to this office. Brewster's grandfather hung out here most of the time, talking to his favorite grandson, willing him to mend fences with his father while there was still time for them to have a decent relationship, something he'd never managed while he was alive.

That was the key with the dead. Ignore them long enough, and they'll give up. Oh, they won't stop talking . . .

ever, but they'll stop expecting you to respond, figuring what they took for awareness was just a fluke.

"You retarded little pervert," Brewster spat. "You don't know anything. My father is a good man." He charged around the desk toward me.

I tensed, ready to move, and faked an easy shrug. "I'm sure he is. He'd probably be horribly disappointed to hear his son got fired for trying to choke a student."

Brewster froze.

"What do you think you're up to, kid?" Grandpa Brewster demanded. He'd recovered enough from his shock to slide off the edge of the credenza and stand over me. "Messing with my Sonny like that?"

I met Brewster's glare without flinching. "Give me my music back, and none of this happened." It was a gamble, but he'd backed me into a corner.

His jaw clenched furiously, and I could see him working through the alternatives. "No one else saw anything. There are no marks on you. It'll be my word against yours."

"True," I said, pretending to consider the possibility. "But at this point, I wonder if it'd take much more than words to convince the school board? I heard it was a really close vote last time."

Brewster stared me down, but I refused to look away. Then, the pungent stench of something burning reached my nose.

Automatically, I glanced to the floor, searching for Grandpa Brewster's cigarette, and found the rubber edge of my Converse high-top smoldering, a tiny blue flame lapping at the side. "Shit." I jumped up, twisting my foot against the carpet to put the fire out.

"Will you look at that?" Brewster's grandfather said with a note of awe in his voice. "I'll be damned."

"No kidding," I muttered. With the smoke from my shoe lessening, I paused long enough from my extinguishing efforts to grind out the cigarette beneath my heel. A cigarette Principal Brewster couldn't see.

I stopped and looked over to find him watching me, disgust spreading across his face.

"Pathetic," Brewster sneered. "Do you really think I'm going to fall for your 'crazy' act?" Of course. From his perspective, I'd jumped up from my chair to scuff my shoe against the carpet for no apparent reason. Story of my life.

Brewster shook his head. "You tell the school board anything you want. No one is going to believe you."

Unfortunately, he was right about that. I had a slight credibility problem these days.

"I could call my mother." I winced inwardly. God, there was just no way to utter that sentence with any kind of dignity.

"If you do, you'll know she'll pull you out of here in an instant and dump you in the nuthouse." His gaze dropped down to my feet and the carpet. Only Grandpa Brewster and I could see the scorch marks. The damage to my shoe was real enough in this world, but unless someone touched the melted rubber on the side of my sole to find that it was still warm and freshly burned, it could have happened anytime. "I'm beginning to think that's where you belong."

"Then let me have my music back. It . . . helps." I stole a quick sideways glance at Grandpa Brewster, who still stood next to me, silent for once as he watched our exchange. That couldn't be good.

Brewster smiled, an expression of his I'd learned to dread. He turned ("About-face!") and strode to his office door, pulling it open. "Mrs. Piaget!" he barked.

Something crashed, and I heard the sound of pencils or pens clattering as they hit the desk and rolled off onto the linoleum floor. "Uh, yes, sir?"

"Write Mr. Killian a pass to class. Tell his first-hour teacher he is not to have any kind of distraction during class, including music. Then, make sure the rest of his teachers know as well."

"But, sir, he has—"

"That will be all." He closed the door with a snap.

"I could skip class," I pointed out as he returned to stand behind his massive desk. It wasn't like I'd never done that before. I still managed a 3.4 GPA.

"I could recommend expulsion," he said.

Dr. Miller, my psychiatrist, would be thrilled. It would give him just the excuse he needed to make the more permanent arrangements he felt I needed "to be safe." Translation: a steady lithium drip and a kid who eats gravel as my roommate.

"What is your problem?" I demanded. "I've never done

anything to you." Until today, obviously. But he'd held this grudge from the first instant I'd met him.

"Isn't it obvious, Mr. Killian?" He began shoving my books, notebooks, and folders back into my backpack any which way, crumpling pages and tearing paper. "You are an insult to every student here making a real effort. You're a bad influence on otherwise responsible and well-behaved children, like young Miss Turner."

I felt sucker-punched at the mention of Lily, but I refused to let it show. "That was a first-tier party." No way in hell I was there. She shouldn't have been either.

Brewster ignored me. "Not to mention, you're a disruption and a distraction with all of your 'special needs.'"

"You say that to all the sick kids?"

He paused, sensing trouble from a new direction. Public schools weren't allowed to discriminate . . . for any reason. "You're not sick, Killian. You're troubled, maybe, and desperate for attention anyway you can get it, including manipulating your mother and digging through my trash to find out about my personal life. But you are not sick."

I rolled my eyes. Why did people always think it was the garbage? Like they wouldn't have noticed someone headfirst in one of their trash cans at the curb. I couldn't remember how many times I'd had this argument. "What could you have possibly thrown away that would tell me your father is gay and—"

"You think you're so clever. It's my job to teach you that you aren't, prepare you for the real world." He chucked my now full backpack at me, but I caught it before it slammed into my gut.

"What if I'm telling the truth? Did you ever consider that?"

"It's just a bunch of nonsense you've sold to that quack your mother takes you to."

Actually, Dr. Miller had diagnosed me as schizophrenic—a real disease that was in the medical books and everything—but that wasn't what was wrong with me. The voices I heard and the things I saw . . . they were real, even though no one else could see them. As far as I knew, medicine didn't recognize that condition. Popular culture did, thanks to TV shows like *Medium* and *Ghost Whisperer* (Jennifer Love Hewitt is hot, but that show sucks ass) and various movies. But try telling one of the three adolescent psychiatrists in the dinky town that is Decatur that you see dead people. See what happens. It's called a twenty-four-hour involuntary commitment.

"We're done here." Brewster stepped out from behind his desk and jerked his door open. "Get to class."

As much as I hated being in his office, it was safer here than the hallway or even the classrooms. The fewer living people in the room, the fewer dead follow. In here I only had Grandpa B. to deal with, but out there, I'd be surrounded, engulfed, drowning in a sea of people dying to be heard. One of them in particular also seemed willing to kill me to get his point, whatever it was, across.

The thought of confronting him without Marcie or

anything else to serve as a distraction made my palms damp with sweat. If he found me here and now, exposed like this, I'd be lucky if I ended up in the psych ward.

"Look, I only have a few weeks left here." Focusing on a splotch of white on the nubbly carpeting where someone had obviously tried to bleach out a stain, I forced the words out, keeping my gaze down. I couldn't stand to see him gloating. "I want to be out of here as much as you want me gone. Just let me have my music back. Please."

"Means that much to you, hmm?" His highly polished black shoes, within my range of vision, rocked back on their heels and then forward again.

"Yes—" I grimaced and forced the next word out "—sir."

"Good. Then the consequences of going without will hold some significance for you."

I jerked my gaze up from the floor to stare at him in shock. "Bastard."

"Watch it, kid," Grandpa Brewster muttered next to my ear.

An arrogant smile spread across Brewster's face. Without taking his gaze from me, he called to the outer office again. "Mrs. Piaget, set Mr. Killian up with an after-school detention as well."

"Oh . . . okay," came the distant and faintly dismayed reply.

He gestured to the open doorway. "Time to collect your winnings, sport."

In the process of hitching my backpack over my

shoulders again, I stopped dead. Of all the stupid little names he could have chosen . . . "Don't call me that."

"What?" Brewster looked confused for a second before understanding dawned, along with an evil gleam in his eye. Never give a bully more ammunition, I know, but I couldn't let that one go. I just couldn't.

"What's wrong with sport, sport?" Triumph rang in his voice. He'd found a weapon to get under my skin, and he wielded it with glee.

"Don't."

"Why not . . . sport?"

I could have told him the truth—that had been my father's nickname for me, and hearing it from him with such disdain and condescension made me want to beat his face in. But that would have only given him more to work with. I could also have gone the human rights way—I'm a person with a name, use it—but he wouldn't care about that. So, instead I went for the more direct route.

"Don't call me that, or I'll tell you things that'll make you wish to God you'd turned your service weapon on yourself that night instead of chucking it in the Sangamon River."

His mouth worked helplessly, but no words emerged.

Brewster had nearly offed himself thirty-some years ago, a few years after he'd come back from Vietnam, a young man who'd seen and done too much in a jungle half a world away. He eventually chucked his gun into the river instead, embarrassed about the fact that he'd even thought about suicide—a quitter's way out. His grandfather—dead only a couple of years at that point—had been right beside him the whole time. The dead see everything, man, whether you want them to or not, and they tell a lot of it to me, even if they don't know I'm listening.

"That's nothing you should be talking about, kid." Grandpa B. sounded alarmed.

I ignored him and pushed past Brewster to collect my pass, detention slip, and a sympathetic smile from Mrs. Piaget in the outer office.

I was opening the door to the main hall before Brewster recovered enough to emerge from his office, eyes wild, hands clenched at his sides.

"Let's see how you survive the rest of the year without your special privileges, you little freak," he spat at me, but he didn't come any closer. Good enough for me.

"Bob!" Mrs. Piaget turned to stare at him.

Ha. It would be a miracle if I could make it an hour. But at least, when they carried me out, he wouldn't be calling me sport. I nodded. "You're on."

## ❦ 3 ❦

# Alona

The surface beneath me felt way harder than my bed and nowhere near soft enough to be a cloud. I reached out a hand without opening my eyes, and my fingers brushed over . . . was that gravel?

Opening my eyes, I found myself—where else?—just to the left of the yellow line on Henderson. Not a dream, not heaven, just right back where I'd started from. Dead in the middle of the road.

I sat up, swallowing the urge to start crying again. I mean, clearly I was trapped in hell, right? Doomed to live on, unseen and unheard, while my best friend makes out, goes to college with, and eventually marries my boyfriend. Just the thought of it made me want to curl up in a ball right there in the road.

So I did, resting my cheek against the warming asphalt. What, like I had somewhere else to be? Like someone would see me? Then I remembered how many times I'd seen hick guys spitting tobacco out the car window on their way to school—gross!—and I moved to the curb.

Behind me, the tennis courts filled with the sounds of life, people laughing, tennis balls bouncing, and the chain-link fence clanking. I turned around, startled. It was Mrs. Higgins's first-hour gym class—I used to see them trooping across the softball field to the courts when I was in government and staring out the window in utter boredom, wishing I was anywhere but there.

It was halfway through first hour, already? This was not the way things usually worked. For the last three days, whenever I'd gotten tired—yeah, that still happened—I'd made my way home, curled up on the couch in my dad's study, and closed my eyes. Then, presto. When I'd opened my eyes it was 7:00 a.m. again—I could tell by the buses going by—and I was on the road. Literally. It was like some giant reset button got pressed every day.

But this time . . . I didn't know what to think. I'd never been "reset" in the middle of the morning before. Of course, I'd never disappeared before, either. I shivered. Where exactly had I gone? I couldn't remember. Did it matter? Not really. I was still stuck here, that much was clear. Stuck here and helpless.

I stared past the tennis courts to the window where my government class went on without me. Now I would have killed for the chance to be bored by Mr. Klopinski. To be alive. To take Misty down in front of the entire caf. Then we'd see who laughs at Alona Dare. Nobody, that's who.

Except for maybe Will Killian.

Frowning, I stood up and started pacing, just in time for Jesse McGovern's green and nasty hooptie to pass right through me as he sped from the parking lot to his loser classes at the trade school in town. I ignored the cold shuddery sensation, trying to focus on a vague memory struggling to come to the surface. I remembered hearing Leanne and Miles bitch about me and seeing Misty kissing Chris, that was clear enough. After that, though, everything started to get a little fuzzy. The bell had rung, and people had started walking into the building, and then . . .

Will Killian's mocking smile and pale blue eyes appeared in my head. He'd laughed at me. He'd looked right at me and grinned, delighting in my misery. Any other day I would have been worried that someone like *him* was making fun of *me*, but today, all I could think about was, to do that, he had to have been able to see me. Hear me, even.

If Killian could see or hear me, maybe other people could, too. Maybe I wasn't really dead. At least, not all the way. Though what I'd seen at my funeral would indicate otherwise. I'd watched them lower the casket into the ground and—

I shook my head, sending my hair flying across my face. No. I wouldn't think about that now. Being dead and trapped here forever, unable to *do* anything, that wouldn't be fair.

There had to be another explanation, and Killian probably knew all about it, freak that he was.

All I had to do was make him tell me.

Too easy. After all, he could *see* me, right? Freak or not, Killian was still a guy.

I flipped my hair back over my shoulders, smoothing it down. After another quick second to tug my shorts back down into place—evidently getting hit by a bus gives you a semipermanent wedgie—I was ready to go. I couldn't do anything about the big tread mark that ran diagonally across my white shirt, though I hated it, and my favorite M·A·C lipstick was probably still in the locker I shared with Misty. If she hadn't taken that for herself, too.

I looked pretty good for a dead girl, though, if I did say so myself. Not that I could see my reflection or anything, but when I'd first woken up here days ago, I'd immediately checked my arms and legs for gaping cuts and bones sticking out and gross stuff like that. I found nothing but a few bruises and scrapes that went away, like, the next day. My face, which I'd explored cautiously with my fingers, appeared similarly undamaged. Apparently, according to the coroner, I'd died of massive internal injuries. But nothing you could see out front. Awesome. Killian didn't stand a chance.

For the second time today, I headed around the edge of the tennis courts and up toward the school building. Unfortunately, I didn't get much farther this time than I had the first. Double doors, big glass ones with that chicken wire stuff threaded in between the panes, blocked the main entrance. Typically, they stood open when everyone got here in the morning, but now with classes in session, Principal Brewster had locked everything down tight. All the better to keep a random psychopath out, never mind the ones in the student body that were locked in by the same measure.

I reached for the metal handle, just to jiggle it to see if the door might pop open, and my hand passed through it. I yanked my hand back and cradled it against my chest until the cold tingling feeling passed. It didn't make sense. Cars and people passed through me, yeah, but I still managed to walk on the ground, sit on a chair at the funeral home, and—

Suddenly the doors in front of me seemed to shift and grow larger. What the—?

I looked down and found my feet sinking into the concrete sidewalk, like at the beach when you dig your toes in and the wave washes more sand over you until your feet seem to be gone. Only this was the real thing.

Oh, no, no, no. I squeezed my eyes shut tight. *The ground is solid, the ground is solid.* I just kept repeating it to myself until I could feel, once more, the sensation of concrete beneath me.

I cracked one eyelid open to check and sure enough, I was back on the ground instead of in it. Unfortunately, my shoes and socks did not make the transition. My toenails, painted in Very Berry, sparkled up at me, under a light layer of dust. Great.

Whatever. At least I'd learned something.

"The ground is solid but the door is not. The ground is

solid but the door is not." I stepped forward, prepared to feel like an idiot when my head smacked the glass. Instead, the cold tingling sensation I'd felt in my hand when it passed through the handle spread through my whole body.

Then suddenly, I was on the other side of the door in the overheated little vestibule between the outer doors and the inner ones, standing on the rubber-backed mat they'd left out from the last rainy day. Yes! Finally something was going my way.

Following the same technique, I walked toward the second set of doors, and in seconds, I found myself barefoot on the cold linoleum in the main hall.

"All right!" I took a second to dance around like an idiot, tossing my hair the way a certain traitorous former friend of mine and I used to when it was just us and we were being stupid and watching videos on MTV2. In some respects, being able to do what you want without worrying about someone seeing you was kind of refreshing.

"Glad to see someone's having a good day," a morose voice said somewhere to my left.

I jumped and turned to see a janitor, dressed in a dark blue jumpsuit, approaching me slowly as he pushed one of those buckets on wheels. The school was set up like a giant *H*. The main hallway, where I stood, was the crossbar in the *H*. He was coming from the first left branch of the *H*, where the library and the English classrooms were.

"You can see me?" I whispered, hardly daring to believe it.

"Of course I can see you." He paused, lifting the

mop into the wringer thing at the top of the bucket and squeezing it. Dirty nasty water flowed out. "You're tracking prints all over my nice clean floor."

I turned around to look at the ground behind me and saw nothing but gleaming tile. "Uh, okay. Whatever." I shook my head. "If you can see me, too, that means I must not be dead. At least, not completely, right?" I bounced on my toes in excitement. Forget the fact I was talking to the janitor—a thirty-year-old guy with bad skin who never left high school? Hello, his picture was the *definition* of loser—I finally had proof that things weren't as bad as I thought.

He let out a bellowing laugh, revealing snaggly teeth and a serious need for whitening strips. "Honey, you're definitely dead. You just ain't the only one here."

He pulled the mop from the bucket and plopped it on the floor, the carpeted floor. Only the main hall was tile. All the branches of the *H*, including the one where he still stood, had that gross, government surplus, every-color-and-no-color-at-the-same-time carpeting.

"I don't understand," I said.

He ignored me, shoving the mop back and forth across the floor. "Damn kids, always leaving a mess."

The carpet didn't get wet, though, at least not that I could see, and then he was pushing past me with his mop.

"Watch it." I jumped back, expecting a cascade of cold yucky water to reach my toes, but the water seemed to puddle only directly under his mop. Weird.

"Never thinking about what they do, what kind of work

it makes for the rest of us," he muttered, rolling his bucket past me.

"Wait." I turned to follow him. "What did you mean I'm not the only one? I mean, yeah, clearly I'm not the only person who's ever died but . . . Oh, my God." Even as I watched, the janitor walked right through the trophy cases in the main hall, still mopping and mumbling to himself. Why would he do that? There was nothing behind that wall except the courtyard and . . .

I inhaled sharply. The old gym. The entrance had once been there. Before they built the new addition . . . way back in, like, 1992. It was *soooo* before my time, but Maura Sedgwick, suck-up that she was, once did this big history project on the school. Total snoozefest, but the old pictures were kind of cool. You should have seen the way people ratted their hair back then. Totally gross. My mom . . . I mean, someone once told me that back in the sixties women used to use sugar water to make their hair stiff, and they'd wake up to find cockroaches nesting in there. *Ewww*.

Tragic hairstyles and bugs aside . . . did that mean the janitor guy was dead, too? He could walk through walls and stuff, just like me. But he could see me and hear me, just like Killian. Killian wasn't dead. He just dressed like it.

I frowned. Answers would be good here. Unfortunately, none of the ones I came up with made any sense. That left me only with my original plan. Find Killian and make him tell me what was going on.

Before I could even pick a direction to start walking,

though, the PA system speaker on the wall gave a preemptive staticky buzz. Cranky old Mrs. Piaget—she was, like, forty and totally hated me for looking like I do; I mean, hello, a little moisturizer wouldn't kill her—was coming on to make announcements. Crap. That meant I only had a few minutes before second hour ended and everyone filled the halls. Given how cold and shaky it made me feel when one or two people passed through me, I had no interest in being trapped in the hallway with four hundred milling human bodies.

"Attention, attention." Mrs. Piaget's voice boomed into the main hall. "Mark Jacobsen and Tony Briggs, please report to the office before the start of third hour."

Panicking, I ran toward the gym, the second right branch of the *H*. The auto body shop, a small outbuilding, was attached to the far side of the gym through a temporary walkway that they'd never gotten around to making permanent. It reportedly flooded every time it rained, not that I had much occasion to be over there, anyway. The auto body shop was where all the weirdos, outcasts, and burners lived, always getting a pass from the shop teacher, Mr. Buddy—no really, that was his name—for permission to leave the regular classes to finish up some "project."

As I bolted past the office, also part of the main hall, I heard the sounds of a commotion nearby. People crying, yelling, even what sounded like begging. Oooh, a fight, maybe? Ask me when I was alive, and I would have totally denied it, but there was nothing more fun to watch than a girl fight.

Intrigued in spite of myself, I slowed to a stop, my feet slipping a bit on the tile, and peered down into the second left branch of the *H*, where all the noise seemed to be coming from. There, looking like the latest hip-hop star to be pulled into court, was Will Killian, staggering down the hallway, his head tucked under his sweatshirt hood and his shoulders hunched. Joonie Travis, the weird psycho goth girl with the dyed black hair from my psychology class, stood under his arm, helping him walk.

A crowd surrounded Killian, people I'd never seen before. A man in an old-timey military uniform, some chick in a (gag) pink polka-dot prom dress, a young guy in a baby blue tuxedo with a ruffled front (maybe polka-dot's date?), some dude dressed as a basketball player, only his shorts were *waaay* too short and his socks were pulled up all the way to his knees, two girls in poodle skirts (no lie!) and those black-and-white shoes . . . and those were just the ones I could see. The mass just kept shifting and moving around him, making it impossible to see all of them, and the racket was unbelievable.

"Tell my granddaughter that—"

"—My parents need to know it was an accident."

"I'm sorry, kid. I didn't know this would happen. Listen, though, if you can tell my boy—"

"Did I make it? Did we win? I can't remember—"

"Thank God, you can see us. We've been waiting so long to tell someone—"

I stuck my fingers in my ears to block the voices.

Childish, I know, but it was either that or scream. There were so many of them, and the pleading and the crying ate away at my last nerve. Why wasn't Mrs. Pederson, the Brit lit teacher, out here breaking this up? She hated "hallway disruptions," and they were right outside her classroom door. Who were these people anyway? Some of them looked young enough to go to school here, but I'd never seen them before. And with their clothes—can you say fashion crisis?—I would have totally remembered them.

Then I saw a familiar face in the crowd. He'd ditched his mop and bucket somewhere along the way, but I'd recognize that disgusting blue jumpsuit anywhere. My friend, the creepy janitor, was talking to Will.

I lowered my fingers from my ears to try to hear him.

"I didn't mean to hurt anyone," he whined, pawing at Will's shoulder. "You got to tell them that. Those kids . . . they were asking for it, teasing me like that. Didn't give that judge no right to kill me."

Holy crap. He *was* dead . . . at least as dead as me. That meant they probably all were: polka-dot girl, tuxedo guy, basketball-player dude, all of them. And every single one of them had gotten to Will Killian before me.

Ugh. I hate waiting in line.

## ❧ 4 ❧

# Will

All I had to do was make it through the day. Not easy, but possible. I'd survived for years before Dr. Miller had taught me the music trick, something he'd found helped his real schizophrenic patients. Once I got home this afternoon, I'd casually mention that Brewster took away my medically authorized privileges for being under a minute late. The tardy thing would be the only excuse Brewster could offer without adding credence to my "wild stories." For that, my mom would be on the phone with the school in a flash. It was all about looking like I didn't *need* it. Ridiculous, but I knew it would work.

Trouble was, that meant about six hours of torture stood between me and my goal, and Grandpa Brewster wasn't helping.

"I always knew there was something different about you."
He followed me out of the office, sounding overjoyed. They
all do, at first. "I need you to do something for me."

I tucked my head down and started walking toward my
Brit lit class, ignoring him.

"Now, don't go and do that, kid." He chased after me.
"We both know you can hear me. I just need you to deliver a
couple of messages."

That's how it starts. Just messages. It sounds simple
enough, but wait.

"First, my son, he lives in Florida. I need you to go there
and talk to him for me. I want him to know that I'm sorry
for all the things I did and said to him. . . . I didn't know. I
didn't understand."

Uh-huh. See? Now not only am I flying out of state,
I'm also supposed to talk to a man I've never met to explain
to him that his dead father wants forgiveness. When I was
younger, I used to try to help them, all the ones that talked to
me. Obviously, flying out of state to deliver a message wasn't
possible then, either, but I did what I could. It only made
things worse, though. The people who didn't believe me
inevitably ended up screaming at me or calling my mom, or
worse yet, the cops. The people who did believe would have
kept me there for days, crying and pleading with me to stay
as a stand-in for their loved one. As a kid, that freaked me
out more than the people who shouted at me. No thanks.

"Then, I need you to tell him not to give up on Sonny. I
know you and Sonny don't get along real good, but you have

to talk to him, too. Tell him it's not too late. He doesn't have to screw it up the way I did."

Me talk to Sonny, as in Principal Brewster, voluntarily? I don't think so. I hitched my backpack higher on my shoulders and turned down the hallway to Mrs. Pederson's class. Maybe she'd have a movie today—something I wouldn't have to concentrate on while trying to tune out good old Grandpa whispering in my ear.

"It's important," Grandpa Brewster insisted. "Please. You're the only one I've found who can do this."

My resolve wavered a bit. The nice ones were always harder to ignore. I felt bad for them, stuck in that in-between place, watching the world and the consequences of their mistakes but unable to do anything to fix them. I couldn't get involved, though. They would land me in a mental ward yet, if I let them.

Pulling Mrs. Piaget's note from my pocket, I pushed open the door to Mrs. Pederson's classroom, interrupting her midlecture. Great. I couldn't catch a break today.

I handed her my pass and slipped toward the back of the classroom to my seat. Joonie, in the seat in front of me, turned her head slightly back toward me, pretending to examine the broken and chipped black polish on her fingernails. "Everything okay?" she muttered. Up close, I could see the dark smudgy makeup smeared under her eyes, and the safety pins in her lower lip flashed as she spoke. Today she was dressed in her standard uniform of a military surplus jacket, black T-shirt, a raggedy looking plaid skirt, torn stockings, and black Chucks. In addition to the safety pins, she also wore a variety of earrings in the outer shell of her ear, all the way from the bottom of the lobe up to where her ear touched her scalp. One of those earrings was a small silver hoop that matched the three in my left ear in virtually the same position—we got them at the same time. We'd been friends since freshman year—back when her name was April, her hair was blond, and she was the better student—so she knew the score with Brewster even if she didn't know why.

I kept my gaze pointed down at my backpack while I pulled out the Brit lit textbook and my folder. We'd learned, the hard way, that Mrs. Pederson wasn't as likely to catch you talking in class if she didn't see you looking at each other. "Same old," I said.

That wasn't exactly true. Grandpa Brewster stood about a foot and a half off my right elbow, glowering at me, and the other dead in the room were taking notice.

In every room full of humans, you have about half as many dead. Some are associated with particular people, some are associated with a particular place, and some are just wanderers. In Brit lit, there were only about seven or eight on a regular basis. Most of them stayed tucked back out of the way—they hated the sensation of being walked through— and they didn't usually cause a ruckus. That would change, rather quickly, though, if they found out someone could hear and see them.

In class today, we had a few grandfathers and grandmothers—I could only tell because of the clothing styles: out-of-date military uniforms, June Cleaver wide-and-puffy skirts with stiletto heels, and really short and wide ties on the men wearing suits. When people die naturally—of old age or whatever—and their energy stays here, that energy usually appears in the form of how the people thought of themselves. No one ever thinks of themselves as old, so they usually revert back to their early twenties, and the clothing changes, too.

At the front of the room, you had Liesel Marks, Mrs. Pederson's high school best friend, and Liesel's boyfriend, Eric. I hadn't yet managed to catch Eric's last name. Liesel did most of the talking. I wasn't even quite sure why Eric was still hanging around. He seemed bored most of the time. Liesel and Eric had died in a car accident sometime in the late seventies while on their way home from the prom, hence her long polka-dot dress and his blue tuxedo. The ghosts of people who'd died violently and/or unexpectedly were essentially stuck in their moment of death.

From what I'd gathered during Liesel's incessant rambling, Liesel had ditched plans with Claire, Mrs. Pederson, to go to the prom with Eric, a boy Claire had liked herself. Now, she was convinced that those two things, along with the sex she'd had with him in the backseat, had damned her to this in-between place until Claire forgave her.

Jackson Montgomery, however, was tied to the school rather than any particular person. He'd died unexpectedly on the basketball court here at school in the early eighties, thanks to one of those hidden heart defects you sometimes hear about on the news. He'd been a star forward, leading the team to the state finals when he fell to the floor in the middle of the deciding game. No defibrillators on-site back in those days. He'd died and the team lost, but Jackson, or Jay, didn't seem to be aware of either of those things. Today, like every other day, he occupied an empty desk, his feet tapping against the floor in his eagerness to be called to the gym for the pep rally before that last game.

And, of course, we had Grandpa Brewster. "You can't ignore me forever. I saw what you can do with my own eyes," he said far too loudly.

I did my best not to wince. Damn Brewster for taking away Marcie.

One of the young-looking grandfathers fired a glare at Grandpa. "Hey, buddy, you mind keeping it down over there? My granddaughter's trying to learn here."

"She can't hear me. Hellooooo?" Grandpa B. cupped his hands and shouted at the girl—Jennifer Meyer, one of Alona Dare's cheerleading cronies, as a matter of fact. Of course, she didn't even blink. If anything, she looked like she was about to doze off.

"Stop that," Jennifer's grandfather ordered. He was wearing a suit and one of those goofy-looking short ties— he looked like a mobster out of an old movie.

Grandpa B. ignored him and turned back to face me. "Do you see what I have to put up with, kid? Just do this one favor for me, and I can leave this way station to hell." He glared over his shoulder at Jennifer's grandfather, who, surprisingly, responded by flipping him the bird.

It sounded good, easy even, but experience had taught me otherwise. Half the time, the dead didn't even know why they were still hanging around. Just because he was eager to deliver messages to his son and grandson was no guarantee that he'd be free afterward. Actually, it might be the opposite. The few times I'd witnessed people "moving on," it had only been after doing or admitting something they'd put off as long as possible. Even in death, people were in denial.

I stared resolutely toward the front of the room, trying to concentrate on Mrs. Pederson.

"Some say that Shakespeare didn't write all of these plays," she droned on.

"You want to go visit Lil this afternoon?" Joonie whispered from the corner of her mouth.

"It's only Thursday," I said without thinking. For the last eight months, we'd gone to the hospital on Friday—the only day my mom worked the afternoon shift at the diner and therefore wouldn't freak when I didn't come home right away.

Joonie twisted around in her seat, her bright blue eyes flashing with anger. "You have a problem with going more than once a week?"

"Don't take none of that attitude from her," Grandpa advised over my shoulder.

I caught myself shaking my head at him and forced myself to stop. "Of course not," I told Joonie, taken aback a little by her sudden fury. "It's just—"

". . . Isn't that right, Ms. Travis?" Mrs. Pederson came to stand at the head of our aisle, glaring down at us.

"Yeah," Joonie answered sullenly.

"Yes, what?" Mrs. Pederson taunted.

"*Romeo and Juliet* was written as a tragedy, not a romance as most people think." Joonie had an amazing ability to parrot back what she'd heard, even if her attention was occupied elsewhere. My life would have been so much easier if I had that gift.

A few people snickered.

Mrs. Pederson's mouth pursed, and she twirled her finger in the air—the sign most of us would associate with saying "big deal" in a sarcastic manner. Only in here it meant "turn around."

Once, Joonie would have rolled her eyes at me and we would have laughed about it, but now she just turned away from me in disgust and flopped back in her seat.

I waited until Mrs. Pederson moved on, her eyes focused on some other part of the room. "Joon," I whispered.

She ignored me, fumbling to pull her battered book bag onto her lap.

"Come on . . ." I pleaded.

She ducked her head and dug around in her bag, resolutely pretending I didn't exist.

"She won't talk to you, but I will," Grandpa B. offered.

Great. At the rate things were going with the few friends I had left, basically Joonie, I might have to take him up on that.

Before Joonie had morphed into the mass of black clothes and bad attitude she was currently, she'd been the weird girl who refused to shower after gym class, whose clothes didn't quite match, and whose hair stuck up in odd places, like she'd never bothered to brush it before leaving the house in the morning. She had two older sisters—one a doctor and one with a full scholarship to some snooty women's college on the East Coast—who could do no wrong. Joonie never measured up, and her father, an ultraconservative Baptist minister in town, always made that very clear.

Back then, I'd been pretty much the same guy I was now—the weirdo often caught muttering to himself or flopping on the floor in some kind of bizarre seizure. Then, at the end of my freshman year, when my dad . . . did what he did, that only made things worse, in every way imaginable.

In the beginning, Joonie and I had eaten together, walked to class, and partnered on projects together, because that meant we weren't alone. Now we were friends. We still didn't have that much in common, but our friendship worked. At least, it used to.

That changed when Lily moved here. Lily Turner had lived in some little town in southern Indiana until halfway through her sophomore year when her mom got a job transfer here. She's a line manager for one of the Caterpillar manufacturing facilities.

Joonie'd found Lily looking lost and close to tears in the cafeteria on her first day and ventured a wary "Hi."

Lily later told us that her school at home had consisted

of about a hundred kids total. Her accent was heavy, and her clothes were all wrong. She wore church clothes every day— a long patterned skirt and a high-necked shirt or sweater.

The Jesus Club kids wouldn't take her because Joonie, clearly a devil worshipper by the way she dressed, had talked to her. The braniacs were angry with her because she was smart enough that her arrival might screw up the class rankings. She didn't play an instrument, nor did she have an unnatural love for math or science. The first-tier elite didn't even know she existed. In short, she didn't belong anywhere. So Joonie had taken her in.

Something about Lily made everyone, especially Joonie, light up. She was just so . . . uncalculating, so refreshing in her honesty. She was fascinated by our choice to rebel against the mainstream, not really understanding, I don't think, that it wasn't so much a choice as a process of elimination. She'd never seen anyone with lip piercings before except on television. She laughed, and blushed, easily.

Within weeks, she'd revealed her own dirty secret. She was addicted to soap operas and celebrity dramas. *People* was her book of choice . . . as long as no one saw her reading it. With the size of her old school and having known almost all the kids there from birth, she'd never experienced anything as convoluted and complex as our social structure. For her, the first-tier kids held an allure equivalent to movie stars with whom she could rub elbows. She tracked their comings and goings, their breaking up and making up, with a fervency that was unnerving.

That probably should have been a clue for us.

Regardless of whatever signs might or might not have been there, the end result was the same. Lily . . . was gone, and these days, Joonie might as well have been. Which left me on my own, except, of course, for my supernatural buddies.

"Why do you keep talking to him?" Liesel asked Grandpa Brewster from her perch on Mrs. Pederson's desk.

"This one can hear me," Grandpa Brewster proclaimed proudly.

Damn. This was exactly why I should have kept my mouth shut in Brewster's office.

I looked reluctantly at Joonie. Her cell was a knockoff of the iPhone. If she had it with her—she was forever leaving it at home in the charger—and wasn't too mad to let me borrow it, I could probably hide it in my pocket and snake the headphones up under my sweatshirt. Mrs. Pederson might still notice, but it was worth a shot.

"Joon?" I whispered. "Got your phone on you?" I sneaked another glance at Liesel to find her frowning at me. That couldn't be good.

Joonie lifted her head slightly, but she wouldn't look at me. "What's wrong?" She sounded cautious, like she wasn't sure if she should still be angry or not.

"Nobody can hear us except us," Liesel said to Grandpa B., but she didn't sound completely convinced. Things were about to go from bad to worse.

"I need music." As in immediately.

"Where's Marcie?" Joonie didn't know the exact nature of

my medical condition—it wasn't something you announce at the lunch table—but she knew that I had permission to have my iPod with me and on at all times.

"Brewster."

"He can't do that, can he? You have a note," Joonie said.

Liesel hopped off Mrs. Pederson's desk in her pink cloud of a dress and headed straight for me. "I don't believe you," she said to Grandpa B., who was still at my side. "Prove it."

"He's not supposed to . . . do you have your phone or not?"

Joonie shook her head. "It's at home." She turned to face me, her earlier anger forgotten. She looked worried, and her tongue clicked the safety pins against her teeth, a nervous habit. "Are you going to be okay?"

Grandpa B. leaned down next to my ear. "Hey, kid, come on. Just tell us if you can hear us. Make this dumb broad"—he jerked his thumb toward Liesel—"shut up."

Not good. I raised my hand.

"Yes, Mr. Killian?" Mrs. Pederson sounded annoyed.

"Can I have a bathroom pass?" Screw Brewster. If I could get out to my car and home without being followed, I'd be home free. The dead weren't omniscient any more than I was. Unless they had my address, they couldn't find me. The trick was getting out of here in one piece.

"Oh, great, now you've spooked him," Grandpa B. said.

"Will, you arrived twenty minutes late to my class. You have only twenty minutes left."

"I know, but—"

"But nothing. I won't tolerate this kind of disruption in my classroom. The pass you gave me"—she stepped back and pulled it from the metal podium that held her notes—"states that the privileges normally allotted to you have been revoked."

"I'm just asking to go to the bathroom." I tried to keep my voice calm, but even still, a wave of giggles and whispers swept over the classroom. God, I hated this.

"Hurry up," Liesel urged Grandpa B. "She's going to let him go."

"No, she's not," Jay Montgomery offered from the other side of the room. "She's evil."

"Hey, watch it," Liesel snapped. "That's my best friend you're talking about. Trust me, she's going to fold. Claire hates it when she thinks the kids are mad at her. She is so insecure." She gave a dramatic eye roll.

I shook my head, trying to ignore all the competing voices. It was getting harder and harder not to scream at them to shut up. "Please, Mrs. Pederson. I'm really not feeling good." I wiped my damp palms down the legs of my jeans to dry them off.

She frowned at me, and sure enough, under the disapproving stare, I saw her expression soften slightly. "If you're ill, go directly to the office, Mr. Killian. Don't bother going to the bathroom to sneak a cigarette. I'll check, believe you me."

No use in trying to explain to her that I didn't smoke. At least, not cigarettes and definitely not on school grounds with Brewster checking me every five seconds. "Thanks." I gathered my book and notebook and stuffed them back into my bag.

"See? I told you." Liesel folded her arms across her chest. "He's no different than anyone else and—"

As I stood up and slung my backpack over my shoulder, Grandpa Brewster gave me a little shove. I should have been expecting it, given what he'd seen with the cigarette in Brewster's office. But they were normally so reluctant to touch us. . . .

I staggered sideways, like an insta-drunk, and tripped over my own feet, going down to one knee.

Both living and dead gasped.

"Oh, my God," Liesel whispered.

"Mr. Killian, are you all right?" Mrs. Pederson stepped toward me.

"Will?" Joonie half stood in her seat, clutching her bag to her stomach.

"He can see us? Does he know the final score of my game?" Jay asked.

"You okay, kid? I didn't mean to push you so hard."

"Can he get us out of here?" Eric asked.

"I just need him to talk to my wife," Jennifer's grandfather jumped in. "She's thinking about marrying that old geezer who owns the park model next to ours in Arizona."

I yanked my hood over my head and covered my ears with my hands on top of it. "I need to leave," I shouted over the din. *Too loud, Will, too loud.* The wide-eyed look of fear on

Mrs. Pederson's face confirmed that. To her, of course, I was yelling for no reason. "Joonie . . . I mean, April, take Will to the office now," came her muffled command.

To her credit, Joonie jumped from her seat, nearly overturning her desk. She yanked the strap of her book bag over her head to rest it on her opposite shoulder, and took my wrist in her cool hand.

"Come on. Let's go." She helped me to my feet, her words a distant murmur over the ringing in my ears.

We headed up the aisle and across the room. Mrs. Pederson stepped back behind the safety of her podium, and as we made our way out the door and into the hall, every pair of eyes followed us.

Unfortunately, so did my ghostly fan club.

"Dibs," Liesel announced.

"Don't be ridiculous. You can't call 'dibs' on something like this," Jennifer's grandfather said.

"We've been waiting the longest. Eric and I should get to go first. You, like, just died a couple of years ago."

"I'm the one who found him," Grandpa B. pointed out. "The rest of you just get in line behind me, especially you, chickadee."

"All I want to know is the score. How hard can that be? Did we win? You got to know, man." Jay's fingers clutched at my other arm.

"Lost by two," I said, though I knew, somewhere inside, he already knew that.

Joonie turned her head to stare up at me, her face, framed

by her jet black hair, even paler than normal. "Will? You still with me?" Despite having seen this kind of thing from me before, she was scared. I couldn't blame her. It scared me every time, too.

He pulled harder on my arm. "I don't believe you."

I tried to shake his hand off, causing Joonie to stumble and list heavily to the left. Her shoulder collided with the edge of the lockers in the wall, and she winced.

"Joon, you okay?"

She nodded, though tears made her blue eyes more sparkly and bloodshot. "You have to hang in there, Will. After what happened to Lily . . . I can't deal. I can't."

"You're lying, man. You're lying. We won. I know it," Jay insisted.

"Check the trophy case, and leave me the hell alone," I told him before turning my attention back to Joonie's pleading gaze. "I'm trying. Brewster wouldn't believe me and—"

"Don't blame this on him." Grandpa B. bumped into my side, jostling for position with the others.

I caught a flash of movement from the corner of my eye, and suddenly, Evan, the ghostly janitor who mopped the floors all day, every day, appeared next to me. He shoved Grandpa B. out of the way.

"I didn't mean to hurt anyone," Evan pleaded, tugging at my shoulder. "You got to tell them that. Those kids . . . they were asking for it, teasing me like that. Didn't give that judge no right to kill me."

"Just let go, please," I said.

But it was Joonie who listened to me, Joonie who let go of my wrist with a hurt look on her face. With no support on my other side, Evan managed to pull me down to one knee. Other hands began grabbing at me.

I resisted the urge to fall to the floor and curl in a ball to protect myself. "Joon—" I began.

"Hey!" an unfamiliar female voice shouted. "Listen up, you dead people."

That got everyone's attention. The ghosts stopped clamoring and pulling and arguing to look around. I followed suit and found myself staring at a pair of female legs so smooth they gleamed. Sleek muscle curved beneath the lightly tanned skin, especially at the calf, where imagination easily supplied the sensation of my hand resting there. Despite everything, my heart thumped a little harder.

Then I raised my gaze a little further and found . . . red gym shorts, a white T-shirt with a big tire tread mark across it, shiny blond hair falling across one shoulder. I groaned. Alona Dare.

Frowning, Joonie knelt next to me. "Are you okay?"

"Yeah, I just . . ." I shook my head and stared at Alona, standing in front of me, her hands on her hips, like she was preparing to lead some kind of cheer. "I thought for sure you were going straight to hell."

Alona glared down at me. "Hey!"

Joonie looked stricken. "Me?"

"What? No, never mind. Can you just help me up?" Alona's appearance had managed to distract the deadly dozen—well, half dozen—and I wanted to take advantage of it while I could.

Joonie knelt beside me and lifted my arm across her shoulder again, but she still seemed shaken.

"Are you new?" Liesel asked Alona. Then, turning to Eric, she whispered, "She must be new."

"All of you, step back and go haunt somebody else," Alona said. "I found him first."

Her pronouncement produced a chaotic burst of sound from the others, but at least it was directed at her instead of me this time.

"You can't—"

"Hey, new girl, some of us have been waiting for—"

"—Just want to know the score."

"Let's get out of here," I whispered to Joon.

Still pale, she nodded. We stood up together and started to edge through the cluster of ghosts. If Joonie thought it was weird the way I moved to avoid invisible-to-her obstacles, she said nothing. She was used to occasional strange behavior from me, and it wasn't something we ever discussed. There were lots of things we didn't talk about. It was easier that way sometimes.

"Look, here's the deal," Alona declared. "I'm not having a very good day, so I'm only going to say this once. I found him this morning. If he's helping anyone, he's helping me first. He's mine. End of story."

The moment she finished speaking, a strange blast of wind carried through the corridor, tumbling Alona's perfect hair and sending a chill over my skin. An odd sense of something having clicked into place fell over me.

I stopped. "Did you feel that?" I asked Joonie.

"Feel what?" Joonie repeated.

"The wind. It—"

Joonie took a cautious step back from me, her eyes wide. She slipped both hands into her bag, like the temperature had just dropped to below zero and it was her only shot at saving all of her fingers from frostbite. "Are you hearing something?" she asked, her voice trembling slightly.

I shook my head, hating the confusion and naked fear I saw on her face. "Never mind. Forget it. Let's just go."

But she didn't move. Her gaze was fixed on me, and her hands fumbled inside her bag for something, maybe the phone she'd forgotten she'd left at home? That she would feel like she needed to call someone because she was scared of me . . . that hurt. "Joonie? I don't—"

Movement flashed near the corner of my eye, and I automatically turned toward it, expecting another sideways assault from Evan the janitor. Instead, a dizzying black cloud of energy hovered about three feet away. The edges of the thing rippled the air, like the shadow of heat escaping from a closed-up car on an August day. It grew larger, taller, wider, and darker, until it blotted out the overhead lights.

My heart sailed into my throat, and I couldn't breathe. It'd been a few weeks since I'd seen it last, and just like every time before, I'd hoped it would be the last time. As in the last time it came around for me, not the last time I survived it.

"Will?" I heard Joonie's voice distantly. "Are you okay? Are you still hearing . . . the wind?"

The ghosts scattered—Liesel ran screaming with Eric on her heels, Grandpa B. hightailed it past me, presumably to the office again. Jay and most of the others just turned and walked silently through the wall of lockers.

But not Alona. She remained rooted to the spot, staring upward at the horrible cloud. "What . . . what is that thing, Killian?" Her voice still sounded remarkably normal, despite the tremor in it.

This "thing" was the reason I knew Alona Dare hadn't committed suicide, no matter what the rumors were. When you killed yourself, all the negative energy—the sadness, the self-loathing, the fear, and the desperation—remained. Most of the ghosts like that were just sad and silent wanderers, vague shadowy outlines of who they'd once been. In this case, the negative energy was so strong, it had consumed any hint of who the person had been, leaving little more than a physical manifestation of pure anger. I'd never seen anything like it before, but that was okay. I didn't need any hints to figure this one out.

"Hey, Dad," I said, trying to sound calm. "What are you doing here?"

## ❧ 5 ❧

# Alona

**D**ad? This nasty black cloud thing was Killian's father? On one hand, that made sense. I could maybe see now why Killian was so messed up. On the other . . . damn, I thought I had problems at home.

At the sound of Killian's voice, the mass of black smoke rose up and launched itself toward him. Unfortunately, it had to pass through me to reach him. Cold air rushed over me, like tiny slivers of metal slicing open my skin.

I screamed and tried to curl into myself, only to find I'd disappeared, again, from the waist down. Twisting my head around, I managed to catch one last glimpse of Killian. He shoved Joonie out of the way and stood there, pale and resolute, just watching this . . . *thing* rush at him.

It engulfed him and threw him hard to the left into the lockers. Killian's head bounced off the metal with a sickeningly loud clunk. He slid to the floor, his eyes closed, and his body motionless.

So much for Plan A. I wondered if Killian would still be able to help me if he were dead. Surely, even dead he would have more knowledge than the average . . .

The now familiar tingling sensation rose up through my neck and into my face. I sighed. *Here we go* . . .

*. . . Again.*

I woke abruptly, expecting to feel the gravel biting into my shoulder blades once more. Instead, I found myself sitting in the backseat of an unfamiliar car that seemed to be traveling at excessive speed and taking corners a little too fast for even my comfort.

What was going on? First, the whole disappearing thing, and now a different location? I did not like this. Did the first four days of my afterlife experience mean nothing?

Not that I was complaining too much. Waking up in a car was more comfortable, at least, than waking up in the road. Whether it was better depended on whether I would die—again or more?—if we crashed. We were coming around the front of the school on Elm Street (I know, right?), just passing the turn for Henderson, where I'd died. Elm veered right sharply, to avoid cutting through St. Paul's Cemetery, and people were forever missing the curve and cracking into the light pole. "Hey, you want to slow it down?" I shouted at the dark-haired driver, whose face I couldn't see.

To my surprise, the driver turned slightly at the sound of my voice, revealing her identity. Killian's friend, Joonie. Or, the High Priestess of Pain, as I liked to call her. She wears *safety pins* in her *face* for heaven's sake.

"Will, you doing okay back there?" she asked, sounding nervous.

Killian? Aware suddenly of a warm weight pressing against my lap, I looked down. Hey, my shoes and socks were back . . . and Killian's head was resting on my legs! His hair was softer than I would have thought . . . and I could feel it. That was weird.

"Ew." I shoved at his shoulders and actually made contact. My hand touched his sweatshirt, and I could feel the heat and solidity of his body beneath it. Well, that explained how those other ghosts were hanging on him. Something was definitely weird about Killian, and it wasn't just his obsession with the Walmart sale bin (or wherever he bought his clothes).

Pushing at him didn't do much good, though. Just made his head loll away from me. He was completely out of it, his body limp. A large red bump had risen on the side of his head, one I could see even through his dark hair. That couldn't be good.

"Will?" Joonie called again.

A horn blared, and with a muffled curse, she spun around to face forward again.

Oh, my God, I knew exactly where I was now. I was

riding in the Death Bug. Joonie Travis had taken a cute little VW Beetle, one of the old ones, and painted it black except for the white skull and crossbones she'd spray-painted on the door panels. Say it with me: FREAK. Right? I mean, how twisted do you have to be to take something so happy and turn it into something so gross and goth? I thought longingly of my graduation present, a silver VW Eos convertible, sitting in my dad's driveway, waiting for me to come back for a drive. I frowned. Unless my dad had sold it already . . .

"You want to wake up again and tell me exactly why I'm not taking you to the hospital?" Joonie called over her shoulder, without turning around again, thank God. If she'd paid enough attention, she would have seen that Killian's head appeared to be floating a few inches above the seat rather than resting on it—at least from her perspective.

Will did not respond. His head remained on my thigh, his left shoulder nuzzled right up next to my hip. I wondered, for a brief second, whether I'd been here, though not aware yet, when he'd decided on this arrangement, or whether he'd simply fallen into this position and I'd rematerialized underneath him, just by chance.

Huh. Seemed an awful lot to put on chance. "Killian, get up." I reached over his chest and shook his shoulder. "Despite all the brain cells you must have burned up, your head is really heavy and it's putting my leg to sleep."

Plus, it was making me a little uncomfortable. His head in my lap suggested an intimacy that I hadn't even shared with Chris. The thought of Chris, sudden in its attack, made it hard for me to breathe for a second. No, I hadn't been planning to marry him or anything. As a matter of fact, I hadn't ever planned on marrying anyone. I'd witnessed the fallout from my parents' divorce at close range, and I'd have sooner . . . well, died, than go through that myself. But still, Chris had been *mine*, you know? Yeah, he'd talked about wrestling way too much and seemed happiest when I wasn't talking at all, but still. I'd miss some things about him. The smoothness of the back of his neck under my fingertips, the way he always chewed gum before kissing me so that he would taste all minty and fresh . . . Tears welled up in my eyes. None of that belonged to me anymore. He was Misty's now, that evil slut.

I sat up straight, jostling Killian's head in my lap. Had she promised him sex? Is that what this was all about?

Killian groaned, turning himself in the seat until he was on his side . . . with his hand tucked under my knee!

"In your dreams." I slapped at his shoulder.

"If you don't talk to me, I'm taking you to the hospital and calling your mom," Joonie threatened.

Whether it was the effect of my actions or Joonie's words, I didn't know, but he seemed to wake up a little then. He left his hand behind my knee but rolled his head back to look up at me with a dopey smile, his eyes half glazed. "No hospital. Home, please." He was slurring worse than a freshman left in Ben Rogers's tender care. Lovely. He'd be all kinds of help in this condition.

His eyes drifted shut again almost immediately, and his

body went limp . . . again. And his head was STILL in my lap.

In the front seat, Joonie relaxed, letting out her breath in a loud rush. "You were starting to scare me there."

Um, starting to?

"You were talking to people who weren't there . . . again," she said with a shaky laugh. "Anyone we know?" Her gaze flicked to the rearview mirror as though she were expecting him to sit up and have a chat; desperation flashed through her eyes. "Will? Are you awake?"

"Yes, he's just doing a lot of intense staring at the back of his eyelids," I muttered.

"Dammit," she said.

I sighed. "Chill out, psycho. If you're not going to take him to the hospital—which is probably not the brightest choice you've ever made, but then again you're wearing deliberately shredded tights, so whatever—can you please take him home where he might have a chance of waking up and helping me? Seriously, I'm having, like, the worst day."

As if she'd heard me, Joonie turned the Death Bug off the main drag in Groundsboro—called, believe it or not, Main Street—and back into the neighborhood behind the post office. Little boxy houses with even tinier lawns lined both sides of the street.

I'd been in this neighborhood before. Ilsa, our cleaning lady, used to live over here, and a long time ago, before the divorce, my mother would drop me off to play with Ilsa's daughter when my dad was on a "business trip" and she needed "an afternoon." A "business trip" translated to a weekend away with Gigi, his assistant then and his wife now. "An afternoon" meant a little quality time with Jim, Jack, and Smirnoff. Sometimes I felt I lived my whole life between invisible quotes.

Ilsa always had fresh snickerdoodles, and her house perpetually smelled like cinnamon. My mouth watered at the memory, but my stomach didn't make so much as a peep. The good news about being dead was I could probably eat whatever I wanted and not get fat. Finding food that I could touch, and therefore eat, might be tricky, though. Something else to ask Killian about when he decided to rejoin the land of the living . . . or wherever we were.

Mumbling under her breath like a true psychopath-in-training, Joonie slowed about midway down the block, pulling into the gravel driveway of a cute but worn-looking brown one-story house, with white shutters and a red door. The garage, almost as big as the house, stood off to the right. A rusted and bent basketball hoop hung over the dented and battered door.

I braced myself against the Bug's side window, which felt surprisingly solid given my previous experience passing through metal and glass, and wiggled out from under Killian. His head hit the seat with a muffled thump.

"Thank God," I muttered, though, honestly, standing half crouched in the backseat of a VW Bug was no picnic, either.

Joonie slowed the car to a crawl, pulling behind the house. Uncomfortable and impatient, I shuffled around, taking tiny steps on the floor, until I faced the passenger-side door. I stepped forward, fully prepared to do the whole cold tingly passing through solid objects thing . . . and my elbow caught on the headrest of the passenger seat.

*What the hell?*

"The car is not solid, the car is not solid," I repeated over and over again. But the plastic, metal, and let's face it, probably asbestos, held me back just as it would have if I'd attempted this in my prebus days.

Joonie jerked the gearshift into park, popped open her door, and jumped out of her seat, flipping it forward to be able to reach Killian.

"Will." She leaned into the car, bracing her hand on the edge of the seat, and shook him gently. "Come on. Let's go."

*This is ridiculous. I did it once. I can do it again.* I concentrated, imagining the feel of the gravel beneath my shoes, the smell of the fresh air instead of burned oil and old pot. Just one confident step forward and I'd be . . .

My knee connected solidly to the side of the car, shaking the whole thing. I stumbled back, clutching my knee. Only my superior balance and coordination kept me from falling onto the seat and Killian.

"Dammit," I shouted. "What is going on here?" I put my foot down, wincing as my now sore knee bent—yeah, still dead and yet I felt pain, where was the fairness in that?— and turned to find Joonie staring wide-eyed at the car as it bounced on its crappy-ass shocks from my movement.

"Hello?" she said in faint voice. What little color she

had drained from her face. Great. If she thought her car was haunted or possessed or something, she'd probably never get in it again to leave Killian's house.

"Boo," I said sourly.

She didn't budge, just continued to look around, her dark eye makeup and pale face making her look like a frightened albino raccoon. I sighed.

"Not so loud," Killian groaned without opening his eyes.

Frowning, Joonie turned her attention back to him. "Come on, let's get you inside."

"Home," he mumbled.

"Yeah, you're home." She leaned over and grabbed his arms. Then, bracing her feet against the ground, she pulled him into a seated position and then with another great tug, she yanked him to his feet.

I thought for sure he'd fall and take her with him—he was, like, a foot taller than her—but they seemed to have this routine down. He stumbled forward but managed to stand while she shifted to the side of him, pulling his arm over her shoulders. Aw, she was like a little safety-pin-encrusted crutch.

After Joonie took a quick look around at the surrounding houses—yeah, check now that you're already out of the car and *obvious*, that's a good idea—the two of them staggered toward the house.

Thank God she'd left the car door open. Otherwise, I might have been stuck in there forever. Amazing how I just kept finding new circles of hell.

I stepped out onto the driveway, relieved to be free and breathing (or whatever) fresh air, and followed them at a leisurely pace. At the door, there seemed to be some confusion about the key, which key, who has the key, something that had Joonie first digging in her pockets and then—ew— Killian's.

So . . . more waiting. Seriously, is there anything to the afterlife, or whatever this is, besides waiting? With a sigh, I leaned against the side of the house . . . and fell straight through.

Wood siding, drywall, and—was that a piano?—flashed by in a cold rush. I landed on the floor—this awful brown and cream marbled carpeting—with a thump I felt but couldn't hear. Stunned, I lay there for a second, staring up at the black upright piano and my legs stuck in the middle of it.

Clearly, this business of walking through walls and such was a lot more complicated than I'd first thought. How come I could fall into the freaking house by accident, but I couldn't step out of the car, no matter how hard I concentrated? It made no sense.

Unless it didn't always have to do with me. Maybe it was something else completely. Like, maybe because the house was wood, not metal like the car, the molecules were farther apart and I could slip through more easily or something . . . I had no idea. Just one more thing I had to figure out.

With a grimace, I curled my legs up toward my chest, half expecting to feel the wall and piano scrape my skin. But it didn't hurt.

Once all of me was in the house, I rolled to my side and got to my feet. I brushed myself off—again, not strictly necessary, but comforting somehow—and took a look around. Definitely the living room. There was no television, heavy curtains covered the big picture window on the other side of the room, and a feeling of emptiness and nonuse filled the room. Cheap silver-colored photo frames covered the top of the piano. One man, who looked just like Killian only way older, dominated the spread. His father, probably. He looked significantly less dark, twisty, and cloudlike in these pictures.

On my left, two dark wood bookcases held a variety of delicate-looking tea cups and ceramic figurines with a few hardbound books for decoration. On my right, a barf-ugly but perfectly preserved peach-and-teal-plaid sofa from, like, 1993 occupied the wall. Next to it were two matching swinging doors with that awful cheap wood louvering. They were closed, but they appeared to be the only way out of the room.

As if to confirm that fact, I heard a commotion through the wooden slats, a sudden thump-stumble and the jingle of keys, and figured that Killian and Joonie had finally made it through the back door, into whatever room lay behind the swinging doors.

I strode toward the doors but stopped just short of trying to walk through them. If they turned out to be solid and I came busting through, Joonie would definitely see it. Not me, but the doors opening. While it might scare her off, she struck me more as the type who'd stick around and demand an explanation from Killian, which I so did not want. So, I waited until their unique shuffle-drag sounded farther away. Then I reached out for the doors and my hand slipped right through. Perfect.

The rest of me followed my hand without an issue, and I made it into what turned out to be the kitchen—bright orange paint and HUGE orange flowers on the wallpaper; was somebody color-blind? I mean, seriously—just in time to see Killian and Joonie stumbling out another doorway on the other side of the room.

I followed at a distance, turning right out of the kitchen into a tiny hall. Three doors led out of the hall, not including the kitchen. That was it. This was NOT one of those houses that looked bigger on the inside than it did from the outside.

Ahead of me, Joonie and Killian chose door number two, which turned out to be, no surprise, Killian's room. It wasn't nearly as disgusting as I expected. No moldy food laying around or gothlike black paint or Marilyn Manson posters. Just a normal-looking guy bedroom: off-white walls, beige carpeting, blue-and-green-plaid curtains to match the blue-and-green-plaid flannel comforter and sheets on the twin bed. One of those cheap, assemble-it-yourself bookcases, crammed full of books and comics, stood next to the left of the bed. A matching nightstand was on the right. Across from the foot of the bed, a battered-looking desk held more books, and the desk chair, turned to face away from the desk, was covered with several layers of black T-shirts and raggedy-looking jeans.

I took a tentative sniff of the air. It smelled like fresh laundry and boy in here. Not sweaty, old-gym-socks boy smell, but that good clean scent I sometimes used to catch when I kissed Chris's neck and he'd forgotten to put on his cologne.

Not that Will Killian smelled good. No, no, no. I wasn't saying that. Just that his room did.

"Here." Joonie helped Killian toward the bed, and he practically fell face-first onto it.

"Thanks, J," he said, sounding muffled by the pillow.

Oh, God, I hoped he didn't suffocate. Then again, that might make this conversation happen more quickly.

I tapped my foot, waiting for Joonie to leave, but she just stood there, still breathing hard from the effort of moving him, and watched him. Yeah, because that's not creepy or anything.

The sound of Killian's deep even breathing—not quite snoring, but certainly not that almost silent, barely there breaths he'd been taking before—filled the room. Still, she did not leave.

She tugged at one of the piercings in her lip, like a nervous twitch or something, and I winced.

"I have to go," she said finally, speaking to Killian's sleeping backside. "If I miss PE again, Higgins will fail me and I won't graduate. And you know"—she gave a weird little laugh—"I have to get out of that house."

Okay, descending to new levels of freakiness here.

"I need you to be honest with me, Will. I think you're

lying to me, trying to protect me."

A tiny *ping* sounded, and I looked down in time to see one of her safety pins skitter across the hardwood floor. Gross.

"You have to tell the truth," she said, sounding close to tears. Blood now dotted her lip where the safety pin she'd been playing with had escaped. "Otherwise, this is never going to work, and I need this to work. Okay?"

I groaned. "Have some pride, will you? Begging someone to like you is so pathetic. Begging for Killian to like you is . . . I don't even have a word for how sad that is."

"I do love you, you know." She sniffed and wiped under her eyes, her finger coming away black with eyeliner. "I'm sorry that you got hurt."

"Be glad you're sleeping," I told Killian. "I wish I was."

Fortunately, that last declaration seemed to end Joonie's need for dramatic and imploring speeches. She took a deep breath, nodded, and with one last look at Killian, she finally left. A few seconds later, I heard the back door shut.

I dropped into the desk chair, exhausted. All of this to have a conversation alone with someone I didn't even like. Being dead sucked.

## ❦ 6 ❦

# Will

The familiar pattern of yellowed water stains on my bedroom ceiling greeted me when I opened my eyes. Home. Safe and in bed, if the soft comfort beneath me was any indication. I had vague memories of stumbling to and from Joonie's car with her support, but not much more than that. Encounters with the twisted and ghostly remains of my dad always left me weak, drained, like he absorbed energy from me. Add to that whatever damage Grandpa Brewster and the others had inflicted first and . . .

*Grandpa Brewster. Principal Brewster. Expelled.* Each word triggered the next, like a series of lights clicking on in sequence until the whole picture was revealed. A sense of horror dawned inside me. I'd ditched school—albeit for a good reason, not that that would matter—less than an hour after Brewster threatened me with expulsion. Expulsion meant a call to my mother, who would in turn call Dr. Miller, and by this afternoon, it would be, "Welcome to Ivythorne Psychatric Hospital, Mr. Killian."

"Shit." I bolted into an upright position and sagged not five seconds later when my head gave a ferocious throb and darkness crowded the edge of my vision. *Too fast, too fast.*

"Finally. Do I need to ask you what year it is, who's president, that kind of thing?" a strangly familiar voice demanded. More than a hint of imperiousness colored her tone, so definitely not Joonie, and—

"Because you have been acting all kinds of freaky. Not"—she sniffed—"that that's anything new for you."

"No. No, no, no, no." This was not happening. I refused to believe it, but my eyes opened of their own accord. My vision cleared enough to reveal Alona Dare, *the* Alona Dare, as she probably referred to herself, sitting in my desk chair atop layers of clean laundry, her sleek cheerleader legs drawn up against her chest. She looked paler than usual. Not altogether surprising for someone who was, in fact, dead.

"You're here."

She scowled. "You don't have to get pissy about it. I don't want to be here anymore than you want me here."

"Good. Go away." The clock on my desk said 11:33. I'd lost more than three hours. Plenty of time for Pederson to report in to Brewster and Brewster to make the call to my mother. The only reason I was still here was because Sam, my mom's boss at the diner, didn't let her keep her cell phone on her while she worked. Mainly because he knew she'd be calling to check on me every five minutes. I had the diner number if there was a real emergency, and Sam's "rule" gave me some semblance of normality and freedom. I liked him for that.

"Is this any way to treat someone who just saved your life?" Alona demanded.

"He wasn't going to kill me. Not yet," I said grimly. "He was just . . . making a point." I stood up slowly, waiting for the rush of dizziness to pass, and the rest of her words sank in. "*You* saved my life? What planet are you living on?"

"Exactly. That would be the question." She nodded with satisfaction.

I stared at her. "Sorry, maybe this is the head injury talking, but . . . what?" She opened her mouth to answer, and I shook my head. "Never mind. Forget it. I can't do this right now." My mom's shift ended at noon. She'd be on the phone checking messages at 12:01. Figure ten minutes to get a hold of Dr. Miller and explain the situation, twenty minutes or so for them both to drive over here from town . . . yeah, I had probably about forty-five minutes of freedom left. Plenty of time.

Right.

I knelt beside my bed, careful to keep my head level, and felt for my duffel bag behind the dust ruffle my mother had insisted on to hide my version of storage—otherwise known as, cram everything under the bed and hope you don't need it again anytime soon. I had to leave for a few days. Let things calm down. Wait until I could talk to my mom alone . . . and try to figure out a way, again, to explain what had happened without telling the truth. Erickson's parents, both lawyers, were always gone. I could crash there for a few days and they probably wouldn't even notice. Hell, Erickson might not even notice.

"I'm serious, Killian." Alona kicked her legs out and stood up. The chair, which was wobbly and on wheels, didn't even wiggle. She must have been out of range.

Despite the fact that I should have been concentrating on finding my stupid bag and getting out of there, I watched her come closer, sort of hypnotized by the movement of her long, tanned legs.

"Where, exactly, am I? How come you can see and hear me? Am I dead, alive, somewhere in between? Am I stuck here for good? How do I make the white light come for me? Where's the food?" She ticked off the questions on her fingers as she approached.

I shook my head to clear it. "It's hard to believe, but I think you were less annoying when you were alive. Did you not hear me say I can't talk to you now? Go haunt somebody else." My fingers closed over the edge of a strap, and I yanked the bag out, bringing a cloud of dust along with it.

"Trust me, I'd find someone else if I could. You're just mad because I never talked to you when I was alive."

"Yeah, the waves of regret are washing over me." I started to stand but had to stop on one knee, brace my hand against the side of the mattress, and close my eyes again. The sudden change in position made my head swim. Another twenty-four hours to sleep, which I didn't have, and I'd be fully recovered, if my previous experiences were any indicator. I'd seen my father, rather what was left of him, ten or twelve times in the last eight months, ever since that night at St. Catherine's after Lily's accident, when I told my mom and Joonie I was leaving after graduation. He'd been pronounced dead at that hospital, and I guess some part of him still remained.

Apparently, he was not happy with my decision to leave. Not surprising, given that the last time I'd ever spoken to him, he'd made me promise to take care of my mother. I hadn't realized at the time, of course, that he meant in place of him, forever. It had been just a regular Monday morning. He'd kissed my mother good-bye and told me to take care of her, just as he always did. Then he'd driven three miles away to a railroad crossing that hadn't been upgraded yet with lights and barriers, parked on the tracks, and waited. He'd worked for the Southfolk Northern train line for the last year and half, making repairs, so he'd known the train schedule and that the engineer wouldn't be able to stop in time.

Sometimes, right after it happened, I tried to imagine what he was thinking while he was waiting there. Then I realized I didn't want to know.

"Hello? Earth to Killian?" I heard Alona moving around, and then suddenly, the foot of my bed sank with her weight. "Whoa," she whispered. "That's weird." She was quiet for one blissful second. Then she started up again. "Did you know that sometimes—"

"When you're near me, within a few feet, you have weight and substance again." I opened my eyes again and forced myself to stand up the rest of the way. "Everything responds to you as though you were alive and in your physical body again. Yeah, I know." I dropped my bag on the bed beside her and unzipped it.

She gaped at me. "*You're* doing that? How? And it's not that much weight," she added rather testily.

I shook my head. "My God, you're just as shallow as ever. Even dying didn't change you."

"Does it change most people?" She curled her slim legs up under herself, her perfect toenails painted some bright girlie color between red and pink. "From what I saw today, it seems more like it freeze-dries them in place, making them just like who they were before they died."

I frowned. That was a relatively decent observation. Maybe she wasn't as dumb as I'd thought. I moved carefully, in deference to my head, around the bed to the desk chair to grab a couple handfuls of clothing.

She glanced from the bag to me and back again with mild interest. "Where are we going?"

"*We* aren't going anywhere." I returned to the bed and jammed the clothes into my bag.

"Really?" She stretched her legs out full length on my bed—my bed!—pushing aside my bag with one shapely and toned thigh. I swallowed hard.

"That is so cool," she said in wonderment, more to herself than me.

"Alona—" I began.

She leaned back on her elbows. "Look, here's the way I see it, Killian. You can either help me out and tell me what I want to know, or I can just follow you around everywhere." She gave me that fake sweet smile I'd seen her use so often at school. Her gaze stayed as sharp and merciless as ever. "It'll be so nice to have someone to talk to, twenty-four hours a day. You know, I don't sleep anymore. At least, I don't think I do. I've never really—"

I groaned. "All right, all right." I did owe her something. She'd dispatched Grandpa B., Liesel and Eric, and the rest of them with surprising efficiency. Of course, nothing stood in Alona's way when there was something she wanted. One advantage to being a social leper—it afforded me plenty of time for uninterrupted observation. From what I'd witnessed, Alona Dare was single-minded, determined, and ruthless. If high school was a zoo, she was the lioness running the hunt on the hapless tourists who'd wandered into the wrong enclosure.

She studied people, learned their weak spots. And then she pounced, offering sweet smiles and fluttering eyelashes, or biting comments and a raised eyebrow of disgust, whatever was most effective. It worked, too. People caved and cowered. Some pretended not to care, but they were back at her table, begging for scraps in a matter of weeks. The fact was, unless you were Misty Evans—her best friend and the only seeming exception to Alona's all-powerful reign—you bowed and scraped and got the hell out of her way.

It was disgusting. And yet, some part of me admired her for it. Knowing what you want and that you'll get it if you push hard enough—even money couldn't buy that kind of confidence. Of course, I'd also heard countless tales of innocent bystanders eviscerated by Alona's particular brand of "charm." A good thing to keep in mind.

I checked the clock again. "You have ten minutes," I told her.

"Deal." She sat up again swiftly, tucking her legs underneath her again. I wondered if she'd stretched them out deliberately to get my attention. I wouldn't put it past her.

"Okay, first question." She steepled her fingers. "Why are you the way you are? Why can you see and hear me and nobody else can?"

That was an easy one. "I don't know."

She gave me a withering look. "You must have some idea. I mean, seriously, you have all these books about dying and weird stuff." She swept her hand toward my bookcase. She'd been snooping around my room? Great. "They must say something, and I know you've got at least a theory."

"What makes you think that?" I felt slightly flattered that she would think so.

She shrugged and flipped her glossy hair behind her shoulders. "What else do you have to do with your time besides think about stuff like this? It's not like you're real heavy into extracurriculars. Besides, you're all, like, goth and into the dead, right?"

Alona Dare, queen of the insult-compliment. "Wow. Thanks. Anyone ever tell you you're good with people?"

She frowned. "No."

"Good. I'm not goth."

"Your hair is black, you have piercings, you wear black all the time and act all freaky—"

"My hair is naturally this color. I have three earrings in one ear, that's it. This shirt"—I tugged at the fabric across my chest—"is navy blue, and if I act weird all the time, it's because of *ghosts* like you."

She rolled her eyes. "Okay, Killian, whatever. So, you're not a goth. Don't be such a baby . . . and don't call me a ghost," she added with a scowl.

"Why not?"

"Hello? Do you see a bedsheet and chains on me?" She gestured dramatically to herself.

That brought to mind all kinds of other, nonghostly images . . . I shook my head to clear those thoughts away. "What would you prefer, then? Living-impaired?"

She sighed. "Just shut up and explain your theory already, okay?"

"Fine." I sat down on the opposite end of the bed. If she was going to make me go through all this, I wanted to save my strength for getting out of here when our "talk" was done. "The best way I can figure it is this: the living occupy a dimension, a particular location in time and space, right?

When you die, your energy transitions out of that dimension into another one." I paused. "You are familiar with the idea of different dimensions, right?"

"Oh, yeah, sure," she lied, shifting a little uneasily.

The bed wiggled in response to her movement, reminding me once more that the most beautiful girl I'd ever seen in real life was in my bedroom, on my bed, just feet from me. Shimmery hair, full mouth, long graceful neck, and was that lace beneath the tread mark and her almost-see-through white gym shirt?

Of course, unlike the occasional fantasy I'd entertained, she was dead and we were talking about the afterlife and different dimensions instead of her batting her eyelashes and pouting while she offered to do "anything" if I helped her pass her English final. Still, the similarity was a little mind-blowing.

"Killian?" She waved her hand to catch my attention. "Are you spazzing out or what?"

Back to reality. My chances with Alona Dare, dead or alive, were about the same, somewhere in the negatives. I cleared my throat. "The dimensions overlap a little bit, I think, and when people die, sometimes they get stuck in between. Like this." I reached back and rummaged through my nightstand drawer for a piece of paper and something to write with. I came up with a receipt for the latest *Manhunter* and a decades-old broken stub of a pencil. Good enough.

I drew two entwined circles and labeled all the pieces appropriately.

I handed her the receipt. "Does that help?"

She studied it intently for a long moment before raising her gaze to meet mine with a frown. "So, you're saying I'm stuck here." She held up the receipt and tapped at it. "In between. Like purgatory."

I held up my hands. "I don't do religion." I'd seen enough dead people of all religions and no religion to know better than to explain it in those terms.

"You said you thought I went straight to hell," she pointed out.

Damn, she was definitely sharper than I'd thought. "I meant gone for good."

She lowered her hand with the receipt, staring down at it. "When I disappeared this morning, both times, I don't know where I went. I don't remember anything. Time passes, I guess, based on when I wake up back here. But I'm just . . . gone." Her green eyes met mine defiantly, but they sparkled a little more than normal, like she was close to tears.

"Are you saying I'm in hell when I'm not here?"

"I don't know." I folded my arms across my chest. "Does your hair smell like brimstone when you get back?"

Her forehead furrowed. "How do I know what . . ." Her eyes widened as she caught on. "Oh, you're an ass!" She tossed the receipt back at me. "I'm being serious here."

"I don't know, okay? People disappear in Middleground all the time. Sometimes they come back, most of the time they don't." I frowned. "Usually, though, the ones that stick around have unresolved issues, things they need to work through."

"Yeah, and . . . ?" Her eyes flashed dangerously, like I was perilously close to saying the wrong thing.

I shifted uncomfortably. "What kind of issues could you have, anyway?" *Other than being a bitch.* I kept that little gem to myself, but it didn't seem to help.

Her head jerked back like I'd slapped her, her mouth falling open slightly. Then her green eyes narrowed, and she pushed herself off the bed, her feet landing with a thump on the hardwood. "I don't have issues? I don't have issues?" She grabbed for the closest thing at hand—which was, unfortunately, my half-packed bag—and chucked a T-shirt at my head. "You don't even know me, you . . . freak."

"Hey!" I held my hands up in a defensive position.

"I'm dead, and I'm stuck here. I totally have issues!" A pair of jeans sailed at my face.

"Just because everything looks okay on the outside"— she paused to reload, stepping forward to grab from the bookcase this time—"doesn't mean"—several books flew at my head, and I ducked—"that it is."

*Tobin's Spirit Guide* thwacked into my headboard and tumbled off, landing on the floor with a solid thump. "Watch it," I said. "You could have taken my head off with that thing."

"Would anybody have missed it?" she taunted, grabbing another armload of books.

"Stop!" I slid off the bed, under her line of fire, wincing at the resulting throb in my head. "I'm sorry, okay?"

"Not good enough," she said from between clenched teeth, each word punctuated by a book. At least she'd moved on to the paperbacks.

Marshaling what remained of my strength, I grabbed her around the waist and hauled her away from the bookcase, trying to ignore the fresh flowery smell of her hair and the way she squirmed against me. Then, she lashed out with one of those long legs I'd been admiring earlier and caught me behind the ankle.

We crashed down onto the bed, which gave off an ominously loud crack and thump as we hit it. Again, not exactly part of the fantasy.

## ❧ 7 ❧

# *Alona*

*I* sat up, tossing my hair back from my face in a single movement, and found Killian beneath me. In the tangle— all his stupid fault, by the way—I'd ended up sprawled across his chest, which was actually broader than it looked. Navy blue *is* a slimming color, I guess.

His hands, also bigger than I'd thought, rested lightly on my legs, and I felt the heat of his skin and the soft fabric of his T-shirt rubbing against the inside of my knees when he breathed.

Three days isn't that long to go without human contact, unless everyone you touch turns your insides into a cold, shaky mess. Then it feels like forever . . . and touching Will Killian actually felt pretty good.

He stared up at me, and I noticed that his creepy pale blue eyes had a darker ring of blue around them, like the edge of some mountain lake that's not quite frozen yet. He licked his lips nervously, revealing white and even teeth that I'd never really seen before because—hello?—he wasn't much into the smiling thing. Yeah, I have a thing for good teeth, so what? It's not like a foot fetish or something nasty like that. Just because I happen to like the work of a good orthodontist doesn't mean I have to like the person who *has* the teeth or anything—

"Um, Alona?" he asked tentatively.

I snapped back into myself and the moment. What was I doing? This was Will Killian, for God's sake. I slapped at his shoulders. "Get off me."

He yelped. "You're on me!"

"You planned this." I tried to push myself off him, but his body pinned my left foot to the bed beneath us.

"Oh, yeah, I set it all up, starting with you throwing books at me—"

I stopped struggling for a second to glare at him. "I wouldn't have thrown books at you if you hadn't—"

His whole body suddenly tensed under mine. "Do you hear that?" His eyes going wide, he sat up. His movement freed my foot but sent the rest of me sliding toward the floor. He caught my arms just below the shoulders and pulled me upright, so now I really was sitting in his lap.

"Killian," I warned.

"Shut up. I'm trying to listen."

The urgency in his voice seemed genuine, so I clamped my mouth shut. If that black shadowy thing was back . . .

But all I heard was a car outside. It sounded like it might be turning into a driveway nearby. Nothing supernatural about that, but Killian sure seemed freaked by it.

He lifted me off his lap and set me to one side—fine, so he *was* stronger than he looked—before pulling himself the rest of the way onto the bed and standing on it to peer out the window, high in the wall behind his headboard. He craned his head hard to the left, looking toward the driveway. "Shit." He lowered himself down carefully, first to the bed and then the floor.

"What's going on?" I demanded. "My ten minutes aren't up yet." He wasn't seriously going to walk away from me, was he? "I only got to ask one question, which you didn't even really answer. You were just guessing."

He ignored me, bending over to scoop up the clothes I'd tossed at him and jam them back into his bag.

I stood up on his bed, wobbling a little, and made my way to the window to see for myself. A car, total blah-brown sedan of some type, pulled to a stop in Killian's driveway. As I watched, the two front doors popped open. A tiny woman with Killan's same dark hair climbed out on the passenger side. Her eyes were visibly red, even from this distance, and she was twisting something white, a handkerchief or a wad of Kleenex maybe, in her little hands. A short, thick man with a full beard and one of those jackets with the leather patches on the arms came around from the driver's side to put his arm around her.

"Your mom and your stepdad," I guessed. "What's the big deal?" Other than his stepdad's excruciatingly bad fashion choices. He was wearing those old man dress shoes with the thick rubber soles. I didn't know anyone actually wore those—I thought they were just the shoe equivalent of the bogeyman. Ugly, horrendous, reported in legend but never clearly seen in real life.

"My mom never remarried." He zipped his bag shut and threw it over his shoulder.

"Okay, so . . ." I hopped down off the bed and followed him as he left the room.

"You have to go. Now." Killian ignored me. He moved down the hall, past the kitchen to a door that I'd missed seeing the first time. Probably the front door to the house.

"We had a deal!"

He stopped so abruptly I almost ran into his back.

He turned to face me, bright spots of color in his otherwise pale face. He was sure worked up about something. "That guy out there?" He jabbed a finger toward the driveway. "That's Dr. Miller, my psychiatrist. He wants to lock me up for seeing things that aren't there. Get it?"

Not exactly. "But I am here."

"Not to him, and you'd have a hell of a time proving it to anyone but me. So, if you want the rest of your ten minutes, you have to shut up and stay out of the way until I can get out of here." Killian lined himself up next to the door. With great care, he pulled the dead bolt back, making a face when it made a loud grinding noise against the housing. Evidently, they didn't use this door very much.

The raw panic in his voice took away some of the insult of his words, but it also gave me an idea. I sidled closer. "Promise me you'll help me."

"What?" He looked up at me, his hand frozen in a claw on the doorknob. Behind us, through the kitchen, I could hear the sound of voices. They were talking outside on the driveway. Clearly, Killian was counting on them coming through the back door while he went out the front. It could work, but the right timing would be crucial.

"If I can't go back to what I was"—and trust me, after what I'd seen in the coroner's office, nobody was getting back in that body—"then I want to move on. Angels, harps, clouds, tossing down lightning bolts on Misty's head, Krispy Kremes three times a day without getting fat—I want it all. Staying around here is just . . . depressing." I tilted my head to one side and lowered my eyelashes to give him the look that once made Chris drive all the way to Peoria to buy me a peppermint mocha latte when the ONE Starbucks in town ran out of the peppermint syrup. "I'll stay quiet and out of your way. Just make the white light come for me."

He shook his head with a tight smile. "I can't do that."

"Why not?" I demanded.

"It's not up to me."

I rested my hands on my hips. "Well, who is it up to?"

He didn't answer, just cocked his head to the side with a

frown, listening to something, and held his hand up for me to be quiet.

Oh, yeah, right.

"I'm serious, Killian," I continued. "I can't stay here, not like this. I need help. You're not my first choice, of course, but I need—"

He let his breath out in a frustrated hiss. "All right, all right. I'll help you," he said in a harsh whisper. "Just shut up already. Please."

It was the "please" that got me. He sounded angry, but scared, too. It wasn't any fun to mess with him when he was like that—no matter what you may have heard, I'm not into torturing people. Besides, I'd gotten what I wanted.

So, I shut up . . . for now.

Through the kitchen, I heard the rapid tap-tap of footsteps and the jingle of keys. Someone was coming up the sidewalk to the back door.

Killian waited a second longer than I would have—but hey, it was his great escape—and then he twisted the doorknob and pulled the door open just as his mother stuck her key in the back door lock.

It would have been perfect. They would have had no idea of how long he was gone, probably wouldn't even have bothered to search outside the house.

Except . . . when Killian pulled open that front door, Dr. Miller stood behind it, his hand up and poised to knock. I couldn't have said which one of them was more shocked.

Boogeyman rubber shoes, supernatural in their silence, strike again.

They got him back to his room and in bed, quick as a flash. It only took me a couple seconds in their company to see that while Killian's shrink might have been the one with the power to send him away, it was his mother who ran the show. Not by pleading or whining, not like my mother. She was broken, by the loss of her husband and the pending loss of her son, and clearly struggling to keep it together. A request from her left Killian scrambling to obey, his face naked with guilt. He'd dropped his bag at the door and followed her without question. If she'd handed him a straitjacket, he'd have buckled himself in with a smile.

Fabulous. This was going to go well. I know all the talk-show hosts blab on and on about having involved and caring parents, but I still think there's something to be said for uninvolved and apathetic parents. It's a lot easier.

I parked myself on Killian's desk chair again to watch the show. I had a vested interest here.

"Where were you headed, Will?" Dr. Miller paced at the foot of the bed while Killian's mother hovered near the door, probably not wanting to crowd the great doctor. Whatever. I hated therapists. Useless lot, all of them. Always asking you to talk about your feelings. What good does that do anyone? Just makes you think and feel more about the things you can't change.

"Just somewhere to think."

"Do you want to talk about what happened at school today?" Miller took his hands from his pockets to cross one arm over his waist and rest the elbow of his other arm on it. Seconds later, his chin settled into the cup of his hand. The guy stepped away from his desk for a few hours and he couldn't support his own head. A chin-rubber. Great. I rolled my eyes.

Killian shrugged, a little too defensively. "Nothing to talk about."

Miller frowned. "Principal Brewster wanted to expel you. I'd say that's something."

"You talked to him?" he asked.

The doctor paused for the first time, hesitation flashed across his face. "I was with your mother at the diner when she got the call," he said finally.

Killian flashed a look at his mother.

Oh . . . something going on between his mom and the shrink? How revolting.

"William, I'm worried about you." His mother took a step inside the room, her thin, pale hands wringing one another. "Things have been getting worse and—"

"Mom, I'm fine." Killian threaded his hands through his hair. I saw the wince when he touched the knot on the side of his head, but he hid it pretty well. "Brewster was just being a jackass again. He took Marcie and—"

"That's the only reason you're not expelled. That, and your mother's efforts with Principal Brewster on your behalf." Miller didn't sound so happy about that.

Killian stiffened, no doubt imagining the pleading conversation that had gone on. Brewster was a hard-ass, that was for sure, but he enjoyed having power over the powerless. The smartest thing to do was just to respect him to his face and keep on his good side from the beginning. Clearly, Killian had blown that.

"It's all right," his mother said gently. "It wasn't as bad as all that." She gave him a weary smile.

I could see, though, that it wasn't all right, at least not with Killian.

"We've talked about this, Will." Miller blundered on in his calm I'm-the-therapist-so-I-know-best voice. Every word out of his mouth made me hate him more. He and Dr. Andrews must have gone to the same shrink school. "Your music is meant to aid you, but if you're relying on it too much—"

"I'm not," Killian protested. I could have told him it didn't matter. Miller had already made up his mind.

The good doctor strolled closer. He lowered a hand to hitch his pants up, obviously intending to sit on the foot of the bed. Then he noticed the tilt of the bed, the left side three or four inches lower than the right. Oops. The bed had broken our fall, and we'd broken it.

Miller straightened up with a frown. "What happened here?"

"Nothing," Killian said again.

"He's not buying it," I said. "Make something up."

He gave the tiniest shake of his head.

"Julia, the boy's bed is broken," Miller pronounced.

"What?" His mother hurried closer, her tiny feet moving soundlessly on the carpeting. Clearly, Killian had gotten his size and height from his father. "What happened here, William?" She sounded aghast, staring down at the bed. If the awful couch in the living room was any indication, he was probably going to end up sleeping on his tilt-a-bed for years to come.

"Was it the spirits again?" Miller asked. "Did they attack you?"

He was good. You could almost miss the eagerness behind the thick layers of fake concern.

"No, no. Nothing like that." He shook his head vigorously in response to Miller's question.

"Then what?" Miller prompted.

Killian shifted uncomfortably in his bed. "It was a girl, okay?" He looked to his mother with pleading eyes.

"She attacked you?" Miller sounded astounded, and far too excited.

Killian only hesitated for a fraction of a second. Then he stretched his arms out again, tucking his hands behind his head with a cocky and lazy smile and looking for all the world like a guy who'd just gotten some. "Yeah, I guess you could say that."

"In your dreams," I protested.

Miller's face fell. "You mean an actual girl."

"How many other kinds of girls are there, Doc?" Killian asked, still smiling. Oh, yeah, I was so going to hit him when the stupid doctor got out of here.

His mother frowned, confused. She stared at the bed, probably trying to remember if it'd been broken the last time she'd been up here. "When did this happen? I don't like the idea of girls visiting your room—"

"Now, Julia, peer interaction is good. Let's just try to keep it to the living room, okay, Will?" Miller reached down and patted Killian's leg in what he thought, gag, would be a fatherly gesture. Then he paused dramatically, and I flinched in advance. Four years of therapy with Dr. Andrews, king of the chin-rubbers, had taught me what to expect next. Show some tiny little spark of happiness, something that might lead you away from your regular weekly appointments, and watch out.

"What do you think Lily would make of this?" Miller asked casually.

Killian's smile disappeared like the doctor had reached over and ripped it off.

"Who's Lily?" I asked.

"She would want me to be happy. We were friends once," Killian said defensively.

"No." I stood up, alarmed. "Calm down. You're giving him an opening." Hadn't Killian been paying attention at all in therapy? Guys like Miller lived for this stuff.

"You're right. That's good. She wouldn't want you to feel guilty. She would want you to live your life happily. It wasn't your fault that you didn't answer the phone." Miller's words and tone managed to convey opposite things. It was a shrink thing. No idea how they did it, but it was their secret weapon.

"She knew I didn't always answer my phone. I can't hear it if I've got my headphones on. She could have called Joonie, her parents, anyone for help." The unspoken phrase that hung in the air was *But she called me.*

I watched Killian pull back into himself, tucking his arms beneath the covers. Great. At this rate, he was going to be too depressed to get out of bed, let alone help me. I didn't know who this Lily chick was, but she was screwing everything up.

"Come on." I moved to stand on the other side of Killian's bed with an exasperated sigh.

His mother frowned. "Did you hear that?" she asked the doctor. "It sounded like footsteps."

Killian shot me a warning look. Oops.

Dr. Miller gave her an overly patient look. "No, Julia."

I took advantage of their distraction. "Miller is messing with your head," I whispered to Killian, just in case, though it didn't seem like anyone else could hear my voice, or they'd have been freaking out a long time ago. "He wants you to feel bad because when you feel bad, he gets paid." I thought about it for a second, and then added, "Indirectly. But you get the idea. Snap out of it."

"No, he's right. Lily deserved better than what she got. She deserved better friends."

I sucked in a breath, watching Dr. Miller's face change as he recognized that Killian was not speaking to him. Was that greed that flashed so lightning quick?

"Smooth move, Killian," I snapped. "He's on to you."

Killian stiffened, and without a glance in my direction, he pushed himself upright again in bed. "I'm sorry. I meant, you're right, Dr. Miller."

"William, what happened to that girl . . . that was not your fault." His mother's voice held only the faintest quaver.

Ooooh. Now in spite of everything, I was intrigued. "Why? What happened to her? Did you get her pregnant? Shove her down a flight of stairs? Help her evil twin abduct her and take her to Mexico for some kind of face-altering plastic surgery?" Hmmm. My addiction to daytime television— thank you, TiVo, gift to people with lives everywhere—might have been showing through a bit there.

Everyone, including Killian, ignored me. Surprise, surprise.

"I know," Killian said, but the words rang hollow. He didn't believe it, and he didn't expect them to, either.

"You should get some rest," Dr. Miller said in that same patronizingly gentle voice. "A night at Ivythorne—"

"No," Killian and his mother said simultaneously.

Miller frowned. "Julia, I strongly encourage you to—"

Killian's mother hesitated for a long moment.

"Mom," Killian whispered, and I could see the fear in his face. She was all that stood between him and a life in lockdown.

Then she straightened her shoulders and met Dr. Miller's gaze straight on, and I saw the woman she must have been before all this tragedy rained down on her life. In that second, I envied Killian a little. My mother would have been fighting me for the opportunity to go to Ivythorne, probably hoping it would finally gain her some attention from my dad.

"I'm sure you would agree that this is an isolated incident triggered by Principal Brewster bullying my son," Killian's mom said. "He's a full-grown man who should know better than to torture a troubled boy."

Miller shook his head. "I know that you would like to believe ..."

"Max, I said no."

"Good for you. Finally, somebody in this family with a little spine," I said.

"All right." Miller held his hands up, surrendering less than graciously. "It's your decision, of course. I brought something else to help, just in case." He reached into his suit coat pocket to produce a capped syringe. "It's a mild sedative," Miller went on. "Just so you can get a good night's sleep tonight."

"And halfway into the next century," I protested. "Tell him no. You promised to help me."

Killian ignored me and looked to his mother. "I don't need it."

Her mouth curved in distaste when she looked at the syringe, but she nodded at him. "You need the rest."

"A sedative on top of a head injury?" I said. Any first-year watcher of *House* could tell you that was a mistake. "You people *are* crazy." Granted, his mother didn't know about the bump to his head, but still ...

Killian offered up his arm reluctantly.

I lunged to yank his arm down, but the bed was in the way, and Miller, after years of doping up patients, moved faster than I did. The needle was in Killian's arm before I could reach him.

I straightened up. "You're such a coward. I take back all the nice things I thought about your chest."

"You're right," Killian said. Then he looked up at me with a frown. "What?"

"I said, I want you to get some sleep," Miller repeated, a little louder. He removed the syringe from Killian's arm, recapped it, and dropped it in his pocket.

Killian's glazed eyes found mine. "What nice things did you think?" he asked, already sounding muzzy.

"Oh, forget it," I snapped.

Miller backed away, clucking his tongue. He nodded at Killian's mom, and the two of them stepped out into the hallway. I followed, narrowly escaping before Mrs. Killian closed the door.

"Now, Julia, I don't want to alarm you, but with your family history . . ."

She flinched.

He took her by the shoulders, enfolding her in a much-closer-than-professional embrace.

"A skeevy chin-rubber. Even better." I wrinkled my nose, imagining the dusty smell of his tweed jacket and the lingering odor of pipe smoke.

"It may be nothing at all, but any sudden change in

behavior is something we should keep an eye on." He hesitated dramatically, setting her away from him but still keeping his surprisingly fat and stubby fingers on her shoulders. "With this latest incident, we should consider hospitalization again—"

"He's doing better," she said firmly, as if she could make it true by the force of her words.

Oh, God, I couldn't even stand to watch this. The chin-rubber would have Killian in restraints within a week, and there was nothing I could do to stop it.

"I know, I know, and you may be right, this could be an isolated event, but the last eight or nine months . . . I care, Julia. So I'm worried." He hugged her again, his bulkier body nearly swallowing her smaller one whole.

"Skeevy bastards, that's what they all are. Wake up, Julia," I shouted right at her.

Disgusted, I pressed against the wall to scoot past them. Seriously, what was I supposed to do now? My one and only brilliant idea was currently gorked out of his brain and probably drooling on his pillow. And the information he'd given me? Not so much of a help.

I stomped soundlessly down the hall through the kitchen and into the living room to flop onto the plaid couch. As eye-piercingly ugly as it was, it felt pretty comfortable. Maybe that's why they'd ignored all good sense and kept it around.

I needed a plan. Killian was out of the game, probably indefinitely. Bargain or no bargain, he wasn't going to risk helping me, not with his freedom on the line. I almost couldn't blame him. Unfortunately, the other dead people I'd met didn't seem to have any clue about how to get out of here or else they'd have already done it, so I was on my own. No biggie—I'd been going it alone pretty much since I was thirteen. Though, paying the bills and keeping my mother sober enough to attend parent-teacher conferences once a semester didn't quite equal determining the fate of my eternal soul, but whatever. I could do it. I always got what I wanted, one way or another, right? You just had to keep pushing until someone or something gives in. She who quits last, wins. I used to have a cheerleading camp T-shirt that said that.

First things first. I needed a pen and some paper. Things always look more manageable when they're written out. I didn't win homecoming queen three times without a little effort and planning, you know. Kicking my legs out, I let the momentum pull me off the couch and to my feet. In the process, one of my ankles passed through a beat-up brown leather briefcase leaning partially against the side of the sofa.

Miller's. It had to be. It hadn't been in here when I'd first come in . . . well, fallen in. The main zipper pocket strained around a massive number of manila file folders and black-and-white composition notebooks, all jammed in unevenly and at odd angles. The nylon carrying strap had broken off on both sides, and the remaining bits of strap had sprouted tufts of brown fuzz. The briefcase looked like some kind of strange creature caught in midchew.

I grinned. Perfect. No good chin-rubber would ever be caught without a notebook and a multitude of pens. With just a bit of concentration . . .

Bending down, I focused on the briefcase, imagining the worn leather under my fingertips and the cool metal of the zipper teeth.

The briefcase creature flopped on its side and promptly barfed up its contents. Pens, the thick expensive kind, rolled free, along with a multitude of files. I grabbed for the least battered-looking composition notebook . . . and my hand passed through it.

"Dammit."

I tried again with the same results. This time, concentrating on making the notebook solid, I reached for it and my hand touched the corner of it, but only for a split second.

"Oh, forget it." If it was this hard to pick up a notebook without Killian right next to me with his personal voodoo or whatever, how would I manage to hold a pen, let alone write? "This sucks," I said aloud to no one in particular.

All right, so no pen and paper. I could still work strategy in my head. I sat down on the floor, crossing my legs. Killian said this was about unfinished business, issues I needed to resolve. Actually, he'd said I didn't have any issues. Showed what he knew.

But how was anyone in my *condition* supposed to resolve anything? No one could see or hear me, other than Killian, and I didn't seem to have gained any sort of afterlife-related super powers, like haunting people's dreams or whatever. I did have the whole passing-through-solid-objects thing working for me, but that seemed decidedly less than useful at the moment.

I drew my knees up to my chest and wrapped my arms around my legs, blinking back the sudden and unwelcome sting of tears. It seemed kind of an unfair test. Sure, you can move on to heaven if you can do the impossible. Otherwise, you're stuck here . . . forever. Alone.

No. I shook my head and straightened up. I wouldn't let this beat me. There had to be a way to win. I *always* won.

Thinking, I chewed on the side of my thumbnail for a second before catching myself. Dead or not, ragged and spit-covered nails are unacceptable.

If Killian hadn't been unconscious, I could have given him messages to deliver for me. I imagined him walking up to Chris and passing along the fact that his dead girlfriend was not so happy with him these days. Yeah, Killian would really need a stay in the hospital after that.

Staring down at Miller's tipped-over bag and the mess of files, folders, and papers on the floor in front of me, I got an idea. Maybe I was thinking too literally. Communication from the great beyond, even if it was actually not-so-great and not-so-beyond, should be subtle.

Concentrating on the topmost file, I gave it a shove, and it slid down the mountain of paperwork before settling on the carpeting. From there, moving it across the carpet and into position with little jabs was actually pretty easy. I figured I'd need about five or six more files to make my point.

Fortunately, Miller was the long-winded type—no surprise there. They'd started down the hall toward the kitchen a while ago, but he'd stopped there to schmooze further, and I could hear bits and pieces of their conversation as I worked.

"... Encourage you to reconsider, Julia."

"I appreciate that, Max, I do. But he's my son and ..."

"What if he'd been driving during this last attack? Have you considered that?"

Julia's response was a low and seemingly angry murmur that I couldn't hear. Good for her. Therapists aren't the be-all and end-all of knowledge. Sometimes they're just another way to lose money.

Out of breath from the effort required, I shoved the last composition book into place—I'd mixed it up a little between notebooks and folders for effect—and stepped back to admire my work. Very nice, but maybe a little more was needed? A little artistry perhaps?

Kneeling down again, I pushed at another folder. Only this one, much heavier and thicker with more paper than the others, spilled its contents instead of sliding across the floor. The uppermost document looked like a letter and the rest were ... chapters? Neatly typed pages with dialogue and headings ...

I leaned closer for a better look. The letter on top was from Page Seven Books and addressed to Dr. Miller.

*Dear Dr. Miller,*

*We are most intrigued by the partial of your book,* The
Dead Don't Speak. *We like the illicit romance between
the psychiatrist and the afflicted boy's mother as well
as the mystery of whether the boy, young Billy, is truly
haunted or just mentally ill. Did his father commit suicide
or was he killed by the same spirits that now haunt his
son? We also think you have an excellent platform, as a
psychiatrist who has treated many of these kinds of cases.*

*Please send a complete manuscript at your earliest
convenience.*

*Regards,*
*Roger Fillmore*
*Senior Acquisitions Editor*


Oh, my God. Unbelievable. Miller was turning his life
into a book. No wonder he was pushing so hard for Killian
to be put away. He needed to write the end. Not to mention
the freedom to openly mack on Killian's mom. Ew!

I reached over to flick aside the letter and read the chapters
beneath, but then I heard Miller's voice getting closer.

"I'll just collect my bag and be on my way now. I have
other patients waiting," Miller said stiffly. Evidently, Killian's
mom had put him in his place, at least for now.

With a little effort, I managed to push the publisher's
letter and the first chapter or so under the couch. Then I was
out of time.

Miller stalked through the kitchen and into the living room, stopping dead when he saw his spilled bag. "What—?"

Then he turned and saw my display. Two manila folders represented eyes, and a third held the place of a nose. Then, five composition notebooks, with their black-and-white covers, formed a menacing—as menacing as one can be with paper products—scowl. All in all, it was a big giant frowny face made out of his stuff in the middle of the living room carpeting.

Miller's face went white, and I laughed.

"J-J-Julia," he sputtered.

"What is it?" She appeared in the living room doorway with a frown. Then she caught a glimpse of my work. Her mouth fell open, and her knees sagged, forcing her to cling to the wall.

I winced. This wasn't supposed to be a strike against her.

"Did you do this?" Miller demanded.

"Idiot," I said to him. "When did she have time? She went with you, remember?"

But Mrs. Killian wasn't thinking that clearly. "It's Danny," she said, looking faint. "He always pulled tricks like this, moving things around. Once I found my kitchen timer in the freezer. He swore he didn't do it, but . . ." She sank to her knees and started to cry.

"Don't be silly," he snapped. "Your husband is dead. He's gone on to a better place. He's not fiddling with notebooks and sending you messages. If you didn't do it, then it's that boy." He glared in the direction of Killian's room as though he could see through walls.

"Oh, yeah, because after you doped him up, he slipped past you in the hallway, did this, and then sneaked back in without you even noticing." I rolled my eyes.

Julia lifted her chin and wiped her cheeks with the back of her hand. "You gave him a sedative, Max."

"This is ridiculous." He snatched up his bag and began cramming the contents back inside. "Ghosts are part of people's imagination, designed to comfort them in times of loss. Period. End of story." But his hands shook when he bent down to scoop up the folders and notebooks from my frowny face.

"Oh, Max, don't spoil the ending for us," I taunted. "You've still got to write it."

He rushed toward the kitchen, nearly knocking over Killian's mom in the process. "What about our next appointment?" she asked between sobs.

"I'll call you," he said curtly.

Then the back door slammed, and Mrs. Killian's shoulders slumped even further, shaking with her crying.

"You should listen to your son," I told her. "He's telling the truth." The high of my first successful communication was wearing off a little in light of her weeping. Actually, I was feeling a little light-headed and woozy, sort of like this morning when . . .

I looked down and found I could see through my arms folded over my chest. In fact, I could see all the way through to the bookcase behind me.

Aw, crap.

# ❧ 8 ❧

# Will

"**D**id you know about this?" My mother's voice intruded on a dream in which a large animated eggplant named Bob teetered on the edge of a cliff with thoughts of suicide and Parmesan.

I woke slowly, without opening my eyes. My eyelids felt gummy and stuck to my eyeballs, my head throbbed worse than it had yesterday, and my back ached from sleeping for hours without moving. I could feel the sunshine beaming in through the open blinds, warmer and brighter than yesterday. It had to be morning again.

"William, I'm speaking to you. Wake up!" Her voice held an unusual edge.

I peeled my eyelids up and squinted at her. She stood at

the foot of my now-lopsided bed, a fistful of papers in her hand. "What are you talking about?" I mumbled.

"This." She stalked forward and held the papers, fanned out in her hand, in front of my face.

The top one appeared to be a letter to Dr. Miller about a book. . . .

I sat up straighter, ignoring the various aches and pains. "He was writing a book about us? Where did you find this? Did he give this—"

"No, no." She shook her head. "I found it yesterday under the couch when I was cleaning after that stunt you pulled."

The cleaning part made sense. My mom always cleaned when she was upset. The year my dad died, she wore out three vacuum cleaners. As for the rest . . . "What are you talking about?"

She shuffled the papers together in her hands and gave a nervous laugh. "Oh, don't try that on me. I've been your mother too long, and besides, your father used to pull the same tricks before you. Moving things around when I wasn't looking and claiming to know nothing about it."

Alona. I flopped my head back on the pillow. It had to be. She was the only one who'd been here yesterday, at least as far as I knew. "What trick did you find yesterday?" I asked cautiously.

She rolled her eyes. "Are there any others more obvious? Dr. Miller's papers spread all over the room and that frowny face made from the folders and notebooks. He was quite frightened." She stared down at the papers in her hands, her mouth tightening in displeasure. "A scare he richly deserved in my opinion."

"Oh," I said. "That trick." Wow. It must have taken a huge amount of energy from her to move all of that around without me nearby. The dead can touch things in our realm briefly—hence all the ghost stories about pictures falling off walls, doors slamming, lights turning off or on—but only with intense concentration, and it really drains them.

My mom perched on the side of my bed, bracing her feet against the floor to keep from sliding off. "That was you, wasn't it?" she asked hesitantly. "You found out about the book somehow and wanted to punish him? You called a friend to come in while we were upstairs. Joonie, maybe. The back door was unlocked the whole time, I checked."

She sounded so hopeful, the way she had it all worked out without any ghosts or supernatural elements involved. My father's words to me when I was six echoed in my head. *She doesn't understand. She doesn't want to understand, Will. It scares her.* He'd drummed his fingers on the steering wheel, while we waited for my mother to join us in the car. She was crying in the bathroom. I'd just ruined a rare night out for us in a restaurant by announcing that Grandma Reilly said not to order the fish because it looked old. Grandma Reilly, my mother's mother, had died six months earlier of a heart attack. *It's a curse, sport, and I'm sorry that I've passed it on to you. Do the best you can to live a normal life, and try not to let it hurt the ones you love. That's all I can say.*

Except my father had screwed up on that one. I didn't

know how my mother would have reacted to hearing that her husband spoke to the dead, but I was willing to bet that she would have preferred that to him *being* dead. Still, he was my dad, and he was gone, so I did my best to abide by what he wanted.

"Yeah," I told my mother. "It was me."

She exhaled loudly in relief. "I thought so. Why didn't you just tell me what was going on? Why all this staging and drama?"

Good question. Alona could have just told me what she'd discovered. When I woke up from the drugs that I'd allowed Miller to administer even over her protests. Okay, fair enough. Maybe she had reason to question my potential for follow-through on something like this. That still didn't explain her sudden compassion for someone else's problems, which was the true mystery.

"I didn't think you'd believe me if I didn't have proof," I said to my mother. A reasonable enough explanation, if not the truth.

She sighed. "You'll put me in an early grave yet. Next time, just tell me."

"Okay, okay."

She stood up and started for my door.

"What are you going to do about Dr. Miller?"

She looked weary suddenly. "I don't know. You're not going back there. I guess I need to report him to someone, and get a recommendation for another doctor." Except Miller had been the most affordable option out there and the only one with an immediate opening for a new client on a regular basis. Now, maybe we knew why that was.

*What an asshole.* I wished I could have seen his face when he got a load of Alona's handiwork. That was actually a fairly clever move on her part for one so newly dead. I was beginning to suspect that she hid a fairly sizable intelligence beneath her pretty face and bitchy attitude. Granted, it was an intelligence directed mostly toward popularity contests, backstabbing, and self-promotion, but intelligence just the same. Her move against Miller, whether for my benefit or her own amusement, had given me the reprieve I needed. It would take a few weeks, maybe even a month, to line up another psychiatrist, barring any more major incidents like the one yesterday, and I had a plan, maybe, to handle those, if Alona would agree. I felt pretty sure I could come up with an incentive to make that happen.

I shoved back the covers and got out of bed, feeling better than I had since before my dad died.

My mother's mouth fell open. "Where do you think you're going?"

"School. You talked to Brewster so I could get back in, right?" I crossed the room to rifle through the laundry on the chair and the pieces that had spilled over onto the floor, thanks to Alona, searching for a clean T-shirt and boxers.

"William, you don't have to prove anything—" she began gently.

"Mom, I'm fine. I can do this." I did a quick sniff test under the arms of my favorite black T-shirt. It said in plain block letters across the front, THERE IS NO SPOON. No one else got it, but it worked for me, reminding me that reality was always up for question.

"What about Marcie? Your music?" She frowned. "Brewster gave you an in-school suspension for the rest of this week."

"Don't worry. I'll be fine. I have a plan." Technically, I had bribery, and a dead homecoming queen who wanted my help. Close enough.

I doubled back to kiss my startled mother on the cheek and then headed for the shower.


Alona Dare died during zero hour on the Henderson Street yellow centerline, just twenty feet or so from the edge of school property. Zero hour was notoriously easy to skip, particularly if you put in the effort to show up in the first place, as Alona had that day.

Rumors continued to fly about why she'd come to school only to leave again, in such a hurry that she didn't bother to look both ways. Some people said she never looked where she was going, expecting everyone and everything to get out of her way. So, it wasn't so much an accident as her arrogance that had done her in. I suspected those people were seeking to make sense of the world by turning her into a cautionary tale, the lesson being, Look both ways. And don't be such a bitch.

Other people whispered about suicide, pointing to her boyfriend, Chris Zebrowski, who was already tangling tongues with Misty Evans, Alona's best friend. A subset of this same group claimed to have witnessed a private showdown between Misty and Alona that left Alona running from the building.

Either way, the result was the same. Alona was dead, Chris and Misty were publicly hooking up an indecently short amount of time after Alona's funeral, and the population of Groundsboro High had something to gossip and whisper about for at least another few weeks.

I pulled the Dodge over to the side of the road on Henderson, next to the tennis courts, flipped the hazard lights on, and waited. Alona hadn't committed suicide, I knew that. The girl had enough arrogance and self-esteem to choke a horse. She had, however, died a violent and unnatural death, which probably meant she was still tied to the exact place of her death. In this case, the middle of Henderson Street. Even though the bloodstains had long been scrubbed away, something of Alona likely remained, calling her back here over and over again at the time of her death. As a bonus, I'd only have to wait a few minutes to see if I was right.

Cars en route to the high school went by, people staring out the windows at me as they passed. Whatever. By now, they'd probably heard about what happened yesterday, and they were probably staring as much for that as for me sitting here. Still, I rolled down my window and pulled my cell phone from my front pocket and held it in my hand to give me the air of authenticity. Waiting in my broken-down car for a tow, that's me.

"Hey, Will Kill."

I looked up automatically, responding to that stupid nickname someone in the first tier had tagged me with.

Ben Rogers hung his head out the open window of his Land Rover. "Classes are held inside the building, freak."

I smiled tightly, my cheeks hurting with the effort. "Really? Thanks a lot." *Dickwad.* For the millionth time, I wondered what Lily had found so fascinating about him and his kind.

Someone behind Rogers, waiting to turn into the school parking lot, laid on the horn.

Looking disgruntled at my lack of reaction, Ben pulled his head back in and accelerated abruptly, his tires screeching when he rounded the corner into the parking lot.

"God, I hate it when he does that." Alona's voice suddenly sounded next to my ear, and I jumped. "What does he think this is, *The Dukes of Hazzard*? He is so not Johnny Knoxville."

I turned to find her in my passenger seat. She stretched her arms over her head with a big yawn, seemingly unconcerned at her sudden and unexpected arrival.

"What are you doing in here?" I demanded. "You died *out there*." I jerked my thumb back toward the road.

She lowered her arms and glared at me. "Thank you, Mr. Obvious. How should I know? Yesterday, whenever I disappeared, I kept waking up in your room. Like that wasn't a pain in the ass." She rolled her eyes. "I had to keep walking everywhere. Also? You snore."

I gaped at her. "What are you talking about?"

She ignored me. "What are *you* doing here, anyway?" she asked with a frown. "I thought you'd be tugging at your chains in the crazy house by now."

I held my breath and counted to five before responding. This was just who Alona was. She didn't mean to be demeaning and . . . actually, yeah, she did. "You helped me, I came to say thanks," I said through gritted teeth.

She frowned again. "You mean scaring off the chin-rubber?"

I raised my eyebrows, confused, until she furrowed her brow and nodded in mock thoughtfulness while her hand came up to support her chin, the top two fingers tapping just below her lower lip.

Startled by her cleverness once again, I shook my head with a reluctant smile. "Chin-rubber, yeah."

She nodded. "He's one of the worst I've ever seen."

I grimaced. "We found the papers about his book. You left those for us?"

"He's skeevy." She lifted a shoulder. "Figured you might want to know about it."

"Thanks," I said cautiously. So, she'd actually done me a favor? Maybe she wasn't quite as bad as she seemed. *Maybe.*

She heaved a deep sigh. "Yeah, you're welcome, I guess." Her head drooping, she slumped down in her seat and stretched her long legs out in front of her.

I cleared my throat, trying to drag my eyes away from the sight. What can I say? I'm a leg man. "What's the matter?"

"Aside from the obvious?" She threw her hands up in the air. "I don't know. I thought I had it figured out yesterday."

"Had what figured out?"

"The afterlife. What I'm supposed to do to . . . move on, find the light, whatever." She waved her hands dramatically.

"And that is?" It didn't bode well for my plan if she'd found her own way to fix her situation. I'd have no value to her then, and Alona Dare did not do favors. At least, I wouldn't have thought so until today.

A horn honked and Alona automatically looked up, a smile starting to form and her hand lifting to wave . . . until she realized they couldn't see her. The smile disappeared and her hand fell back to her lap. "This bites," she muttered.

"What did you figure out?" I asked, reminding myself to be patient.

She turned toward me, tucking one leg underneath her. "Okay, so I thought about what you said and . . ." She stopped, frowning. "Aren't you worried about what people will think, seeing you out here talking to yourself?"

"Actually, I—"

She held up a hand. "Wait, never mind. I mean, they already think you're crazy. Talking to yourself might be one of the more normal things you'd do."

My jaw tight, I held up the cell phone in my hand. "Speakerphone."

She arched an eyebrow. "You have speakerphone on that old thing?"

"No, but they"—I gestured to the people in the cars

waiting to turn at the stop sign— "don't know that." Cell phones with speakerphone or, even better, Bluetooth were the best invention yet for disguising conversations with people no one else could see. It became so normal to see someone seemingly talking to the air that half the time I suspected people didn't even think to check for the phone. Plus, it saved me the effort of coming up with a less believable lie. Back in sixth grade, I told my mother I was rehearsing lines for a play when she caught me. My dad knew better, but my mom kept asking, for the better part of the year, when the first show was and could she buy tickets.

"Oh." Alona thought about it for a second. "Pretty smart."

I bit back a sarcastic reply. For the moment, I needed her, and I didn't want to run her off just yet. "So what were you saying about figuring it all out?"

"Oh, yeah." She promptly became more animated. "So, I thought about what you said, about resolving my issues and moving on to the *spirit* world." She emphasized her chosen term and leveled a warning glance at me.

I held up my hands, protesting innocence. If she didn't want to be called a ghost, fine. Even if that's what she was.

"Except it didn't work out very well. I tried communicating. You know sending signs of my presence, tipping things over . . ."

My mouth fell open. "You tried haunting people?"

"No, I tried *communicating*. It's not my fault if they got scared. Besides, it was only a few people, and they totally deserved it," she said defensively.

"When did you do this?" I demanded.

"Yesterday when you were in la-la land."

I rubbed my forehead. The fact that she was still here was a miracle, then. For ghosts, nothing drains their energy like trying to cause harm. And when their energy dips low enough, they disappear . . . for good. "What exactly did you do?"

"What does it matter to you?" she shot back.

"Just tell me." I'd have to figure out damage control. If she was going to be sucked back up permanently any second now, then my plan was history.

She picked at the edge of her thumbnail. "Among others, I may have visited a former friend's house and knocked over a few things while she was making out with"—she grimaced in distaste—"her new boyfriend."

"Chris and Misty." I sighed. "They're not your unfinished business."

"How do you know?"

"Because, unless I completely misunderstood what I saw, you didn't even know about them until yesterday. As in three days after you were already dead and stuck here." I could see she didn't want to believe me. "Whatever. Did you scare them?"

A cocky smile emerged on her face. "Yeah, a little." She hesitated and then leaned closer to me, excitement making her whole body tense. "It was so cool. I only knocked down pictures with me in them, right? That way they'd know it was me." She frowned. "But there weren't that many pictures of me up anymore, so really I only got to push down one, and they didn't even notice because the music was so loud—"

"Alona," I tried to interrupt. Even as she spoke, the tips of her fingers were turning translucent.

"But then I decided to find her yearbook because—"

"Alona!"

"What?" She looked over at me, decidedly irked.

I grabbed her wrist and held her disappearing hand up in front of her face.

Her green eyes grew wide. "Oh, crap, not again. It's getting worse. Yesterday whenever I tried to communicate, I kept being pulled away . . . to that other place." She shuddered. "The one I can't remember."

"Do you think that might have been a clue?" I muttered, releasing her wrist before it dissolved, too. "Say something nice," I commanded.

She narrowed her eyes at me. "In your dreams."

"It doesn't have to be about me," I said with some exasperation. "It's probably better if it isn't, because it has to be genuine."

"What are you talking about?" She stared at me.

I resisted the urge to shake her. "Look, I don't have time to go into a whole lot of explanation on this. Your ankles are already gone."

She glanced down at her footless legs and squeaked in horror.

"Say something nice," I repeated, feeling a growing sense of panic. If she'd been "communicating" all day yesterday, this might be it, her final visit to Middleground.

"Why are you helping me?" she asked with a frown.

"Why do you care?" I snapped. "Just do it."

"Will? Is everything okay?" Joonie's voice came from my right.

I looked over to find Joonie's beat-up black VW Bug, requisite skull and crossbones etched in the paint on the driver's side door, stopped in the road, just ahead of the stop sign. Joonie had her window rolled down, all the better to stare at me more clearly.

"What happened, the Dodge finally give out on you?" Joonie asked, her painfully thin black brows drawing together over her bloodshot blue eyes. I always wondered, with her eyebrow piercings, if it hurt for her to make certain expressions.

"Sort of."

"What does saying something nice have to do with anything?" Alona, now a torso only, demanded.

"Are you waiting for a ride?" Joonie asked, disbelief coloring her tone. No wonder, considering I probably could have crawled to the school on my hands and knees and still made it on time.

"Tow truck?" I offered as a possible explanation, though when she saw my car in the lot later, it might trigger a few questions. "Do it, unless you want to be gone forever," I said to Alona, out of the side of my mouth.

"This is bullshit," Alona muttered. "Fine." She took a deep breath and said loudly, "I'm happy to be here." She threw up her arms, now missing from below the elbow. Nothing happened.

I fake coughed. "Has to be genuine."

"Are you sure you're okay?" Joonie frowned at me. "You seem a little . . . disconnected."

"Stop being my mom, J. I get more than enough of that at home," I said gently.

She stiffened, her mouth opening to rip me a new one, no doubt, when she caught herself. "Sorry," she said with a forced grin. "You bring out the mama bird in me, I guess." Her expression clouded. "Especially when I have to drag your half-conscious ass out of school the day before."

"I'm fine. I promise." Or, at least, I might be fine, if I could get Alona to say one genuinely positive thing.

"It's a warm spring day, and that makes me happy," she shouted angrily.

*Riiight.*

"Listen." Joonie leaned out of her window. "I went by the hospital yesterday. Saw Lily."

Next to me, Alona stopped shouting random and fake compliments to everyone ("Your friend's tongue-piercing is very shiny") and everything ("The tennis courts look really . . . green today") and looked at me. I felt her gaze, but I kept my focus on Joonie, trying to maintain a neutral expression. Alona didn't need any more ammunition against me. "Yeah?"

"We need to talk."

I shifted uncomfortably. Joonie held herself responsible

for Lily's accident, for the fight that had, in theory, driven Lily away. But Joonie blamed me, too, and I didn't know why. I mean, she was right, of course, but she didn't know about Lily's call to me, the one I'd missed. I couldn't tell her because I knew once she thought about it she'd realize that I would have been Lily's second choice for help. She was always much closer to Joonie . . . until that stupid fight.

Last summer, a few weeks before school started, Joonie had shown up at my house without Lily for movie night. When I'd asked what happened, Joonie had waved it away and eventually, at my pressing, said they'd had a fight.

"About what?" I'd asked.

She'd looked away, staring out the window instead of at Arnold Schwarzenegger tearing it up on screen as the Terminator. "Boys."

I still didn't understand how a fight about boys could be that bad, particularly since neither of them had been dating anyone. But understanding girls, even ones I had as my friends, wasn't exactly something I had a great deal of success with, so whatever.

The problem was, now, I didn't know how to feel guiltier and more shamed than I already did, and I couldn't apologize for something Joonie knew nothing about. In short, it was horrible and destroying whatever was left of our friendship.

"Yeah, okay," I said finally, not sure what else to say.

Another car, Kevin Reynolds's old Geo Metro, pulled up behind Joonie and honked.

Joonie responded by tossing him the finger. "If you're not

in Pederson's class, I'm coming to find you," Joonie warned as she shifted the Bug back into gear.

I shook my head. "I've got in-school suspension this week, apparently."

She frowned.

"I'll catch up with you, I promise. You better hurry up. Brewster will be looking for you to be late."

The Bug stuttered and then revved, pulling up to the stop sign, where Joonie conscientiously came to a full stop, prompting another honk from Kevin.

"Your friends seem to care about you," Alona said next to me, her voice holding more than a trace of wistfulness. "Like they'd really miss you if you were gone."

I looked over at her, a bobbing head three feet above the passenger seat, like some kind of green-screen movie magic, and watched as the rest of her body took shape and filled in again. She really meant what she'd said, and while not exactly a cheery sentiment, she'd intended it as a compliment.

I flopped back in my seat, exhausted. "There. Was that so hard?"

## ❧ 9 ❧

# Alona

*I* stretched out my newly solid legs, bending them at the knee and rotating my ankles, rejoicing in their, well, there*ness*, and then turned to stare at Killian leaning back in his seat, his eyes closed. "How did you do that?" I demanded. I'd tried everything to keep from disappearing— well, if everything meant screaming, shouting, and cursing for it to stop—and it hadn't even slowed the process a bit.

He opened one eye to squint at me. "I didn't do anything. You did."

"Oh, no, no." I pointed a finger at him. "Don't even try that with me. You knew it would work. How?"

"Positive equals energy," he muttered under his breath.

I frowned. "What?"

He sat up slowly. "Nothing. Forget it."

"I will not forget it. I need to know how you did that."

"Why? So you can scare people and then pull yourself back together at the last second?"

"Well . . ."

"Sorry, it doesn't work that way, sweetheart."

I glared at him for the endearment, but his gaze was already focused on something in the rearview mirror.

"Cops," he said. "Time to go."

Glancing back over my shoulder, I found a squad car doing a slow roll down Henderson. It sped up and pulled even with us just as Killian started the engine.

The policeman, an older, grizzled-looking type, rolled down his passenger-side window.

"Everything okay here?" he asked. His sharp gaze took in Killian's hair, his dark clothes, the car.

"You better smile, or we're toast," I said. "Everything about you screams social malcontent with a grudge and a trunk full of weapons."

Killian's hands tensed on the wheel, and I knew he was dying to tell me off. Instead, he forced a reasonable-looking smile on his face. "Yes, officer. Everything's fine. Just waiting for someone who never showed."

"Oh, ha, ha," I said.

The policeman nodded after a long moment. "The street is not a parking lot, son. Move along."

"Yes, sir." Killian turned off the hazards, flipped on his

turn signal, put the car in gear, and pulled away from the curb—textbook driving.

"Well, aren't you a good citizen?" I smirked.

"Shut up." He kept his gaze on the rearview mirror as we proceeded down Henderson at three miles *under* the speed limit. He turned right onto Elm, cut in front of the school, through the teachers' parking lot, and into the last aisle of the student lot. I knew it as Burner Row. He parked and slumped back in his seat with a loud sigh of relief.

"If he could arrest someone for looking guilty," I said, "you would have been it. You weren't even doing anything wrong."

"Doesn't matter. I can't risk any more trouble right now."

I turned sideways in my seat to face him, grateful for the first time for being invisible to everyone else. Hardly anyone was left in the parking lot by now—all of them moving toward the building and class—but still. Never in my wildest dreams could I have ever imagined a scenario, even life after death, that would have me in Will Killian's car in Burner Row. Though, it did offer a pretty view of the track and the football field. "So, why am I here? And no smart-ass answers, please," I added quickly.

Killian didn't answer right away, tapping his hands restlessly on the steering wheel, pale-skinned but nicely shaped biceps pulling at the sleeves of his T-shirt. Wow, so goth boy found time to work out. Interesting. "I have a proposition for you," he said finally.

To which I responded the only way I could. "I'm not

sleeping with you, even if you are the only one I can touch. I'm dead, not desperate." I flopped back in the passenger seat and checked the tips of my nails for damage, more out of habit than anything else. I'd worked very hard to grow them out for prom and graduation, not that it mattered now.

He made a disgusted noise. "Don't flatter yourself."

"I'm not the one who keeps staring at my legs," I pointed out.

Two red spots rose in his pale cheeks. "What happened to being nice?"

I lifted a shoulder idly. "Break glass in case of emergency, you know?" I waggled my fully formed, noninvisible hand in front of him. "I'm not disappearing yet."

"Unfortunately," he muttered.

"Hey!" I sat up. "I was only disappearing because you wouldn't help me in the first place. You can't take credit for fixing a mess that you made."

He raked his hands through his shaggy black hair, which might actually have been attractive with the right cut. "Whatever. I'm ready to help you now."

I let my hand drop. "What?"

"You heard me." He refused to meet my eyes.

"Why?" I asked suspiciously.

"What does it matter?" he asked with impatience. "Just—"

"Oh, no, it matters. Yesterday, you kept trying to send me away. I had to twist your arm to get you to give me ten minutes of your time, and then you went and got yourself knocked out for the day. Plus," I added with a little extra indignation, "you said you thought I went to hell."

He sighed. "Are you going to keep bringing that up?"

I pretended to consider it. "Yeah, I think so."

"All that matters is . . ." He fidgeted with a gash on the steering wheel plastic, his fingers tracing it over and over. "Look, do you want to get out of here or not?"

"Depends," I said slowly. "Where are you going to send me?"

He made an exasperated sound. "It's not like that. I don't have that kind of influence over . . . You have to understand . . ." He took a deep breath and let it out slowly. Then he turned slightly in his seat to face me, his face serious.

Feeling a tingle of anticipation for what he was about to say, I leaned forward.

"Not everyone who dies ends up here," Killian said, with the air of someone imparting some great secret.

I flopped back in my seat with a sigh. "Duh."

He scowled at me.

"Seriously, do you expect that to be a shock to me?" I shook my head in disbelief. "I've been here for five days, and I have yet to see any of the dead people I know . . . knew." I frowned. "Whatever. Plus, it would be way more crowded."

He looked startled. "That's true. How did you—"

"Just because I care about what I look like"—I took in his black T-shirt and ratty jeans with some distaste—"doesn't mean I'm stupid."

"Fine, fine." He scrubbed his hands over his face. "Just listen, okay? Not everyone who dies ends up here. Some of them go directly to their final destination. Do not pass Go, do not visit your own wake." He gave me a sharp look.

I shrugged. Yes, I'd attended my own visitation and funeral, so what? Who wouldn't? It's literally a once-in-a-lifetime opportunity—actually less than—to see who really cares about you and how much.

Thinking about it now, I did not remember seeing Killian at the funeral home, the church, or the cemetery. Yeah, it had been gratifyingly crowded at each location— the super-intendent had even let everyone out of school early just so they could go—but trust me, you pay a lot of attention to who's coming and going when you're the guest of honor, so to speak.

I felt a weird sort of pang in my chest—almost like hurt. So, I was good enough to argue with, stare at, and fanta-size about—since sixth grade, and yes, it was obvious—but not special enough to warrant a fifteen-minute side trip in the course of his day? Granted, the number of other spirits that probably hang around a funeral home and church might have made it a bit uncomfortable for him, but still.

Whatever. Like it mattered. Who was he to mourn for me? Just a lame-ass social nobody I never even would have realized was missing from my funeral, if I hadn't died and needed his help. Right, okay, a small logic problem with that, but you know what I mean.

He waved a hand in front of my face to catch my attention. "I'm not doing this just to hear myself talk. You with me?"

I swatted at his hand. "I'm sorry, was my glassy-eyed boredom distracting you? Please, keep going."

He gritted his teeth for a long second, but eventually continued. "Like I was saying, for people like *you*"—he made it sound as if nobody was like me, but not in the good way— "who end up here, one of three things happens."

Now this is what I needed to hear. Forcing aside the odd little flare-up about Killian missing my funeral—being dead really screws with your emotions—I sat up straighter and turned toward him again, folding my legs underneath me.

"Most people aren't here very long—"

I frowned. "But those ghosts . . . spirits at the school—"

He let out a breath between his teeth, an impatient hiss. "Hang on, I'm getting there."

"Well, hurry up." Sheesh, wasn't like we had all day. Actually, one of us had much longer than that, but again, listening to Killian babble was not exactly how I wanted to spend the rest of eternity.

He glared at me. "Are you always this pushy?"

"Only when my immortal soul hangs in the balance," I shot back.

"I knew you were Catholic," he muttered.

"Watch it."

He ignored me. "Like I was saying, when people land here, they don't stay very long. For the most part, they're gone in a few days."

"Gone how? That's the part I need to know."

He clamped his mouth shut, and his jaw muscles

twitched beneath his skin. To be sure, he had a nice jawline, firm and square. Too bad he ruined it by being all pale and spooky-looking. "For some of them, someone or some . . . thing comes to get them."

"A bright white light?" I asked eagerly. I'd seen no sign of that around me at all, but at least I'd know what I was looking for.

Killian, for once, didn't seem annoyed by the interruption. He shook his head thoughtfully. "No, not like what you see on television. It's hard to describe. At a distance, it feels sort of warm and welcoming, like someone captured a perfect summer day in a jar and poured it out over your head." His eyes stared off at some point above my head, a faint smile pulling at his mouth.

"How poetic," I said with a smirk.

He snapped back to attention then, glaring at me. "You asked."

"What about the others?" I persisted. "You said one of three things happened. The happy golden light is one alternative. Getting stuck here forever or at least for a bunch of years, like the people at school, that's clearly option number two."

He nodded begrudgingly.

"So what's the third thing that can happen?" I bet he just loved having me pull all of this information from him, making him feel special and important and crap.

"Most of them just disappear," he said, sounding like that's what he wanted to happen to me right then and there.

Alona gone, poof. But for once I didn't feel the slightest bit woozy.

"How long does the disappearing thing go on?" I really hated this sliding in and out of existence. It was annoying, like never being able to finish a sentence before having to start over again.

Killian shook his head. "That's what's weird. For most of them, it's a one-shot deal. When you disappear, you're done." He looked over at me, his pale blue eyes distant and cool, like he was imagining me gone.

"So what happens when you completely disappear? I mean, is it bad there?" I felt tears pricking my eyes. Okay, so maybe I hadn't been perfect, but surely, I didn't deserve to be completely obliterated, right?

"I don't know," he said, lifting his hands palms up. "I've never had anyone come back and tell me."

"But I don't understand—" I stopped, a sense of horror dawning on me as his words made another piece of the puzzle click into place. "That's why you laughed at me yesterday. Before school started. You didn't care if I saw you see me because you thought I was gone for good." I felt the truth in it even without his response.

He glanced away, staring out the side window at the parking lot. "I shouldn't have laughed. That was wrong."

"You're damn right it was." I couldn't believe him, parading around as this nice, albeit freaky, guy when secretly he wanted nothing more than to see me gone . . . permanently. "I've never done anything to you to deserve—"

He laughed bitterly. "Oh, right. The great and golden Alona Dare, the original Miss Perfect."

Stung, I jerked back. "I never claimed to be—"

But he wasn't done yet. "One cross-eyed look or nasty word from you destroys lives, and you take pleasure in it—"

"I've had enough of this." I turned away from him to pass through the car door and into the street, but my foot, followed closely by the rest of me, smacked solidly into metal and plastic. "Ouch." I reached for the car door handle.

"Becca Stanhope."

I stopped, my fingers wrapped around the metal handle. "The fat . . ." I paused and rolled my eyes. "Big-boned girl from pre-calc who wears the baggy sweaters? What does she have to do with anything?" I tossed a triumphant look over my shoulder at Killian. "*She* came to my funeral, and she cried."

"Probably with relief because you were dead and wouldn't be bothering her anymore."

"What are you talking about?"

"You made her cry."

It took me a second to remember what he was talking about. I'd said something to the her, I didn't even remember what. Only that she'd run from the room, crying, her sweater flapping behind her. "Once, and that was, like, months ago."

He gave me an accusing look. "You told her she should buy her clothes in the right size."

"So?" I shrugged, feeling surprisingly defensive. "She should. There are plenty of cute things in the plus-size section. It just takes a little effort and—"

"Her grandmother makes her those sweaters."

"Her grandmother should know better. It's like she's trying to make the girl look even worse." I frowned. "How do you know that? About the grandma sweaters, I mean?"

"Because she cried every day at the end of PE when she was getting dressed for her next class. Pre-calc," he said flatly.

"You've taken to spying in the girls' locker room, Killian? I didn't think you were that desperate." My comeback lacked punch. The image of Becca Stanhope sobbing in the aisles of the girls' locker room made my conscience twinge. I hadn't necessarily meant to be cruel. It just bugged me how little people cared about themselves and how they were perceived. You don't care what the world thinks? Fine, but don't expect the world to accept and applaud you solely for that fact.

"Joonie has class with her. She told me," Killian said in that lofty voice of the morally superior. He sounded like Father Rankin.

"I'm sure Becca and Joonie are close friends, right?" I crossed my arms over my chest. "Joonie probably went right over, gave her a big hug, and told her it was going to be okay." Becca wasn't in my lunch hour, so I had no idea where she sat, but based on the look of her, I'd guess the fourth or fifth tier of caf tables, probably floating between the band geeks and the Spanish club. Nowhere near the courtyard full of burners like Joonie and Killian.

Killian looked away. "She overheard Becca telling Mrs. Higgins."

"Yeah, see, you and your friends exclude people, too." Actually, Becca probably would never have spoken to Joonie anyway, so it was more of a mutual exclusion, but my point was the same. Everyone does it.

Killian shook his head. "We're not deliberately mean."

I gaped at him. "I'm not—"

"Joey Torres," he said immediately, as if he'd just been waiting for me to deny it.

"Pizza-faced Joe?" I frowned.

Killian winced. Whatever. I didn't give Joey that nickname. "He asked you out, and you made fun of his skin. He had to transfer schools because of you."

"That's what people are saying?" I asked incredulous.

He arched an eyebrow. "That's not what happened?"

"First of all, I had a boyfriend at the time, which he knew."

"Not everyone keeps up with the minute details of your social life."

"Fine, then he should have known. Isn't the first rule of asking someone out—make sure they're single?"

"You're saying you would have gone out with him if you didn't have a boyfriend?"

I shuddered. "Of course not. He is so not my type."

"Why, because he sits at the wrong cafeteria table?" Killian sneered.

"No, because he dresses up as a storm trooper on the weekend," I snapped. "He invited me to some kind of sci-fi convention thing."

Killian looked startled.

"The point is," I continued, "it doesn't matter. He asked me out, knowing I had a boyfriend, and hoping he could count on guilt or pity to force me into going. I said no, that's it."

He shook his head. "You are a piece of work."

Now I was getting angry. What was this, Beat Up on Alona Day? Someone should have told my mother she'd created a new holiday. "Oh yeah, how is your good friend Joey doing now?"

"What do you mean?"

"He goes to St. Viator, right? In town?"

Killian shrugged uncomfortably. "I don't know."

"I do." I sounded smug, and I didn't care. "I saw him at a basketball game a few months ago when we played their team. His skin was clear, and he had his arms around a cute little nerdette, very early Jennifer Garner, as a matter of fact."

"You take credit for that, I see."

"Of course not. I was just honest with him and said no. The world is cruel, Killian, and you should know that better than anyone. People don't get jobs if they show up looking sloppy. Having physical flaws doesn't mean you should rely on pity for dates. Just because your life doesn't automatically work out the way you want it doesn't mean you get to give up and expect the rest of the world to work around you. You have to play within the system to win."

"Says the girl with the perfect face, the perfect body, the perfect life . . ." he intoned.

I should have been pleased that he'd bought into my image; I'd spent years cultivating it and countless, exhausting hours refining and tweaking it, buying just the right clothes, planning just the right thing to say, making it look effortless. But instead, I felt this wave of fury building in my chest. He was going to judge *me*? Like all this so-called perfection just fell in my lap and I should have been more *grateful* or something?

"Let's go," I snapped. "Drive." It was still early. My mother would probably still be passed out. The empty vodka bottles I'd painstakingly arranged yesterday into the word *STOP* on the floor would still be in place. Let him get a good whiff of my perfect life.

He gave me a confused look. "Drive where? We're already here. And"—he checked his cell phone with a grimace—"ten minutes late. Brewster's going to kill me."

I reached over and yanked the gearshift down one notch into reverse, and metal on metal shrieked.

Alarmed, he jammed his foot onto the brake. "Alona! The transmission is not—"

"You want perfect?" I said in flat voice I barely recognized as my own. "I'll show you perfect."

# ❧ 10 ❧

# Will

I'd never seen this side of Alona Dare, and to be honest, it was kind of freaking me out. She'd been silent—other than giving me directions on where to turn—and still, except for her foot jouncing against the floorboards, since we'd left the school parking lot. I'd never realized how much of her was movement, energy, and life—even after death—until seeing her this way.

I turned into a cul-de-sac lined with sprawling brick houses and huge yards. Ben Rogers lived somewhere over here. We weren't far from where Lily had . . . had her accident. This was definitely not my side of town.

"Now what?" I asked. I let the car roll forward slowly, hoping it looked like we were lost and checking addresses.

Probably wouldn't take much for people in this neighborhood to call the cops. One shabby-looking car doing an extended drive-by might be enough.

Alona's foot increased its frantic rhythm and then stopped suddenly. "Nothing," she said after a long moment. "Never mind." But her gaze was fixed on one house in particular. It looked pretty much like all the others. Except all the curtains were pulled tight, a piece of weathered-looking plywood covered one of the upstairs windows, the bushes by the front door and under the huge picture windows were scraggly and overgrown, and the trash cans were tipped over at the foot of the driveway, spilling out little black microwave meal trays and lots of glass bottles. Looking closer, I could see two deep parallel lines, tread marks, in the front lawn, like someone had badly miscalculated the driveway's location.

"This was a bad idea," she said shortly. "Let's just go back to school."

I hit the brakes and stared at her. "You dragged me all the way over here, which is going to make me really late and only piss off Brewster even more, just to look at some random house—"

"Not some random house," she snapped. "My house. Home sweet home."

I froze. Her house? I'd had no clue where she was leading me when we'd started our little road trip, but this was the last thing I would have expected. The base of a broken vodka bottle rolled back and forth in the gutter, capturing my attention like a pocket watch in an old-fashioned hypnotist's routine.

She couldn't have lived *here*. I mean, yeah, I could picture it. Nice neighborhood, a clearly expensive house, but something was obviously wrong on the inside. This did not match the Alona Dare I knew. And that, I realized, had been her point.

"Nice, right?" she asked with no small amount of bitterness. "We're aiming for the whole white-trash-meets-skid-row look. I mean, it could use some sprucing up. Clearly, we're missing an opportunity with the car in the garage instead of on blocks in the yard."

As if she'd commanded it, the dented-up garage door on the house rose. Alona stiffened.

A barefoot blond woman in a barely tied, pink silky robe stumbled out, one hand raised against the light, the other dragging a plastic garbage bag, its contents clanking. The resemblance between the woman and the girl sitting next to me was unmistakable. But it was like looking at old Elvis and young Elvis. You could still see the framework of the beautiful woman she'd once been, beneath the puffiness of extra weight, the rays of wrinkles around her eyes, and the general air of being beaten down by life.

"What are you staring at?" the woman shouted at us. Rather, at me, as I was the only one she could see.

She tottered down the driveway toward us, faster now. The bag dragged behind her, seemingly forgotten in her hand. The broken glass from the trash can gleamed brightly on the ground at the foot of the drive, but it didn't look like it was going to stop her. "Stop staring at me!"

"Um, Alona—"

"Just shut up and get us out of here," she said, her voice tight.

I pulled the steering wheel hard to the left, and the Dodge's tires protested a bit at the sudden change in course. "Do you want to talk about—"

"No."

"You want to go back?" I asked.

"No."

I hesitated. "You know, if there's something holding you here, it might be—"

"I said no!"

I held my hands up. "Okay, okay. Back to school, then." I turned out onto the main street in her former subdivision.

She forced a laugh. "Now you can go back and tell all your little friends about how fucked up Alona Dare really is . . . was. I'm sure it'll be the thrill of their pathetic lives." She turned away from me, flipping her hair over her shoulder, but not before I caught a glimpse of her eyes, shinier than normal.

I cleared my throat. "Unfortunately, everyone I know, myself included, has a pretty fucked-up life, so I doubt they'd be interested."

"You can say that again," she said, but her tone lacked its usual venom. She stayed quiet the rest of the way back to school.

* * *

By the time we reached the parking lot again, I was forty-five minutes late for first hour. In other words, right on time for the start of second hour. Brewster might already be outside looking for people skipping. I was running out of time.

I pulled into my same parking space in the last row. "You doing okay?" I asked Alona.

She turned suddenly, her eyes narrowed. "Why are you being nice to me?" she asked. "Do you feel sorry for me?" Her voice held a dangerous note.

*Like that would be such a horrible thing?* But even I knew better than to say that out loud.

"Just because you know . . . stuff about me now, that doesn't make us friends," she added.

"I never thought it would," I said, trying not to grit my teeth. How did she do it? Make me want to comfort her one minute and dump her out of the car in the next.

She eyed me carefully. "Then what do you want?"

*This is it, Killian. Make it count.* "Look, we . . . I only have a few weeks of school left. With Miller out of the way, I might have a shot at finishing. I just need to graduate and get out of here."

She frowned. "And go where?"

"Some place less crowded. Fewer people means fewer gho . . . spirits."

"What does that have to do with me?"

"You got the other gho . . . spirits to back off yesterday, to leave me alone."

153

"Until that thing . . . showed up." She shuddered. Then she glanced at me. "Sorry."

I lifted a shoulder. "Like I said, everybody's got their problems."

"So . . ." She cocked her head to one side. "You want me to be, like, your bodyguard."

I grimaced. "A humiliating but accurate description."

"Uh-huh. What do I get in return?"

"I teach you everything I know about this place and how it works."

"You can make the light come for me?"

"No, I told you, it doesn't work like that. That's all you and your . . . issues," I said, avoiding her gaze. "But I think I can teach you how to stop disappearing before—"

"I'm gone for good?" she asked. "No bright light, no nonvirgin mojitos, no shoe stores," she murmured softly.

"What?"

She shook her head. "Nothing." She shoved her hair back, tucking it behind her ears, and turned toward me in her seat. "Let's say I believe you. How does it work?"

And here it was, the worst part. Who said God did not have a sense of humor? "You have to be nice."

She made a face. "Right."

"I'm serious." Distantly, I heard the bell ring, signaling the end of first hour. I couldn't wait any longer, not without jeopardizing what my mother had done to get me back into school. I got out of the car, my keys and cell phone in hand,

and started across the parking lot for school, hoping Alona would follow.

She scrambled out of the car after me. "Be nice?" she hissed. "You said this had nothing to do with heaven or hell or sin or—"

"No, I said I don't explain it in those terms. Too many pitfalls, too many shades of gray when you look at all the religions."

"But, 'Be nice'?" She threw her hands up in the air. "That's totally the whole 'Do unto others' thing."

"Yeah, but it's also a basic scientific principle," I pointed out. "Ask any of the science club kids, they'll tell you. While you're here, you're primarily a form of energy. Being positive allows more energy to flow through you, helping you stay here. Negative energy, like when you say all those clever and nasty things about people, drains you, eating away at your ability to be here. In simple terms, it's like a battery. Being nice helps you recharge."

She stopped abruptly.

Looking back over my shoulder, I found her standing there, her arms folded across her chest. "I'm a *battery*?"

"I said, in simple terms . . . but, yeah."

Defiance flashed in her eyes. "I'm not going to say I love it when it rains, that ugly people are beautiful, or that I like your T-shirt."

"What's wrong with my shirt?" I demanded.

She ignored me. "I just won't. I've spent too many years lying already." Her expression held a darkness I'd never seen before . . . until today.

I recalled the way she'd frozen when her mother had appeared outside and felt my anger soften. "Look, you don't have to lie. In fact, you can't. It has to be genuine, remember?"

She jerked her head in a nod.

"Now, you said something not nice about my shirt. So say something nice instead."

She arched her eyebrow. "About that shirt? Impossible."

I sighed. "Fine. It's your fate. If you want to spend the rest of your time—"

"You have nice teeth," she blurted out.

I stared at her.

She lifted a shoulder. "What, I have a thing for white, even teeth, okay? It's not a big deal," she said, shifting her arms across her chest.

"Nice teeth," I repeated slowly.

"I would have said you had a nice smile, if I'd ever seen it to know," she snapped, and I couldn't help it, I started to laugh.

"It's not that funny," she muttered when I doubled over, my sides aching. She was right. It wasn't that funny, but it was that last bit of ridiculousness that broke through the tension I'd been carrying around inside of me since yesterday.

"Straight and white teeth are a sign of good health," she persisted. "They can be a very attractive feature." Her mouth started to curve into a reluctant smile.

"Ask you to say something nice," I gasped, "and you picked the smallest, most insignificant—"

"It's not insignificant to me." She strode forward and gave me a gentle push on the shoulder, but she was smiling at least. "Dental hygiene is very important. Who wants to kiss a mouth full of yucky yellow teeth?" She shuddered.

It took a second for her words to sink in. "Who said anything about kissing?" I tried to sound casual while my heart thundered in my chest. Like I said, every guy has his fantasy, and for better or worse, since the sixth grade, mine had always centered on Alona Dare.

She rolled her eyes. "Please. I meant it metaphorically. Besides, how are *you* going to kiss *me*?"

Stung, I stiffened my shoulders. "I've never had any complaints. I'm a good—"

She kept talking like I hadn't said anything at all. "You'd look like a loon. Your head all tilted, tongue sticking out." She threw her hands up in the air, like she was holding on to someone's neck, closed her eyes, tilted her head dramatically, and waggled her tongue around outside her mouth.

I snorted. She looked ridiculous, and she had a point.

She stopped and opened her eyes. "So you do have a sense of humor. Never would have guessed that." Her gaze shifted to something behind me. She cocked her head sideways. "You're going to need it, too. Trouble at ten o'clock."

I turned to my left about a quarter turn and saw nothing but the football field.

"No," she said impatiently. "Ten. Ten o'clock." She pulled my shoulders and yanked me around to the right.

"That's two o'clock."

"For you, yeah! I meant ten o'clock . . . whatever. Just look." She raked her hand through her hair impatiently.

"Time passes clockwise here in this universe. . . ." I trailed off, seeing Principal Brewster approaching, his shiny shoes crunching in the gravel and raising clouds of dust. "Oh, crap."

"Now, just listen to me," Alona said.

"I'm not going to suck up to him," I snapped.

She put her hands on her hips. "Who said anything about sucking up? I'm protecting my own interests here. So just listen." She took a deep breath. "He wants you to say something stupid. Just like the cops want to catch you speeding."

"Hey, I have an uncle who's a cop," I protested.

"It doesn't matter. You know what I mean. They have quotas they have to meet. Brewster has a reputation to maintain as a hard-ass. If you give him the opportunity, he'll use you to do it. So just"—she shrugged—"don't give in."

"That's your advice?" I asked, raising an eyebrow.

"No," she smirked. "This is. Be nice."

I stared at her. "What?"

"Be nice."

"Oh, no."

"What? It works for me but not for you?" she demanded.

"It's not the same, at all."

"Whatever." She rolled her eyes. "You don't have a lot of choices here. Just try it." She folded her arms over her chest and stepped back as Brewster approached.

"Good morning, Principal Brewster," I said through gritted teeth.

He stopped short, his dress shoes sliding in the gravel, and stared at me. Probably because it was the first time I'd ever voluntarily spoken to him. "Mr. Killian. What are you doing out here?"

"No sarcasm," she whispered urgently in my ear, "and say 'sir.' He totally gets off on that."

I turned away from Brewster and faked a loud cough to cover my words to Alona. "Why would I want to do that?"

"Because he'd get even more pleasure from kicking you out," she pointed out.

I took a deep breath and turned back to face him. "Sorry, sir. I overslept, and then I had to finish a phone call." I gave him my best sunny smile and held up my cell phone.

"Not a bad start," Alona said. "Now don't blow it."

A flicker of uncertainty crossed Brewster's face. He couldn't tell whether I was being serious or not. "No loitering. Classes started forty-five minutes ago. You're either in or you're out."

"I do apologize for my tardiness," I said, with a little more edge than I intended. I couldn't help it, the guy just set me off.

"Careful," Alona murmured near my ear. She was so close I could feel her T-shirt brushing my arm. Not an unpleasant experience.

I pulled a folded-up square of paper from my pocket. "Here's a note from my mom, excusing my absence yesterday."

Brewster snapped the paper from my hand, his brows

furrowing. "Surprise, surprise. A mama's note for a mama's boy."

I stepped toward him, my hands clenching into fists.

"Uh-uh," Alona said, placing one cool hand on my upper arm. "See what he's doing? He's pushing a button he knows you'll react to. Look at his eyes."

With a grimace, I looked up and met Brewster's gaze. His dark eyes shone with amusement and eagerness. He was playing a game.

"He wins if you react," she said. "Haven't you ever had a parent pull this kind of crap on you?"

No, I hadn't. My mother, emotional and overwrought as she could be, could never direct her emotions in such a manipulative manner, and my dad . . . well, he had too much going on as it was to mess with my mind. But it certainly gave me even more insight into Alona's home life. Scary.

"Very well, Mr. Killian. We're honored you could join us once again today." Brewster leaned in a little closer. "You will, however, serve two days of in-school suspension under my supervision for your attitude and mouthing off yesterday in my office. And"—he smiled—"there is the small matter of your tardiness this morning."

"I have a note," I protested.

"It says nothing about being late here." He turned the note from my mother over, pretending to look for additional writing.

"You want another note?" I asked dully. This being

cooperative was far more exhausting than simply beating his face in.

He tucked his hands behind his back and rocked forward on his toes. "I think a detention would serve nicely as punishment, don't you?"

An extra hour in this hellhole? "I think you're full of—"

Alona jabbed me sharply in the ribs, and I flinched. "Buttons," she hissed.

Brewster watched me with a raised eyebrow.

"Fine, detention. Whatever," I mumbled.

"Good." He nodded sharply. "After you." He pivoted and extended his arm toward the school in a sweeping gesture.

I swallowed back a sigh and started toward the building again. I hated doing anything, though, that seemed like his idea or his request.

"See?" Alona whispered in my ear. "That wasn't so—"

"Before I forget, Mr. Killian," Brewster said behind me, "I must compliment you on your . . . interesting taste in music."

I froze.

"I expected much more screaming and thrashing about, but Beethoven, Tchaikovsky, and Pachelbel? Not exactly stars of the MTV today."

First of all, it was MTV2 today. They don't even play music on MTV, and it's not "the" MTV. Second, he'd been listening to my iPod? Marcie's clean white earbuds had been in his crusty old man ear holes?

Clenching my fists, I started to turn. Brewster

maybe would get his fondest wish of kicking me out. It would be worth it to hit him just once. To feel his jaw collide with my knuckles and know that the resulting bruise on my hand would be a trophy worth showing off.

Alona was whispering something frantically in my ear. ". . . Falling right into his trap. God, you're terrible at this. Don't you have any self-control?"

"Say something nice," I said to her automatically.

"What did you say?" Brewster drew up even with me, frowning.

"Oh, for crying out loud," Alona muttered. "Fine. I think you're doing the right thing, standing up for yourself against a bully, but this is a game and you have to learn to play by the rules if you want to win."

Technically, I wasn't sure if that counted as something nice given that she was still criticizing me. . . .

As if reading my thoughts, she continued, in a rather grumpy tone. "Your eyes aren't nearly as creepy-looking as I first thought they were. They're kinda . . . nice."

"Gee, thanks," I said.

"What?" Brewster was starting to sound a little annoyed. "Mr. Killian—"

"I said, you said something nice. Thanks for that," I improvised. It was close enough to what I'd actually said that he probably wouldn't catch it, and throwing him off his game even just this little bit had dramatically reduced the urge to hit him. Or maybe it wasn't just throwing Brewster off, but also what Alona had said. "Kinda nice" from the Queen of

Put-downs and Dirty Looks was practically a song of praise.

Brewster looked taken aback.

"I'll burn you a CD if you want," I offered, just to watch him squirm.

His mouth worked silently for a long moment as he stared at me. Before he could pull himself together enough to lecture me on federal laws regarding unauthorized copying of music, Jesse McGovern's car sped past us into the parking lot, throwing up bits of gravel and a huge cloud of dust as he spun into one of the last remaining parking spaces.

Brewster's mouth snapped shut, and he stalked off toward Jesse without another word.

"Not too shabby for a beginner," Alona observed near my shoulder, the ends of her silky hair brushing my arm.

"Thanks." I stood still, hoping foolishly that she'd stay close, but she glided away, just as smooth and graceful as she'd been in life. "That was the easy part."

She frowned. "What do you mean?"

I pointed to the front doors of the school, where even from this distance, I could see a crowd gathering. A flash of a pink dress, the dull gleam of a mop bucket being pushed toward the front, an early-eighties Afro standing several inches above the heads of the rest . . . no question who was waiting for me, even if I wasn't close enough to see their faces.

"Oh, them." Alona waved her hand dismissively. "I can handle them."

I raised an eyebrow at her. "Without being cruel?"

Her shoulders sagged. "But I'm doing a nice thing by helping you out. . . ."

I shook my head. "If you want to risk it . . ."

She gave an exaggerated sigh. "All right, all right. Keep them away from you and not be mean to them." She rested her hands on her hips and tossed her hair back. "I mean, how hard can it be? I was elected homecoming queen three times, you know. Winning people over comes naturally to me."

Right. I should be prepared to run, just in case.

## ❧ 11 ❧

# Alona

"Ready?" Killian asked under his breath as we reached the sidewalk leading to the main doors.

"Sure." I rolled my eyes. He was acting like we were going to war, or something. Whatever. Unless Killian's dad showed up all dark, twisted, and shadowy again, in which case all bets were off, they were just people. Dead people, but still. I am a people person. Let's face it, you can't win popularity contests—which is pretty much what high school is from orientation to graduation—if you don't know how to work the crowd.

Speaking of which, the crowd was now headed this way, swarming through the doors—literally walking through the glass and metal, of course—shouting and clamoring for Killian.

"Here we go," he said under his breath.

The spirits surrounded him, elbowing and shouldering me back out of their way.

"Watch it," I protested, but I doubted anyone even heard me. The noise was unbelievable. All these voices, yelling and pleading, at once.

"You came back. I told you he would—"

"Never said he wouldn't."

"One small favor. Please you have to—"

"My granddaughter needs to know that her mother—"

I realized I could no longer see Killian in the middle of all of them. They'd swallowed him up.

"Hey," I tried. Shouting at them had worked yesterday. "Hey, dead people." The girl in the fugly pink polka-dot prom dress tossed me a dirty look over her shoulder, but no one else even seemed to notice me.

This could be a problem.

I must confess, I'm not exactly used to being ignored. So, I may have gone a little overboard.

Ducking my head, I pushed my way through the crowd, ignoring all the grunts of pain and shouts of protest as I stepped on feet and my elbows connected with rib cages. Killian stood dead center, his shoulders hunched and his eyes closed, looking like he was praying for someone to save him. Well, I didn't know anything about that, but I knew that I would not stand for these loser-y types pushing me around. Killian shouldn't have either, not when he had something they wanted. He should have been the one in control, for

God's sake, but whatever. He couldn't take care of himself, so that left me room to do it for him while he helped me. Everybody wins, I guess.

I spun around to face most of them, putting my back against Killian's. He stiffened for a second before evidently figuring out it was me. "All right, listen up, freaks."

"Freaks? What does she mean by—"

"—Suffering from delusions of grandeur."

"Just ignore her. She doesn't have any say here."

This last bit was from my friend, the creepy janitor, who actually tried to shove me away from Killian while he was talking.

"Oh, no, you don't." I slapped at his hands. "Killian is mine. Mine, mine, mine. You want something from him, you come to me, first."

Then the weirdest thing happened. As soon as the words left my mouth, all the ghosts . . . er, spirits, froze up. They just went totally stiff, no pun intended. Then this blast of wind came out of nowhere and knocked them all back, like they were dresses on a rack. They hovered, wobbling in the wind, about three feet back from us.

I shivered, but the wind didn't move me. "What is going on?"

Killian didn't answer.

I elbowed him in the back, and he grunted. "Ouch!"

"I asked you a question. Open your eyes and tell me what's going on."

His back moved against mine as he straightened up and

looked around. He drew in a sharp breath. "That is so . . ."

"Weird? Freaky? Utterly random?" I tossed adjectives at him, hoping to keep him talking and explain what we were looking at.

"I don't know," he said finally. "I've never seen anything like this before. Except . . ." He paused.

"Oh, my God," I snapped, "talking to you is like pulling a backflip into the splits."

"What?"

"Awkward, painful, and not particularly useful in a routine." I spun around to face him. "Except what?"

"Yesterday," he said slowly. "In the hallway. When you got them to back off . . ."

I frowned, trying to remember. "Yeah, you're right. This weird breeze totally kicked up from nowhere, but it wasn't anything like this." I waved my hand at the stiffened stiffs.

"What did you say?"

I stared at him. "I said, what happened yesterday wasn't anything like—"

"No, I mean, what did you say yesterday when it happened?" Killian looked like a man with an idea.

I shrugged. "I don't know. I don't remember. 'Hey, you dead people, back off'?"

He looked around as if expecting a wind, but nothing happened. He sighed. "What did you say today? Do you remember that?" he asked with some sarcasm.

I made a face at him. "Bite me."

"I'm serious. What did you say?"

I rolled my eyes. "Nothing special. You were right there. You heard me."

"Just . . ."

"All right, all right. I said that they'd have to come through me to get to you."

A light wind kicked up again, blowing Killian's hair back from his face. I held my breath, waiting for it to toss me away like the others, but the air simply flowed around me.

"That is so cool," he murmured. He looked at me, his pale eyes lit with delight.

I folded my arms across my chest, taking in the frozen faces with a shiver. "Don't thank me yet. What does it mean?"

He shook his head, turning in a circle to see them all. "I don't know. I think it might—"

"Second thoughts, Mr. Killian?"

We both spun around to find Brewster striding up the sidewalk, a sullen Jesse McGovern in tow.

"Shit," Killian muttered. Then in a louder voice, "No, sir, Mr. Brewster." He looked over at me with a questioning glance.

"What?" I shrugged. "My work here is done. They aren't going to bother you. Ever again, it looks like." I frowned. "So, go to class or suspension or whatever. Find me when you're done, and you can teach me more stuff."

"You sure?" he asked.

"Yeah," I said. At the same time, Brewster, now a few feet from us, asked, "Sure of what, Mr. Killian?"

Killian gritted his teeth and started toward the building.

Oddly enough, I felt a little . . . sad to see him go. Now that he wasn't being quite so annoying and trying to run away from me, it was kind of nice to have him around, a relief to be not so alone anymore. Even if it was with weird Will Killian. He hadn't even made me feel bad about what he'd seen at my house.

I edged around the frozen spirits to park myself on one of the wooden benches in the Circle. There was something just a little creepy about standing there by myself in the middle of all of them. Like they were just waiting for something to happen and . . .

The doors clanked shut behind Killian, and a ripple spread across the spirit crowd. One by one, they broke free of whatever had been holding them . . . and they all turned toward me. Some of them seemed, perhaps, a little angry. The creepy janitor guy was actually cracking his knuckles in anticipation.

I stood up, surprised to find my knees shaking. Hmmm. "You have to come through me to get to him," I said quickly.

But . . . no strange wind, no freezing in place.

"Gladly," the janitor said, advancing toward me.

I threw my hands up to cover my face and gave a much too girlie shriek. Though, if I'd had a chance to think about it, I would have wondered what they could do to me. I mean, I was already dead.

"What," a disgusted female voice spoke up, "are you doing?"

I lowered my hands slowly and found them all forming

a line, some of them pushing and shoving, but nonetheless, a line with me at the head of it. The polka-dot princess was second behind the janitor and leaning out around him to stare at me.

"Well . . . what are *you* doing?" This seemed a reasonable question to ask.

She frowned at me. "Would you rather we take numbers?"

"Huh?"

"No question," the janitor said, "this one is as stupid as she looks."

"Hey!"

"Look, honey . . ." The young man I'd seen in the hallway yesterday with Will, the one in the old-fashioned blue military uniform, stepped out of line. "Save my spot," he said over his shoulder to a young guy wearing a short stubby tie over his white dress shirt, before he walked toward me. A few boos emanated from the back of the line, but he waved them away. "I ain't cutting. I'm just trying to help her. All of you shut up."

He turned to me. "Sweetheart, we all heard you. We have to come through you to get to him." His voice held tinges of a New York accent, but he looked familiar. . . .

He must have seen me trying to place him, because he offered his hand for a handshake. "Robert Brewster the first."

I shook his hand automatically. "Brewster as in Principal Brewster?" If the principal was being haunted, that would go a long way in explaining his pissy mood.

He beamed. "That's my boy."

"Your son?"

He frowned at me. "My grandson." He waved a hand at his uniform. "This is World War II. Can't you tell how old . . . Oh, forget it. You young people have no sense of history." He shook his head.

I shrugged.

"None of that's my point anyway. This is. You volunteered to be his guide, so you tell us how you want to hear from us."

I stared at him. "I don't . . . I don't understand."

"Told you. Stupid," the janitor muttered.

"That's enough out of you," Grandpa Brewster said over his shoulder, and the janitor shut up immediately. Then he turned back to me. "Look, I'm sure you're a real nice girl and you got no idea what you got yourself into back there, but you're not leaving us any choices or helping us out at all."

"Sorry?" I offered, still having no idea what he was talking about.

He let out a deep sigh. "Okay, look, let's just start at the beginning."

Someone in line groaned.

"Just shut up," he shouted at them. He rolled his eyes at me. "So impatient, you wouldn't think they was already dead, right?"

I nodded. It seemed the best thing to do.

"So here it is . . . We're all dead and we all have last requests. You with me so far?"

I nodded again.

"There are things that maybe are holding us here, keeping us from moving into the light."

"Maybe?" I asked.

He shrugged. "We don't really know. We're guessing."

"Okay," I said slowly. Seemed like kind of a bad thing to guess about, but whatever. I wasn't doing much better.

"Anyway, it's pretty rare to find one among the living who can hear and see us, like your boy Will."

"He's not *my* boy," I protested, and immediately sensed a sudden rise in tension. I looked and found all of them staring at me, as if I were on the verge of denying something important. Shoot. "Okay, he's mine, like in the 'he helps me, I help him' way, but not in the boyfriend/girlfriend way."

Grandpa Brewster shook his head like he couldn't believe what he was hearing. "Whatever. Point is, you claimed him. He's yours. So, if we want him to do something for us, we got to go through you. Plain and simple."

"Go through as in . . ."

"The line, sweetheart." He gestured impatiently to the spirits standing behind him. "We'll all wait for our turn to tell you what we need him to do for us, and then you tell him." He shook his head. "God almighty, I'm beginning to think that bus scrambled your brains into eternity."

"Told you," the janitor muttered.

"Wait, wait." I held up my hand. "I don't understand."

"What a shock," the janitor said, a little louder.

I switched my attention to him. "You, move to the back of the line."

His mouth fell open in protest. "You can't do that."

"She can and she just did," Grandpa Brewster pointed out. "Move it."

Muttering under his breath, the janitor stuffed his hands in his pockets and slouched his way toward the end of the line.

"No calling me bad names," I yelled after him. Then I turned back to Grandpa Brewster. "So if I have all of this power just because I said Killian is mine, how come one of you didn't just claim him or whatever before I did?"

A low murmur rose from the line, the spirits whispering and talking among themselves suddenly.

"What?" I asked. "What did I say?"

"None of us knew about him until yesterday," Grandpa Brewster said, glaring at the people in line over his shoulder. "He was real good at hiding among the others."

"Okay, but you still had plenty of time to—"

"She deserves to know the truth, Bob," the pink-polka-dot girl spoke up. Then she gave me an evil gleeful grin. "Nobody claimed him because nobody wants to be what you are."

"Liesel," Grandpa Brewster said in a warning voice.

I frowned at her. "Everyone always wants to be what I am. What are you talking about?"

"You're a spirit guide now. You're at everyone's beck and call, but especially his, the medium's."

Suddenly, I felt cold all over. I shook my head. "No."

She sighed impatiently. "Been waking up in strange places lately?"

I stared at her. I hadn't woken up on the road since yesterday morning. It had been close this morning, but no . . . I'd found myself inside Killian's car.

"Wherever he is, that's where you are, right?" she prodded.

"That doesn't mean—"

"You tied yourself to him. You're his guide." She eyed me with a nasty gleam of amusement. "Has he started calling you yet?"

"What?"

"If he thinks hard enough about you, concentrates on you long enough, poof! You're dragged away from whatever you were doing, wherever you were, to wherever he is."

I felt a little sick. Could that be true?

Liesel stared up at the sky, her hand tapping her chin. "What is that phrase the kids use today? Oh, yeah. You're his bitch, his spirit-world bitch." She laughed delightedly at her own cleverness.

"Hey, Liesel, you're looking a little thin today, don't you think?" I asked. "A little more see-through than usual?"

Her laughter immediately ceased, and she stared down at herself. "No, I'm not . . . am I? Oh, God. Eric? Eric, where are you?" She wandered out of her place in line, looking for someone else to verify her state of existence.

"That wasn't very nice," Grandpa Brewster admonished.

I thought about that for a second. "Your hair looks . . . great, very healthy," I called after her.

Grandpa Brewster stared at me.

I shrugged. "It's the best I could do and still be honest. Besides which, she was being mean first."

He opened his mouth, as if to protest, and then lifted his shoulders. "Fair enough."

"So, is what she said true?" I asked.

He hesitated long enough that I didn't need to hear his answer.

"Forget it," I said firmly. "I am nobody's bitch, spirit world or not."

"I certainly wouldn't have put it that way," Grandpa Brewster said. "It's very disrespectful, but—"

"But nothing. I don't *belong* to Killian."

"You're denying the connection?" Grandpa Brewster asked casually.

"I . . ." It dawned on me that if I said yes, they'd probably all sail right past me into the school and begin bugging Killian again. He'd get kicked out of school and then locked up in some nuthouse, and I'd be stuck here forever. Then again, if he liked having a spirit guide well enough, it sounded like I might be stuck here anyway. But he'd promised to help me. The question was, did I believe him?

"Well?" Grandpa Brewster's impatience showed through.

Looking at it from a purely selfish perspective, if I didn't help Killian out with these guys, he wouldn't be able to help me, even if he wanted to. Of course, that didn't mean he *would* help me, but he'd seemed pretty willing to do so before, and besides which, even if he changed his mind, I can be *very* persistent. It's part of my charm.

"No," I said finally. "I'm not denying it."

Groans rose up from the line.

"Oh, just quiet down," I snapped.

"All right then," Grandpa Brewster said with a sigh. "Then how do you want us? In a line, first come, first serve? Alphabetically?"

"Oh, no," I said, shaking my head and holding my hands out in front of me in the classic "stop" position. "Just because I'm claiming Killian"—I refused to think of it the other way around—"doesn't mean I've got anything to do with you."

That shut them up for a second.

"You'd turn your back on your own kind?" Grandpa Brewster asked, astonished.

"None of you are my kind . . . except possibly her." I tilted my head toward a pretty blond, pony-tailed girl in a poodle skirt, tapping her saddle shoe impatiently against the sidewalk, about halfway down the line. "If she dressed better."

"Some of us have waited years, decades even, to say our piece," Grandpa B. said. "You think we like being stuck here?"

I frowned. Now that he mentioned it . . . "No, probably not."

"You're going to deny us our one chance to make things right for ourselves?" he asked. "People like Will, the special ones, they don't come along very often."

I felt a twinge of guilt. No one had mentioned *this* part of the bodyguard job. "You don't even know if he can help you. He said he doesn't know what makes one person get stuck and another get pulled into the light."

"But you won't even let us try," Grandpa Brewster pointed out.

"Why does it have to be me?" I tried to sound petulant instead of whiny. Trust me, there's a very fine but important difference between the two.

"What are you going to do instead?" Grandpa demanded. "Spy on the living? That gets old real quick."

"No, I have other things to do. I have a life. An afterlife."

"Like what?" Grandpa asked, amused. "Knocking stuff down, making scary sounds to frighten the bejesus out of the living?"

"How did you know that?" I demanded.

"Trust me, honey, if anyone has that vindictive look, it's you."

"Oh. Thanks?"

"You know pulling those shenanigans will turn you into nothing faster than just about anything else," Grandpa advised.

"I know that . . . *now*." I plopped back down on the bench, not even taking care to cross my legs just right so the little fat dimple on the side of my left thigh wouldn't show. I was too depressed. All of this was depressing.

"Help your boy help us," Grandpa urged. "It's better than sitting around staring at the living. Besides, it'll count as a good deed. Maybe you just need a big one to catch their attention upstairs, so they'll send the light for you."

I looked up at him. "I thought Liesel said—"

He waved his hand impatiently. "Don't listen to her. She

meets one former spirit guide while she's stuck with Claire on vacation in Puerto Rico, and she thinks she's an expert. None of us had ever met one of the ghost-talkers before yesterday. Nobody knows how it works. Everything we know is based on rumors that keep circulating here on this side of things. Plus whatever we see on television." He shrugged. "You may have a shot to help yourself out, kid. Don't blow it."

I sighed. "All right, all right. I'll try. What do I have to do?"

## ❦ 12 ❦

# Will

Normally, being trapped in the tiny, overheated, and infrequently used special ed room with Brewster coming in and out every ten minutes would have been a nightmare. Especially with Grandpa Brewster and the others knowing who I was and what they could do to get my attention. After the first fifteen minutes, I'd have been huddled under my desk, trying to protect myself from their shoves and pinches, and that would not have gone over well with Brewster.

But this morning . . . it was like nothing I'd ever experienced. It was quiet in the little room, which I suspected used to be a supply closet from the lack of windows and the holes in the wall where shelves used to be, and I was alone. Really and truly alone. Not a single ghost popped through to bitch and moan or try to trick me into talking.

Brewster stopped by midway through the morning and tossed Marcie at me. I probably should have been mad that he didn't return her first thing, like he was supposed to. But no way was I using Marcie until I'd completely disinfected her headphones or bought new ones, and besides, I didn't need the music. At times, the complete and utter silence around me actually made my ears ring. It was great. Whatever Alona was doing, it was working.

Then lunch happened.

Mrs. Piaget stopped by a little before noon. "I've got cafeteria duty today. Mr. Brewster is meeting with the superintendent at the regional office now, but he says you can come with me to get some food. You have to come back here to eat, though." She gave me an apologetic smile.

"Okay." I pushed back from my desk, stood up, and stretched. It felt good to be able to sit still and concentrate on what I was supposed to be doing instead of putting so much energy into blocking everything else out.

"You seem better today," Mrs. Piaget said when I joined her in the main hallway.

"Not getting expelled really agrees with me."

"I can see that," she said with a startled laugh.

I followed her down the hall to the caf. Joonie, with her ratty old book bag strapped across her chest, waited right outside the doors, near the start of the serving line. She straightened up when she saw me, but her gaze flicked to Mrs. Piaget and she didn't come any closer.

Mrs. Piaget hesitated and then turned to me. "Remember, food and then back to the room. Don't give him any excuses." No need to specify the "him" in this situation, I guess.

I nodded. "Thanks."

Mrs. Piaget disappeared through the doors to the caf, and I approached Joonie. This close up, I could see something was clearly wrong. Purple shadows of exhaustion looked like bruises under her eyes, dark streaks of makeup were smeared on her cheeks, and one of the holes in her lip was empty and flaked with dried blood.

I resisted the urge to touch my own lip in reflexive sympathy. "What's going on? Are you—"

From down the hall, a group of rowdy freshman surged toward us. Joonie grabbed my arm and yanked me into the caf, off to the side.

"They're going to let her die."

*Who*, the word came to the tip of my tongue, but I shut my mouth in time. I knew who, of course. "What are you talking about?"

She fiddled with the strap of her bag, plucking at one of the buttons she'd pinned to it. This one read, *Let's just say I have a problem with authority.* It was a gift from Lily last year before everything went south.

"I went to visit Lily after school yesterday, and I heard some of the nurses talking." She shifted her weight back and forth, pacing without taking a step. "It's about her parents' insurance or something. They're going to take her feeding tube out and let her starve to death. . . ." Her breath caught in her throat and she had to stop, choking on her emotion. "Or, they're going to take her away, put her in some more permanent facility back in Indiana somewhere."

I took an involuntary step back, her words like a slap out of nowhere. I knew, at some point, this day would come. I just hadn't realized it would be today.

Her eyes welled with tears. "What are we going to do?"

Joonie and I had been there, visiting Lily, since the first day it was allowed. I'd touched her hand, seen her eyes. She was gone. The essence of whatever made Lily Lily had moved on a long time ago. She hadn't even stuck around long enough to haunt her hospital room. Or the place where her car had crashed. I'd checked there, too. Just to be sure. So, there was nothing left to do. "Joonie, we can't—" I tried.

"You don't understand. It's my fault she was there in the first place." Tears rolled down her cheeks, and she didn't bother to wipe them away.

"Why, because you guys had a fight months before and *she* stopped talking to *us*?"

I'd figured Joonie and Lily would work their issues out, and didn't think a whole lot more about it. Until Joonie and I'd arrived for the first day of our senior year, Lily's junior year, and watched as Lily, dressed in a short skirt and tottering unsteadily on high heels, clung to the fringes of the junior-class elite. She'd walked past us like she didn't know us, her nose up in the air. Two and half weeks later, she'd lost control of her mom's station wagon and wrapped it around a tree.

I shook my head. "J, don't do this to yourself. You tried to apologize for whatever happened, and she wouldn't listen. She chose to hang out with those people, and she chose to go to that party. We didn't have anything to do with that."

As I said it, I realized it was true. Maybe I could have changed things, maybe I could have saved her if I'd heard my phone that night. But she was the one who'd chosen to dump us as friends. All I'd done was miss a phone call from someone who hadn't spoken to me in months. She didn't even leave a message.

I felt lighter suddenly, relieved in some way. I would still have given anything to see Lily whole and healthy again, even if she didn't want to be my friend. The fact that I wouldn't, though, was not my fault. It was the combination of a hundred factors, only one of which—answering my phone—I'd had control over.

However, my words did not have the same effect on Joonie. "You don't understand," she said tonelessly, her eyes fixed on some invisible point in the distance.

I caught her by the shoulders and shook her gently. "You have to stop. This wasn't your—"

It was at that exact moment I saw Alona on the stage, surrounded by every dead person I'd ever seen haunting the halls at Groundsboro High, and I knew I was in trouble.

First, if you're wondering why our cafeteria has a stage, it's the same reason we have cafeteria tables on different levels. Our cafeteria doubles as an auditorium, which some flipping genius dubbed a "cafetorium." As you walk out of the lunch line, you're on the same level as the stage but directly across the room from it. Then there are steps leading down to the various tiers of tables. Alona's crowd, the so-called first tier, hang out, ironically enough, on the lowest level, what serves as the orchestra pit when the drama club decides to shed its student-written, angsty, and apocalyptic plays for the rare cheerful musical. It's the farthest from teacher supervision, so no surprise in their choice there. From there, the level of popularity decreases as you go up. Joonie, Erickson, and I eat in the glass-enclosed courtyard when it's nice enough, which puts us completely off the map as far as popularity is concerned. All the better.

But the stage . . . the stage was the holy grail for the first-tier crowd. Clearly, it was a position they felt *should* be theirs—sitting high above the disgustingly average crowd—but this was one benefit they were denied. Ever since some kid, no doubt a first tier, broke his leg jumping off the stage a few years ago, no one is allowed up there during lunch except the members of the drama club, and then only if they're preparing for a production. This winter, everyone got high on the fumes when they painted sets for their spring production, *Death and Sundaes.* I have no idea what it was about, but it involved a lot of black-and-red painted sets and complaining from the first-tier girls when the occasional spatter came flying in their direction.

So, really, I guess it shouldn't have come as a surprise that Alona had taken advantage of her invisible-to-most-of-the-world status to claim the stage for herself. Still, it was more than a little shocking to find her sitting on a barstool behind a section of what appeared to be a 1950s diner countertop (another prop . . . don't ask, I have no idea how it relates to *death* or *sundaes*), taking what appeared to be notes while ghosts waited patiently in a long and winding line for their turn to speak with her individually.

"What the hell?" I muttered.

Joonie snapped out of it enough to look at me, really look at me. "Are you okay?" She rested her cool fingers on my arm. "You look like you've seen a—"

I didn't wait to hear the rest. Pulling away from her light grip on my arm, I started down the stairs, heading toward the stage. I won't be as melodramatic as to say that the entire cafetorium noticed and held their collective breaths, but I did see heads turning. After all, I hadn't been lower than the third tier since starting here almost four years ago. That was just like asking one of the first- or second-tier jocks to hit you, a fight you'd also be blamed for starting.

"Will, what are you doing?" Joonie's loud whisper followed me down the stairs, but I didn't turn back.

However, the second my foot touched down on the first-tier carpet, a ripple of noise and movement spread through the room, people turning to whisper and watch. Normal conversations died down until it grew quiet enough that I could have sworn I heard the rustle of the carpet fibers beneath my shoe when I took my first step.

Alona's crowd did nothing at first but stare. After all, this

186

was their inner sanctum; no one dared to knowingly trespass here, and those who found themselves here by some kind of accident or misunderstanding (new kid; geeky guy under the illusion that because Misty had asked to cheat off his chemistry test that he would be allowed to acknowledge her existence; the occasional utopian fool who thought that popular people "are just people too," etc.) usually broke quickly under the weight of a nasty stare from so many perfect faces, and ran away. But not me, oh, not me.

I stayed away from Alona's friends and edged closer to the table of junior-class elites, the second table pushed up against the stage. They still thought they were better than me, but they'd hesitate longer on starting a fight, waiting for the seniors to react first.

When close enough, I pulled the cell phone from my pocket. "What are you doing up there?" I asked, trying to sound casual. "Who are your new friends?"

At first, I didn't think it would work. How would Alona hear me, let alone know that I was talking to her? In this particular case, though, the ear-ringing silence that accompanied my approach into forbidden territory actually benefited me.

"Will?"

I heard her voice, but I dared not look up at the stage. At this angle, I'd look crazy, staring at nothing. Well, *crazier*.

Seconds later, her white gym shoes appeared, and she knelt down, her blond hair swinging over her shoulders, releasing that familiar, sweet, perfumey scent. "What are you doing down here?" She sounded perplexed. "You're going to get yourself killed."

"What am I doing? What are *you* doing?" I asked through clenched teeth. "You've got half the Groundsboro cemetery up there with you."

She glanced back over her shoulder, as if she hadn't been aware of this fact until I mentioned it. "Yeah, well, they just keep showing up. I think someone's passing out flyers or something." She laughed.

"Oh, ha, ha. It's very funny. What are you doing up there?"

She shrugged. "Taking notes. As your spirit guide, it's my job to—"

"As my what?" This time, I couldn't help but stare up at her.

She rolled her eyes. "Your spirit guide. You know, someone who helps you work with the spirits." She paused thoughtfully. "I'm kind of like your manager."

"My what?" I said weakly. I couldn't seem to stop repeating myself.

"Manager. You know, like you're the talent and I'm the one who hooks you up with the people who need you. Besides, it keeps them quiet"—she jerked her head toward the ghosts behind her—"if they think someone is listening, and it gives me a chance to do something nice, right?" She shifted slightly to stare at someone or something over my right shoulder.

"But I—" I didn't even know where to begin.

"Oh, heads up. Nine o'clock. You're about to get your face beat in." She turned her head and gave me a sunny smile. "See, I'm being helpful already."

I started to turn to my left, but then, remembering Alona's previous difficulty with the clock concept when facing me, I turned to the right instead—three o'clock—to find Chris Zebrowski and Ben Rogers approaching.

"If you get out of here right now, they'll probably leave you alone." Alona pushed herself back up to her feet.

"Wait," I said.

"I can't. Do you see how long this line is?" She rolled her eyes with a sigh. "I'm going to be here all day." She shook her head and started back toward her position at the counter.

"Alona," I whispered as loudly as I dared. Nothing like shouting a dead cheerleader's name in the middle of the cafeteria to get people to stare at you. Not that I needed the help.

"What's up, Will Kill? You lost?" Ben Rogers's oily voice came from behind me.

I turned to find him and Chris behind me, ready to face off. Ben had his hands in his pocket, a deceptively relaxed pose, but tension ran through his shoulders. He might have been a rich, lazy son of a bitch, but he didn't shy away from a fight. Next to him, Chris, Alona's ex, made no pretense that this was anything but a fight. A shorter, stockier guy with years of experience on the wrestling team, he stood with his feet apart and fists at the ready.

"No freaks allowed in the first tier," Chris added.

I held up my hands in the "don't shoot" position, my fingers wrapped around my cell phone. "No trouble here, guys. Just taking a call, and I needed better reception. I'm leaving." As much as I hated their privileged asses, I wasn't about to start a fight on their turf. I'd get blamed for it and I'd lose. Two against one wasn't fair. Sixteen against one, as it would end up being when all the sheep jumped in to follow their leaders, was a bloodbath.

I started to walk around them, back toward the stairs, but I didn't get very far. A small wisp of black smoke appeared out of nowhere in the center aisle, on the second-tier steps. It looked like exhaust from an oil-burning car. I stopped, my heart pounding in dread. Almost instantly, as if it had been waiting for me to see it, the little wisp of smoke grew to a roiling and seething mass of black vapor.

"Um, Killian? Gloomy Gus straight-up noon," Alona called from behind me, tension threaded through her voice.

For once she had the clock right. "Yeah, I see him," I said tightly.

I heard her drop down from the stage, landing lightly on the ground behind me. "So what's the plan?" Her voice shook a little, and yet she was still there with me.

"I don't know."

"You don't know what, Will Kill?" Ben eased around to stand in front of me. He smiled, showing a little too much teeth. Chris followed him, slamming his meaty fist into the palm of his other hand in a rather effective use of a cliché.

Damn, I'd forgotten about them.

Everyone in the caf was watching, waiting to see what happened next. Joonie, at the top of the center aisle, seemed to be praying, her hands tucked securely inside her bag, her eyes half closed and her lips moving silently.

Then Gloomy Gus, as Alona had apparently dubbed him, lurched forward suddenly, pouring toward us in a rush.

"Alona, get out of here now," I said sharply and without thinking. The without-thinking part turned out to be kind of key.

"What did you say?" Chris demanded.

Oh, shit.

Twenty minutes later, I sat in the nurse's office with an ice pack against the left side of my face. Okay, so lessons learned: first, talking to a guy's dead girlfriend in front of him, even when he's moved on to greener pastures, is a big mistake. Second, the entity once known as my father, now known as Gloomy Gus, did not like competition. He disappeared, thank God, the moment Chris hit me. Third, Alona Dare may be my spirit guide, whatever that is, but Mrs. Piaget is my guardian angel. She got Mr. Gerry to break up the fight, and remained firm in her conviction that Chris had taken the first swing. I got another detention, but I could live with that.

I leaned back in the uncomfortable molded-plastic chair in the nurse's office, wincing at the new ache in my ribs, and pressed the bag of ice cubes tighter against my swelling cheek.

The chair next to me wiggled and jolted, sending little shocks of pain through my side.

"What is your deal?" I said to Alona, who couldn't seem to sit still, moving from one position to another. We were, fortunately, alone for the moment. Judging that it would not be wise to stuff both Chris and me into such a small room, Nurse Ryerson had stepped out to take care of him. Yeah, I managed to get in a swing or two. Bloodied his nose, at least.

She shifted her feet to the floor and stared at them for a long second before looking over at me. "You defended me. Why would you do that?"

"That's what's bothering you?" I asked. "Technically, I was just defending myself from your boyfriend's fists of fury." I opened my mouth and wiggled my jaw experimentally. Damn, wrestlers could really pack a punch, maybe even more so than the various football players who'd whaled on me in my younger years.

She shook her head with an impatient noise. "Not him. Though"—a faint smile appeared on her face—"that must have really pissed Misty off to see you two fighting over me."

I rolled my eyes. "We weren't fighting over—"

"Also, smooth move shouting my name in the middle of the cafeteria." She slapped my shoulder hard, and the sensation traveled down to my ribs, making me grunt in pain. "But what I meant was you trying to protect me from Gloomy Gus."

"Oh."

"You were just covering your own ass, right? I mean,

I'm your spirit guide now and you probably love the idea of bossing me around too much to give it up this soon."

The words sounded like something she would say, the bitchy arrogance of them, but beneath that, I could hear the question she wasn't asking, the vulnerability she was trying to hide. Had anyone ever defended her in her life, except for when it benefited them? True, she didn't *seem* like she needed much protection, but everyone wants to feel like someone's looking out for them.

She had her head tipped down, pretending to examine her nails. The glossy curtain of her hair hid her face from me. It was the perfect time to say something classy, something that would convince her that even though she drove me crazy sometimes, I admired her strength, even more now that I knew some of what she must have lived through to get it.

"Um . . ." My heart beat fast in the back of my throat, and the words, any words, seemed to have vanished from my brain.

She made a disgusted sound. "Never mind. Forget it." She tossed her hair back over her shoulder.

"Hey," I protested. "You have to at least give me a chance to—"

The door to the nurse's office edged open and Joonie poked her head in, looking around. It didn't take long. The office consisted of a small desk, two chairs, and a cot. The other door leading out of the room led to a microscopic bathroom. "You alone?" she whispered.

Alona rolled her eyes.

"Yeah," I said.

Joonie frowned at me and slipped all the way into the room. "Then who were you talking to?" She slung her book bag down on the floor in front of the chair next to mine, right on Alona's feet.

Alona yelped. "Watch it, freak."

"Nobody. I wasn't talking to anyone. It's *nice* of you to stop by." I glared at Alona.

"Fine. Fine," Alona grumbled. "She's a good friend. Blah, blah, blah."

"Hello? Killian?" Joonie waved her hand in front of my face. "I'm over here." She moved over to sit in Alona's chair and Alona scrambled out of the way to avoid being sat on. "Are you okay?" Joonie's gaze felt too intense, and I had to look away.

"I'm fine."

"I just saw you walk into first-tier territory to take a freaking pretend phone call. Yesterday you had a seizure in the hallway—"

I waved her words away. "I'm fine, okay?" Out of the corner of my eye, I caught Alona frowning at something on the floor.

"No, not okay." Joonie fidgeted with the silver rings in her ear. "You're acting completely bizarre even for you, and I can't worry this much about you and Lily, okay? There's not enough of me." She gave me a shaky smile. "So, just tell me what's going on."

Alona knelt on the floor near Joonie's feet, her head cocked to one side. "Check this out," she whispered, completely unnecessarily. Then, using the effect of my presence around her, she pulled back the top of Joonie's tattered and broken-zippered book bag. The corner of a flat wooden board, decorated with numbers and letters, stuck out. It looked familiar, but I couldn't place it until . . .

I jumped up out of my seat. "Jesus, Joonie, is that a Ouija board?" Yeah, it was just a creepy but harmless kid's game . . . unless you happen to be playing with one around someone like me.

Joonie stopped, her mouth hanging open midword to stare at me and then guiltily at the floor. Her face flushed red and then paled. "I have to go." She stood up and yanked her bag from the floor before bolting from the room.

"Joonie, wait," I said.

She didn't answer, nor did she stop, and the door to the nurse's office slammed shut after her.

I turned to Alona, who now leaned back against the nurse's desk, her arms folded across her chest and a smug look on her face. "How did you do that? How did you know it was in there?"

Alona shrugged. "I'm dead. I know everything now. Like how you look for a little personal time every morning before—"

"Stop," I snapped, trying to pretend my face wasn't turning red. "Death doesn't make you, or anyone else, omniscient." Which meant she was an alarmingly good guesser or I was shockingly predictable. "Try again."

"You are no fun." She sighed. "The edge of the board stuck out for a second when she dropped her stupid, ugly bag on me. Took me a second to recognize it is all." She shrugged. "What's the big deal anyway? Other than it's total proof of her freakiness that she carries that thing around with her."

I shook my head. "It's more than that."

"You don't think that thing actually works . . . do you?" She arched an eyebrow at me.

"Around me, it does."

"Right."

"I'm serious." I lowered the ice bag from my face so I could see her more clearly. "For regular people, it's no big deal, but for me . . ." I paused. "Okay, imagine you're trying to make a call to someone in another country, but you don't have a phone."

"Am I stupid in this example? How do you call without a phone?"

"Just shut up for a second. I'm trying to explain." I took a deep breath. "You want to call, you're concentrating all your efforts on communicating, but with no phone, nothing happens."

"Duh," she muttered.

I ignored her. "Give someone a Ouija board, and you have a phone but no service."

She nodded.

"Use a Ouija board around me and suddenly, you've got a

phone with the megaservice package. Except instead of just sending voices, it's like opening a doorway between the two places. The Ouija board acts as a focus, helps you concentrate and send your energy, but it can't go anywhere without me. Me, whatever I am, I give it power and a place to go, a conduit to travel. Remember, I'm caught in the middle just like you, but I can interact with both sides. Energy on either side is just energy until it finds me, and then it has weight and substance and form. . . ." A trickle of ice water leaked from the bag and ran across my hand, and I shivered from more than the cold.

"So Joonie calls up a couple of dead relatives to come through the doorway for a chat." She shrugged. "What's the big deal?"

"No," I said firmly. "People who are gone, really gone, can't be reached. And reaching out like that . . . you never know who you're going to get. Just because you're dialing a particular person, so to speak, doesn't mean it's going to be that person who answers."

She frowned.

I sighed. "It's like the telephone is ringing, and anyone walking by can pick it up. And some of those who are stuck in between are not people you want to be messing with." Sometimes people were crazy before they died. Sometimes dying made them crazy . . . or crazier. Grandpa B., Liesel, and the rest of them, they were annoying sometimes, but not particularly harmful. That was not the case with others I'd seen and been careful to avoid.

She gave me a scathing look. "I get what you're saying. I'm not stupid." She paused, lifting one hand to her mouth to nibble at her thumbnail before she caught herself and pulled her hand away. "I was just wondering . . . how many times have you seen Gloomy Gus? I mean . . . you know who."

"Yeah, I know," I said dryly. "Ten, twelve times, maybe."

"What makes you think that's . . . your dad?"

I let out a slow breath, lifting the watery ice bag up to my face. "Because I've seen a few suicides come through here, and they're sort of like that, not whole." I gave her a sideways glance. "That's how I knew you didn't hurt yourself intentionally, no matter what Leanne Whitaker is saying."

"Bitch," Alona muttered.

"What were you doing that day anyway?" I asked.

She cocked an eyebrow at me. "My question came first. Why do you think it's your dad?"

I watched her for a long second, and she met my gaze steadily. I opened my mouth to tell her to forget it, but the story of that last morning with my dad poured out of me instead. It was the first time I'd told anyone, except Dr. Miller and Joonie, and I regretted it even as I was still speaking. But Alona just nodded thoughtfully.

"That still doesn't explain why you think it's him, though. Surely there are other people who've . . ." She made a face.

With a sigh, I continued. "It . . . he seems particularly focused on me. Whenever he shows up, he always comes straight after me." I lifted a shoulder, wincing at the pain in my ribs. "He's the only suicide that I've known personally."

"They all look like that?" She pressed. "Big black clouds of smoke or whatever?"

"No, I've never seen one like this before. He's . . . more waves of emotion than anything else. But I've seen lots of different things over the years. What are you getting at?" I asked impatiently.

"Your dad died, like, three years ago, right? That's what you said." She stared at me, daring me to challenge her.

"Yeah, so?"

"When did you start seeing Gus?"

Suddenly, I didn't like the direction this was heading. "That doesn't mean anything. Sometimes it takes a while for spirits to find their way—"

"When?" She kicked at my shin lightly.

I bent down and rubbed my leg with my free hand. "I don't know, about eight or nine months ago, I guess."

Actually, I knew exactly when I'd seen him the first time. It had been the first night the doctors would allow Joonie and me to visit Lily after her accident. My mom had come with us. And after I'd seen Lily and what my gift had indirectly caused, that's when I'd realized I couldn't stay.

"Right after I told my mom I wasn't sticking around after graduation." She'd fled the hospital in tears. That was more than enough probably to call my father from wherever he'd been residing. I'd promised to take care of my mother—it was the last thing I ever said to my father.

"So you're saying that your dad, who knew you were

a ghost-talker, was just hanging around waiting for *three* years for you to do something to piss him off before he tried to talk to you...or kill you, as the case may be?"

When she put it that way, it sounded ridiculous, but Alona didn't know how things worked. Hell, sometimes I didn't even know how they worked. Besides, who else, or what else, could it be?

"You ever see it when Joonie is not around?" Alona asked quietly.

I froze. Against my will, my mind played back all my encounters with the angry ghost and every time, sure enough, Joonie was nearby, if not standing right next to me. "No," I said firmly. "Not possible."

"Why not?" Alona stood up. "Because she's your friend? Did you not see her in the caf today?"

I hadn't realized Alona had noticed her, too. Joonie could have been praying, like I thought. Or maybe she was trying to concentrate on the Ouija board in her bag . . . No. I shook my head. I wouldn't allow Alona's prejudice to taint my thoughts.

"And I don't even want to tell you the weirdness I witnessed from her in your room yesterday. She's, like, in love with you or something, but . . ." Alona frowned. "No, that's not quite right, either. Something is really wrong with that girl."

"Stop it," I snapped. "You don't know her. You don't know anything that we've been through in the last year."

"Oh, what, the mysterious Lily?" She folded her arms

across her chest. "Why don't you tell me? I've asked enough times."

I shook my head. "It doesn't matter. Joonie has no idea what I can do, so she'd never even think of what you're suggesting. Not to mention there's no reason, even if she did. She wouldn't want to hurt me. She's my friend."

Alona dropped into the seat next to me and twisted to face me, tucking her legs beneath her. "Then why," she asked quietly, "did she run away when you asked her about a stupid board game in her backpack?"

Direct hit. When had I ever doubted Alona Dare's intelligence? "She was probably just embarrassed," I insisted. But I'd seen the look on Joonie's face a few minutes ago. If that wasn't guilt, it was a close cousin.

"Uh-huh." She tossed her hair back over her shoulders. "I may be pretty, but I'm not stupid. She is hiding something."

"It's not . . ." Suddenly, I remembered Joonie's shift in intensity, from worrying about Lily to asking me questions. What was that all about?

"I could follow her, I'm real stealthlike these days." Alona turned in her seat again, stretching her long legs out in front of her, and I found myself staring.

"Hey, my face is up here." She snapped her fingers at me, and I jerked my gaze upward.

"You don't have to follow her," I said. "It's Friday. I know exactly where she's going after school." No way would Joonie miss a visit to Lily, not after what she'd told me today.

"So are we going, too, or what?" Alona idly flicked a piece of . . . ghost lint? . . . off her shorts.

I grimaced. "I have detention right after school." I thought about it. "Actually, I have detention today and Monday. I can't afford to skip it."

She brightened. "Oh, good, then you'll have some time to do a little work."

Alarm bells rang in my head. "What are you talking about?"

She raised the hem of her shirt, revealing smooth tanned skin over a tight stomach, her belly button a tiny divot in the taut surface—cheerleading does a body good—and reached into the waistband of her shorts to pull out a stack of small but neatly folded pieces of paper. "Sorry," she said. "No pockets."

I cleared my throat. "No problem."

She handed me the papers, and I took them, still warm from her skin, and unfolded them. The top one read: *R. Brewster. Wants forgiveness from son for being antigay toward him, and grandson to reconcile with his father. Anon. letters?*

Lifting the first sheet aside, I read the second one, or started to, anyway. *Liesel Marks and Eric . . .* I looked over at Alona. "What is all of this?"

"What does it look like? I met with all your spirits and wrote down what they wanted." She flicked her hair away from her eyes. "Hey, did you know that if you die or transition or whatever with something you get to keep it? Thank God that one girl died with a pen and notebook in her purse or I would have had to remember all of this." Leaning closer to me, she pointed to the papers. "I even negotiated for you and got you out of making personal visits or phone calls." She sat back in her chair with a shrug. "Basically, all you have to do is write some letters, find a few lost items. That kind of thing."

"No," I said flatly.

She whipped around in her seat to face me, her hair hitting me in the eyes as she turned. "Are you kidding? I spent my whole morning on this."

I lowered my ice pack and glared at her. "Oh, gee, I'm sorry. Whatever are you going to do with the rest of eternity?"

She took a deep breath, opened her mouth . . . and then stopped. Holding her hands out in front of her, she inhaled and exhaled slowly.

"What are you doing, meditating?"

"No, I'm trying to calm down so I don't kick your ass," she said through clenched teeth.

I swallowed back a sigh. "I appreciate what you tried to do, really, and you helped me out by keeping them occupied but—"

"Listen, I wasn't cool with this either in the beginning." She tucked her hair behind her ears. "I mean, seriously, who am *I* to be your message girl?" She rolled her eyes. "But if you just listen to what they're asking for, it's not—"

"I'm not getting into this again." I held up my hands, papers in one and the ice bag sloshing in the other.

"All they want is what you have. To be able to speak and be heard. That's it. Apparently, whatever you are"—she looked down her nose at me—"is pretty rare. Except maybe in Puerto Rico."

"What?"

She ignored me. "So, if you walk away, they might not get this chance again."

"Chance to do what? Send me on a bunch of useless errands that don't help anyone? I told you. This doesn't work." I held the papers back out to her.

She folded her arms across her chest. "What if it wasn't you and it was your dad trying to get through and some ghost-talker wouldn't help him?"

I froze. "My dad is none of your business."

"Really? It seems to me that he's very much my business since you think he's the one showing up here, knocking you around, and trying to kill you, which, let me tell you, would put a serious crimp in my plans to get out of here." She shuddered. "I don't even want to know what happens if a spirit guide lets her person get killed."

"Alona, just leave it alone," I said wearily.

She examined the tips of her nails. "I think the whole reason you want that scary black cloud thing to be your dad is because at least then you have some kind of contact with him. Otherwise, he just left you hanging, and you of all people know he could have come back to talk to you if he wanted—"

"Enough," I shouted, and threw the papers at her. They

fell to the ground with a dry raspy sound like dead leaves.

"What is going on here?" Nurse Ryerson burst in through the door. She stopped short when she saw me alone in the room.

"Nothing," I said tightly. "Nothing's going on in here."

"Damn right about that," Alona muttered. She stood up and stepped over the papers on the ground, careful to avoid them.

"I thought I heard . . ." Nurse Ryerson's voice faltered. She poked her head in farther to check behind the door, as though someone might be hiding back there.

"That shouting, you mean?" I asked.

She nodded.

I gave a shrug. "Not from in here."

She frowned and slowly backed out the door.

Alona started to follow her.

"Where do you think you're going?" I demanded in a whisper.

She lifted a shoulder in a shrug. "Clearly, you don't need me, and *I* don't have to go to class anymore. One of the few benefits of being dead."

"What about—"

"The spirits? The ones that have been bothering you? I don't know," she snapped. "I had worked out a deal where if you agreed to help them, they'd leave you alone. I guess that's off the table, though, right?"

I sighed. "Alona."

"Good luck with class," she said with faux cheer. "Hope

you like musicals. I'll make sure to tell them *Annie* is your favorite."

"Wait, just wait a—"

Without another word, she slipped through the closed door, humming "Tomorrow" under her breath.

Great. Not only do I have an angry spirit guide, but an angry spirit guide with a vindictive streak and an unnatural knowledge of show tunes. Better and better already.

## ❧ 13 ❧

# Alona

*I* stalked to the end of the main hall, reaching the double glass doors, and stopped. I had no idea what to do or where to go next. Actually, to be honest, I was a bit surprised to find myself intact still. I hadn't exactly been nice to Killian back there, but then again, I was fighting for the right. He hadn't spent the last few hours hearing all the stories, seeing all the faces . . .

Look, I'm no soft touch for hard-luck stories. You make your own bad choices, you have to live (or not) with the consequences. But most of the people I'd talked to earlier were resigned to their fate. They'd come to talk to me after hearing rumors about Killian's ability—the dead apparently *love* to gossip—on the slimmest possibility of hope. Some of them had been here for *years*, watching helplessly as everyone they've ever known or loved had moved on or spiraled into a half life of misery and regret.

Tricia, the girl who'd given me the pen and paper, had been stuck since 1988 (the leg warmers would have been a big clue even if she hadn't told me). She'd chased after their family's dog, Mooshi, when she went out into the street, but Tricia had slipped on an icy spot and hit her head. She'd died almost instantly. All she wanted now was to tell her "little" brother that it wasn't his fault. He'd left the door open, just a crack, after he and Tricia had come home from school, and Mooshi had nosed her way out. He was only eight, and it was just a dumb mistake. But even now, he still blamed himself for Tricia's death, their parents' divorce, and every bad thing that had come after that. According to Tricia, he'd tried to kill himself twice.

*We*, Killian and I, could change that. We could tell Dave what his sister wanted him to know, helping both of them at once. And yeah, maybe it wouldn't work every time. Maybe some of the spirits were deceiving themselves about what was really holding them here, but what about the one or two or five that *weren't*?

A swirl of black in motion in the *H*-branch to the right caught my attention. I spun around, expecting to see Gloomy Gus coming to shred me for real this time. Instead, it was just Joonie emerging from the bathroom, her book bag clutched tightly to her chest. Her face was pale, except for around her eyes where it was red. She looked like she'd been crying.

Tucking her head down, Joonie scurried toward the library. I followed. Killian had said that there was no need to trail her. He knew her schedule on Fridays. He'd never bothered to explain it to me, though, so I'd have to do the detective work on my own. No problem. Wasn't like I had anything else to do right now.

"Hey, Alona!" Creepy janitor guy waved to me with great cheer as I passed him once more mopping the carpet.

God, if Killian didn't come through on at least some of those requests, my reputation was going to be shot all to pieces. I waved back and kept going, following Joonie through the library doors and to one of the computer stations against the wall.

With a nervous glance over her shoulder, she set her bag, now zipped, carefully on the floor next to her.

"Oh, good," I told her. "Now you worry about who might see it."

In a few clicks, she was on the Internet and then Google. Her search topics? Comas, ghosts, contacting the spirit world, and my personal favorite, reincarnation.

I snorted. No, Joonie wasn't involved in this mess, not at all. I wished I could print it all out and show it to Killian. He'd never believe me otherwise, finding some other perfectly rational explanation for her behavior that did not include raising a really pissed-off spirit or whatever the heck Gus was.

The question was, why? Why would she go to such dangerous lengths? Her last stop on the Web provided one possible answer.

After a quick glance over her shoulder to check on the location of Mr. Mueller, the librarian, Joonie typed in a MySpace Web address. A bright pink page appeared on the monitor, along with the first few crashingly loud notes of some former *American Idol* pop song. While Joonie fumbled for the mouse to turn down the volume, I leaned in to take a better look. To my surprise, the girl in the profile photo looked vaguely familiar. Cute in that innocent farm girl kind of way. Straight, mousy brown hair pulled back in a ponytail (with some blond highlights and a decent cut, it would be acceptable), pale skin (hello, Mystic Tan?), and light brown eyes that would have been striking, if not pretty, with the right application of products. The little box that listed her vital stats put her at sixteen, possibly a sophomore, maybe a junior. That would explain why I didn't know her, even though her page claimed she went to Groundsboro High.

I frowned. Why did I remember her face? Something niggled at the back of my brain but wouldn't move forward into the light.

Joonie clicked to view her pictures, and as the images scrolled across the screen, one major piece of the puzzle dropped into place. A few vaguely out-of-focus pictures of a dog and a much too childlike bedroom with princess wallpaper passed by, and then I saw people I recognized: Joonie sticking her studded tongue out at the camera; Killian with his arm protectively around the girl as she stretched her arms out to take a portrait of the two of them together. Killian grinned into the camera, revealing those perfectly white and even teeth. I'd never seen him that happy. She wasn't facing the camera, though. She'd tipped her head back to look up at him, adoration shining from her plain face.

My gaze snapped back up to the Web address. Lilslife. Lil. Lily. The one I'd been hearing so much about—this was her. She was—what?—Killian's girlfriend? He said they were just friends; I heard him tell his sketchy psychiatrist that. But still . . .

An uncomfortable prickle started in my chest. I wrapped my arms around myself. It wasn't jealousy, though. No. What was there to be jealous of here? A pseudo-goth guy and his plain-Jane maybe-girlfriend? Just because I'd never looked at anyone like that, not even Chris on our best days, and now it was too late because I was dead, and Killian had never smiled at me—

A loud sniffle from Joonie interrupted my thoughts. "I'm sorry, Lil. I'm trying," she whispered. Her black eye makeup ran in streaks down her cheeks. She glanced back over her shoulder, checking on Mr. Mueller's position, then turned back to face the computer, kissed the tip of her index finger, and pressed it against Lily's mouth in the picture.

Whoa. What was going on here?

While I gaped at her, Joonie exited the browser and logged off the computer. She stood up, scooped her bag off the floor, and strode to the library door—her skull necklace clanking—with what appeared to be a renewed sense of purpose.

I, of course, followed, my thoughts all abuzz. If Lily

was *Killian's* girlfriend, Joonie sure had a strange way of showing it. I mean, seriously. I'm not afraid of gay people, guys or girls. I don't think every lesbian in school wants me; I *know* they do, just like all the straight guys. But I also know that they aren't going to trap me in the corner of the girls' bathroom and try to convert me. Please, Alona Dare as a resident of Lesbos? I don't think so. I like the male form a little too much for that. Plus, I hate flannel.

Joonie's behavior was just . . . weird. Also, clearly, something had happened to this Lily chick. When they talked about her, it was in this hushed and holy tone. Was she dead? Then why had Joonie said something to Killian about visiting her in the hospital?

I followed Joonie around for the rest of the afternoon, ditching her only the few times when I saw Killian coming. He didn't look happy with me. Too bad, so sad. The best part was that it had never been easier to avoid him. Not like he could call out after me, right?

Unfortunately, as far as Joonie was concerned, nothing else happened. No bathroom stall séances or blood sacrifices at her locker. Joonie went to class just like normal, or as close to normal as she could get, anyway. Until last hour.

Joonie hauled her bag up tighter on her shoulder and hurried into chemistry class. I frowned, my complete and utter boredom shattered by the small but odd behavior change. In my vast hours of experience with her, Joonie never hurried to anything, especially not a class. Her whole persona was based on an utter lack of caring about anything.

Which is total bullshit, of course. First of all, because she obviously cared about making people think she didn't care about anything. But whatever.

I followed her, watching with amazement as she sat down at her lab table, pulled her chemistry book and notebook from her bag carefully, and lined them up on her desk . . . a full two minutes before class even started.

Mr. Gerry nodded with approval at her from his lab stool up front.

"What is going on here?" I muttered.

The rest of the class filtered in, including Jennifer Meyer, who was wearing the absolute worst plaid miniskirt. I shuddered. Plaid was so . . . mid-nineties.

The bell rang, and for the next thirty-three minutes, I saw a completely different Joonie Travis. She raised her hand on almost every question, volunteered to hand out safety goggles, and even put on a protective glove that no one else had to wear—Mr. Gerry thought the piercing in the web between her thumb and first finger might get overheated near the flames of the Bunsen burner—without complaint.

Now, you're probably thinking, "Oh, how nice. The High Priestess of Pain found something she is good at that is also relatively socially acceptable." Well, let me tell you that . . . she sucked. She got most of the answers wrong, and the ones she didn't, it was only because she flipped through the textbook wildly before raising her hand. She also dropped two beakers—empty ones, thank God—and partially melted her own safety glasses when she leaned too close to the burner's flame. In short, she was a disaster. But she kept trying . . . something I didn't understand. At least, not until the last ten minutes of class.

When the clock reached 2:15, a full fifteen minutes before the end of class and the end of school, Joonie stopped working and began putting all of her equipment away. By 2:20, she was parked on her lab stool, books put away and bag zipped up, staring at Mr. Gerry.

After sighing at another pathetic attempt at the daily experiment by Jennifer Meyer and Ashleigh Hicks, Mr. Gerry finally looked up and saw Joonie, her foot jiggling against the stool legs and her body ramrod straight with tension. He nodded reluctantly at her, and Joonie leaped to her feet, slung her bag over her shoulder, and practically ran from the room.

Caught off guard by her sudden exit—I was entertaining myself by watching Jesse McGovern use the Bunsen burner to heat and bend plastic straws swiped from the caf into swearword sculptures—I had to run to catch up.

Joonie tucked her head down and darted down the hall and the stairs, through the main hall, and out the front doors. Interesting . . . she'd better hope that Brewster didn't catch sight of her. He was exactly the type to bust her for skipping school, even if it was only the last ten minutes.

Breaking into a light jog—I hate sweating—I caught up with her near the Circle and tagged along out to her car, the Death Bug. She tossed her bag in the back, climbed in, and started the car while I was still talking myself into sliding through the metal.

She began backing out.

"Hey, watch it!" I threw myself the rest of the way into the car, trying to ignore the cold shuddery feeling I got from passing through the door. "What is your big freaking hurry?"

Joonie pulled out of the parking lot at, like, the speed of light, throwing gravel everywhere and leaving a huge trail of dust in her wake. She turned right onto Henderson, and then left onto Main. A couple more turns and it was obvious: we were heading into town.

Referring to it as "town" sort of gave the impression that Decatur was the cultural center of the area. It was, however, where most of the jobs were—people just lived in the little towns outside, like Groundsboro, and drove in to work at the factories. On a day with a strong breeze, you could catch a whiff of ADM or Staley's, processing soybeans in town. It smelled like instant mashed potatoes. There'd been days when I couldn't wait to get away from here and that smell. But now, honestly, if I'd caught the scent, I might have felt a little comforted. I'd died, but some things still stayed the same.

Anyway, Decatur did offer a few things—a movie theater, a mall, and a hospital. Actually, the big movie theater and the mall were technically part of Forsyth, another dinky little town clinging to the edges of Decatur, but that probably didn't matter, since I doubted Joonie was going anywhere for fun.

My hunch was confirmed when, twenty minutes later, the Death Bug pulled into the visitors' parking lot of

St. Catherine's Hospital. Joonie had mentioned visiting Lily in the hospital. I sat up straight in my seat. Finally, this was getting good! Maybe now I'd get some answers.

Joonie slammed the gear shift into park, snagged her bag off the floor by my feet, and hustled out of the car toward the hospital. With a sigh, I followed her, albeit at a slower pace. I didn't understand what the big hurry was. If Lily was in the hospital, it wasn't like she had other plans anytime soon, right?

Joonie pushed through the revolving door, and I slipped into the compartment after hers, letting her do all the work of moving the heavy glass and metal. She headed immediately for the elevator and pressed the up button. While we waited—I might have figured out how to pass through walls and solid objects, but levitation seemed a bit more of a stretch and I didn't particularly feel like searching out the stairs—I noticed a lot of nurses coming and going with their lunch bags and jackets. Shift change, probably?

The elevator finally arrived, and Joonie pushed the button for the fifth floor. A short ride later, during which I very deliberately concentrated on thinking about how very *solid* the elevator floor was, we arrived at our destination—the children's floor. The wall opposite the elevator was painted with fluffy clouds, rainbows, and bright yellow smiley faces—the exact same kind you see on bumper stickers with the saying *Shit happens*. I suspected that any kid residing on this floor probably already knew that fact better than most, anyway.

Joonie stepped off the elevator and immediately headed to the left, like she knew exactly where she was going. The nurses manning—*wo*-manning?—the floor desk didn't even glance up, as they were checking charts and talking to the next shift of nurses.

I watched Joonie stop at a door midway down the hall and step inside. A second later, her head reappeared, looking up and down the hallway, before she slapped either a yellow sticker or magnet on the outside of the door and shut it gently.

Interesting. Automatically glancing back over my shoulder at the busy nurses, like they could see me, I headed toward the now-closed door. When I got closer, I could see it was a magnet she'd put on the metal door frame, and it read, BATHING. PRIVACY PLEASE.

"What the hell?" I muttered.

"Don't you know you're on the kids' floor?"

Startled, I looked down to see a little blond girl with pigtails, staring up at me from her old-fashioned wooden wheelchair.

She sighed in disgust and rolled on down the hall, passing through the wall. Yep, dead like me. Maybe it was a good thing Killian hadn't come with me. The hospital was probably full of spirits.

I approached the door Joonie had closed and cautiously peered in, ignoring the chill against my face.

At first, it appeared to be your standard hospital room. Blah beige walls with a matching tile floor, a puke green curtain hung on a rack in the ceiling so it could be pulled for privacy from annoying roommates, and a television mounted high on the wall. That old cartoon *Mighty Mouse* was on, but the sound was off.

The girl in the bed, though, was my first clue that not everything was as it seemed. I recognized her, sort of, as the girl in the picture Joonie had pulled up earlier. I mean, I recognized her, but she only vaguely resembled the person she'd once been. Her dull and glazed eyes stared straight ahead, about three feet below the television. A jagged scar, still puffy and red, decorated the left side of her face from her hairline down to her jaw. There were no tubes or anything, other than an IV, and a monitor with her heartbeat showing, so she was obviously breathing on her own, just not much else.

The weird part was that seeing her this way, as a three-dimensional, albeit damaged person rather than a flat image on a screen, finally made it click for me. I knew where I'd seen her before. Months ago, she'd been one of Ben Rogers's girls, another stupid and willing underclassman. Really, I'd only seen her a few times with Ben before they broke up . . . or at least, that's what I assumed happened.

She was new, as of last year, I thought. Didn't have many friends. I'd never seen her with Killian or Joonie . . . as far as I knew. To be fair, though, until recently they were not a demographic I would have bothered noticing. People like them don't even vote for homecoming queen.

I tried to remember the last time I'd seen this girl, Lily Whatever—Turner, that sounded right. Maybe Ben's back-to-school bash? I did remember something about a car accident a few miles away, one they were going to try to pin on our party, but the driver hadn't been drinking, so they had nothing to hold over us. But that was, like, all the way back in September. She'd been like *this* since then?

The utter stillness about her was the worst part. She still moved—even as I watched, her fingers, resting on the top of the bedcovers, jerked and twitched—but she seemed . . . empty. I'd never thought about life as energy before, at least not until Killian talked about it like that, but now I could see what he meant. Even someone sleeping, eyes shut and not moving at all, would have seemed more alive than she did, and I could see that from across the room.

Joonie, however, did not seem to notice or care, and that was my second clue that something was really wrong. She was racing around the room, setting what appeared to be little silver hockey pucks on the floor at set intervals around the bed and talking to Lily at the same time.

"I'm sorry," she said. "I tried to get Killian to come with me. I thought it would work better with him here, but he . . ." She paused, probably remembering his reaction to the Ouija board. "He wouldn't. I'm so sorry, Lil."

I snorted. He wouldn't. Right. Well, I mean, he wouldn't have, but she didn't even try to explain what was going on or what she wanted him to come to the hospital for. Speaking of which, why did she want him to come to the hospital? This was obviously more than just a friendly, keep-coma-girl-company visit.

"But it doesn't matter," she said firmly. "I'm going to make this right, no matter what it takes." Her gaze wandered to the still form on the bed. "I'm going to get you back where you belong."

Joonie jerked back into motion and her combat-booted foot knocked one of the silver disks toward the door, where I still stood, half in and half out. I looked down and found it to be a little white candle in a metal wrapper, like the kind my dad used to put in my carved pumpkin when I was little.

Candles, living-dead girl, creepy declarations of intent, plus the Ouija board Joonie was packing . . . uh-oh. I knew nothing about magic, witchcraft, voodoo, or whatever else this might be (and I bet Joonie didn't either, given the results so far), but I'd seen enough *Charmed* reruns to know this was trouble.

"Okay, then." I pushed myself the rest of the way into the room. "Hey, Joonie, stop. Whatever your freaky little self is up to, cut it out."

Joonie ignored me, of course, and reached into her bag to pull out the lighter and the Ouija board.

Oh, crap. I paced a step or two and lifted my thumbnail to my teeth—what now? It wasn't like I could march out into the hallway and shout at the nurses for help.

Nurses. Help. *Call button.* If there wasn't a lightbulb hanging in the air above my head, there should have been. If I had the strength to concentrate and shove folders around the floor, surely I could push one little button.

I strode confidently across the room, avoiding Joonie as

she crouched down to begin lighting candles, but I hesitated when I reached the bed. Up this close, Lily was tragic . . . and eerie. The light of the television flashed in her blank eyes, adding a creepy and superficial spark of life. The remote with the bed controls and the nurse call button lay half under Lily's arm, a big sign of someone's wishful thinking.

"Don't be such a baby," I told myself. Trying not to think about the germs that had to be floating around here—it was a hospital after all, full of disgusting sick people—I reached down, intending to scoot the remote out from under her arm with a series of little pushes. My hand should have passed through her arm with little more than a cold tingle, but the second I touched her skin, I *felt* it. An intense heat radiated up my fingers. Then the solidity that was Lily's arm melted beneath my touch and my hand sank into her arm. Not through, but in. My skin, the darker of the two, thanks to my hours in the sun for prom prep, melded with hers.

I sucked in a breath and jerked my hand away. Her arm followed, lifting off the bed. I watched in horror. For an endless moment, the bond between us held tight, then something loosened and let go. Her arm flopped back onto the bed, landing squarely on top of the remote. It didn't push any buttons. Oh, no, that would be too good to be true. It prevented me from another attempt to reach the call button, though, unless I wanted to touch her again.

*No freaking way.* I stumbled back from the bed, clutching my arm against my chest. I didn't know what had just happened, nor did I want to know.

I bolted past Joonie, who, her acolyte duties finally completed, was settling herself on the floor with the Ouija board in her lap. I passed through the door, barely even feeling the tingle of it, and darted down the hall.

I ran for the nurses' station. But what could they do? What could anyone do? I was terrified to even look down at my hand, afraid I'd see Lily's pale skin instead of my own.

When I drew even with the nurses' station, the elevator dinged and the doors opened. Some instinct made me look up and over. Killian, head tucked down and hands tucked in his sweatshirt pockets, strode off the elevator and then down the hall toward me and Lily's room.

"Will!" I darted toward him, relief at seeing him here washing away any of my leftover anger from earlier this afternoon.

He looked up, startled. "What are you—"

"Joonie's in there right now and she's doing something with that stupid board." I spoke as quickly as I could.

He started down the hallway toward Lily's room. I stayed next to him, trying to explain. "I told you, she's the one that's doing it, calling up that creepy ghost, and when I tried to stop her, my hand touched Lily's arm and . . ." I shuddered. "Something is just wrong. I don't understand—"

The air suddenly turned to ice around me, and Killian stopped suddenly. I watched the color drain out of his face as he stared at something down the hall.

I turned away from Killian slowly, knowing already what I would find. The creepy shadow ghost was back. This time, it grew, rippling at its edges, to fill the entire hallway, blocking out the light from the windows at the end of the hall. Inside its misty body, things moved beneath the surface, like snakes sliding under a blanket.

It gathered itself, pulling together at the edges until it hung over us like a wave waiting to crash.

"Killian," I said, my voice wobbly.

"Yeah?" He didn't sound so great either.

"Run!" I shoved him away.

With a roar that should have shaken the building, the shadowy spirit crashed down on me. Slivers of what felt like frozen metal tore through my skin, and I screamed. Then everything went dark.

# ❧ 14 ❧

# Will

I was beginning to think that the universe was united against me in some kind of vast conspiracy. I was supposed to be in detention right now, and I would have been . . . if someone hadn't accidentally set fire to a bunch of straws in chem lab during last period. The fire alarm went off right as school let out for the day. Recognizing the hopeless prospect of keeping all of us delinquents in one place in an area as unconfined as the parking lot, Ms. Bernadino, the detention teacher for today, had canceled detention and rescheduled it for next week. I'd gone there for four years and had had more than my share of detentions probably, but I'd never heard of them canceling it before.

Feeling unexpectedly lucky—really, I should have known

better—I headed to the Dodge, which started on the first try, and then on to St. Catherine's. I knew that's where Joonie would be.

I couldn't forget what Alona had said about her. She, Joonie, had been acting so weird lately. But she'd been my friend, pretty much my only one, for years. Why would she want to mess with me like that? Of course, she'd have no way of knowing what a Ouija board did when I was around. But Alona was right. Why else would she act so guilty? Why run away? Why didn't she just laugh or seem confused at my strange reaction to seeing her with one?

I was afraid I already knew the answer, but I needed to know for sure. I needed to talk to Joonie. If she was involved, that changed everything, including—most likely—the true identity of the entity Alona called Gus. As an angry and despondent ghost, my father might have attacked me to show his disapproval. Maybe. But he wouldn't need Joonie or a Ouija board for that.

I'd gotten to the hospital in record time and found a parking space in the first visitors' row. A waiting elevator, which also happened to be both people- and ghost-free, had taken me directly to the fifth floor. And then my luck had changed with a vengeance.

Rooted to the spot, I watched the shadow ghost collapse over Alona and tear through her, her green eyes going wide with the pain before she vanished.

"No!" I shouted, furious. Why hadn't she run? She knew what this thing could do to her, knew that every time she disappeared there was a growing chance she might not come back.

*Because she was saving me.* The realization knocked me back a step. She'd seen what Gus could do to me, and Alona Dare had just sacrificed herself . . . for me.

My throat grew tight, and the hallway blurred before my eyes. Maybe that unselfish action would be enough to send her to the light, though I'd seen no sign of it before she'd vanished. Either way, I wouldn't let it be in vain.

"Joonie, get out here!" I forced the words out past the lump in my throat.

Rushing footsteps sounded behind me as the nurses' abandoned their station and raced down the hall toward me. "Sir? Sir, you can't yell in here. This is a hospital."

"Joonie, I said come out," I repeated.

The black shadow ghost, having long since dissolved Alona, just hung there in midair as though waiting and watching to see what I would do next.

"Joonie . . ."

"Sir, you're going to have to come with us." Strong female hands grabbed at my arms and shoulders. "Somebody call security, please."

All up and down the hallway, doors started to open, and pale and somber little kid faces poked out to see what was going on. Then Lily's door opened and Joonie stepped out.

"J," I said. "Call it off, you don't know what you're doing."

She shook her head, eyes bright blue and red-rimmed. "I can't, Will. I just . . . can't."

Then she backed up into the room and shut the door.

"Sir, you have to come with us." Those hands on my shoulders and arms began pulling me backward, but it wasn't enough. I knew it wouldn't be.

The shadowy ghost poured over me, surrounding me in deathly cold and tearing me from the nurses' grasp. I struggled, pulling back with all my strength, but it . . . he? . . . she? . . . easily overpowered me, slamming me face-first into the wall. Something in my face, possibly my nose, possibly a cheekbone, cracked, and someone screamed. It might have been me.

"What do you want?" I squeezed the words out.

It gave no response, only a vague howling sound, like wind rushing through a broken window. Then it hauled me away from the wall and tossed me down the hall. I tried to regain my footing and stumbled, bashing my head into the side of a medicine cart left abandoned there, and everything went mercifully black.

I woke up in restraints, my hands pinned to the bed beneath me with Velcro and fabric straps. Never a good sign, really. Before I even opened my eyes, I recognized the antiseptic smell unique to hospitals. So I wasn't in jail—that was a plus, at least.

My whole body ached, and my head throbbed with an intensity that I suspected would only grow worse when I finally decided to brave the light and crack my eyelids open.

"Will!" A vague whisper from my right. "Wake up. I

know you're in there. I saw you pulling against those skanky armbands. I mean, seriously, do you think they clean those after every use? I doubt it. You're, like, sharing skin cells with the last sweaty and depraved lunatic they locked up. Sick people are so gross."

Alona! The disgust in her voice was as distinct as the antiseptic hospital smell. I braved the light enough to squint in the direction of her voice. When my eyes stopped watering and focused, I found her sitting in the visitor's chair next to my bed, her knees pulled up to her chest as if she didn't even want her ghost feet touching the floor. She looked pale and tired, and for the first time, a line of bruises decorated the left side of her face. That meant either she didn't have the energy to project herself as flaw free, or she was really feeling beat up.

"Are you okay?" I asked, my mouth feeling stuffed full with cotton.

She straightened up and flipped her hair over her shoulders when she saw me watching. "I'm fine," she said quickly. "But I'm not the one locked up with a cracked face."

Automatically, I tried to reach up to touch my face, but my effort only tightened the restraint on my arm.

Alona unfolded herself from her chair and moved to sit on my bed. Her deft fingers worked the Velcro and straps until my hand was free. "I'll have to refasten that, you know, or else they'll be locking you up tighter next time they come to check on you."

"Yeah, I know." I traced the swollen lines of my cheek

carefully with my fingers. Puffed up like a pincushion and hot, the right side of my face felt like it'd been microwaved.

"They did X-rays or an MRI or whatever about an hour ago. You have a hairline fracture in your cheekbone. I heard them talking about it before you woke up."

I groaned. Well, that explained the pain radiating down to my jaw and up to my temple.

She pulled her legs up on the bed and curled in closer to me, her hip and backside a steady warmth against my waist. "Why didn't you run? I told you to run."

"I thought Joonie would listen to me, that she'd stop it when I confronted her," I said.

She rolled her eyes. "Good thinking."

"Hey," I protested.

"I'm serious. Now you're stuck in here." She shook her head, and the scent of her shampoo drifted toward me. "They're all convinced that you're schizophrenic and possibly epileptic on top of it. You're on a regular floor for now, but they're going to move you as soon as a bed opens on the psych floor. And the chin-rubber is back."

"No." I struggled to sit up.

"Yeah. He has hospital privileges here or something. Your mom's trying to get rid of him."

"My mom is here?" I reached for the remaining strap to undo it.

"Don't." Alona pushed on my shoulder, forcing me back. She gestured to the mostly closed door. "They're in here about every fifteen minutes. I don't know if I can get you all the way tied up again without getting caught. I'm good, but maybe not that good." She gave me a wan smile, the likes of which I'd never seen from her before, and it startled me.

Over the years, I'd seen all kinds of smiles from her. The kind designed to make all the blood drain from your head and gather behind your zipper. The kind given with cold, cold eyes, showing she was mad as hell but wasn't going to break form to show it. The superior smile was a particular favorite of hers in recent years, like she couldn't help but find it funny that you, a petty, insignificant being, would try to interact with her. None of those even looked related to her current expression. She looked . . . defeated.

"What happened in there?" I asked, not entirely sure I wanted to hear the answer.

Alona lifted a shoulder in a shrug. "She had candles and that stupid board. And she kept talking to coma-gir . . . I mean, Lily." She hesitated. "I think she's trying to fix her."

I frowned. "What do you mean, fix her? Lily is—" I paused to take a deep breath, needing it to force the words out—"brain dead. She has been since the day of the accident." Fifty-four miles per hour around a curve that has a thirty-mile-per-hour speed limit. One tree. No seat belt. Lily, as we knew her, wouldn't be coming back. It never got any easier, that realization. I kept thinking it would, but no.

Alona shook her head slowly. "I don't think she's talking about brain surgery here, Killian. Lily's empty, you know? The lights are on but nobody's home?"

I grimaced but nodded. Alona had quite a way with words.

"So first, I'm wondering what Joonie's trying to do with all the candles and spirits and everything." Alona waved her hand dismissively. "I mean, hello, even I recognize some kind of creeptastic ritual when I see it." She paused, her sharp green eyes focusing in on me as though trying to will me into believing her words. "I think she's been trying to call up Lily's spirit."

That was . . . possible. Joonie had not been the same since Lily's accident. She'd blamed herself for it, a crazy line of thinking that went something like this: if she and Lily hadn't had a fight, Lily would have been with us instead of the first-tier crowd and she'd still be alive . . . in more than just the technical sense.

"But then, I'm like, what does any of this have to do with Killian? I mean, she could try to call up Lily's spirit on the Ouija board without you."

"It won't work, though," I said, "with or without me. Lily isn't here anymore. She's . . . moved on. Like I said before, people who are really gone are gone. There is no reaching them."

"But I bet Joonie doesn't know that," Alona pointed out.

"Probably not," I admitted.

She took a deep breath. "It gets worse."

"How?"

"She's not *just* trying to call up Lily's spirit. I think she's trying to get it back into Lily's body." Alona hesitated. "And she wants you to help."

"No," I said instantly.

She looked at me in exasperation. "What else could 'get you back where you belong' mean? She was staring right at Lily's body when she said it, and she definitely mentioned you."

"No, I mean it's not possible. It's a one-way door. It has to be," I tried to explain. "Once you're out, you're out. Otherwise, you'd see walking corpses everywhere when people like Grandpa Brewster or Liesel got tired of being trapped in between."

"But Lily's still alive." She gave a shudder.

"Not really." As much as it hurt to say that, I made myself keep going. "Her heart still beats and everything, but she wouldn't be able to function, even if you could get her spirit back inside her body. The connection between the two is broken."

She rolled her eyes. "Again, *you* know that. Does Joonie?"

My mouth worked for a second, as I tried to find an answer. "But Joonie doesn't know what I can do. How would she even think to—"

Alona held up her hands. "I don't know. Not my problem. You figure it out. I'm just telling what I saw and heard."

I shook my head, angry at the suggestion. "No, she knows better than to mess with stuff like this." Even if it was possible, which it wasn't . . . as far as I knew, there were so many things that could go wrong. What if Joonie successfully managed to get Lily's spirit back into her body only to discover that it was little more than a prison of flesh and bone?

How would she even know she had contacted the right spirit to begin with?

"Desperate people do really dumb ass stuff," Alona said. "Trust me on that."

"Joonie would never take the chance of hurting Lily," I insisted. What was left of her, anyway. "It almost killed her when Lily ended up here." Joonie had spent most of the month of September locked in her room, not leaving for school or anything until Brewster threatened to keep her from graduating if she didn't return. After that, she'd dragged herself back to school, but it had taken a couple more months for her to show even some spark of her former self.

"I bet." Alona's voice was bland, but her tone hinted at something she wasn't saying.

"What is that supposed to mean?" I demanded.

"You know."

"No, I don't." I ground out the words.

She sighed. "Was Lily your girlfriend or not?"

I shifted uncomfortably. "What does that have to do with anything?"

"Just answer the question."

"No. She wasn't. We were friends. I looked out for her. At least, I tried to." Obviously, I hadn't done such a great job of that.

Alona arched an eyebrow. "I saw the picture of the two of you."

"How . . ." I shook my head. I didn't want to know. "Okay, so she might have liked me a little or something, but it never turned into anything. She had a crush on Ben Rogers, too," I pointed out. Which was probably the reason my friendship with Lily had stayed just that, a friendship. I liked her. She was sweet and funny. Hell, she even made Joonie happy, and that was a true miracle. But obsessing over the popular crowd and their entanglements had been one of Lily's favorite pastimes, one that I did not share. So, it hadn't been that big of a shock, at least not to me, when she dumped us to climb the social ladder after she and Joonie had that big fight.

"Lily wasn't the only one with a crush," Alona said.

"What are you talking about? Joonie?" I laughed. "Joonie doesn't like me like that."

"Not you," she said pointedly.

"What?"

"Oh, my God, could you be more dense?"

"What are you talking about?"

"You know what, just forget it. Even if I tell you, you won't believe me and you'll just get angry, so it's not worth it. I don't know why I'm even here in the first place. You don't listen to anything I say—"

"You're not saying anything!"

"You don't do what I tell you to, you dismiss all of my ideas. I mean, what's the point of having a spirit guide if you're just going to ignore her?"

"Trust me," I said. "You are impossible to ignore. I've tried. As far as I'm concerned, you can't leave here fast enough."

She froze, a wounded look flashing across her face.

I felt like a shit. "I'm sorry. I didn't mean that."

"Yes, you did. I'm done here." Alona swung her legs off the bed. "I don't have the time to waste on you anymore."

"Alona, wait."

She ignored me and pushed her hands against the mattress to climb down. I grabbed for one of her wrists . . . and my hand passed right through her.

I gasped.

Alona glanced back over her shoulder with a sigh, more bruises flickering to life. "Looks like you're getting your wish."

# ❧ 15 ❧

# Alona

Will stared up at me, his face pale except for the black eye he'd gotten from Chris and his bruised and swollen cheek. "What's happening to you?"

I turned away from him, closing my eyes against the tears that suddenly stung them. "Shut up, I'm trying to concentrate." I'd been fighting this sensation of being pulled away since the moment I'd woken in his hospital room. It felt like I'd left part of me behind in the place I couldn't remember, and something on the other side was working as hard as possible to get the rest of me.

"Think positive thoughts." He sounded panicked. "Um, makeup sales, prom dresses, sex in the backseat of a limo."

I shot him a look over my shoulder. "Exactly what

kind of prom night do you think I was planning?"

He raked his free hand through his rumpled black hair, making it stand out even more crazily. "I don't know. I'm just trying to help."

I shook my head. "Thanks, but it's not working."

"Maybe if you think positive thoughts about other people—"

"Killian. I've been here two hours, and I'm fading in and out, no matter how often I think about puppies, rainbows, and your surprisingly large biceps." Ha, let him chew on that one for awhile.

A pause. "My what?"

"Forget it. You were right. There's a time limit for everyone, and mine is just about up." Oddly enough, the thought brought relief. I was tired of fighting this . . . whatever this was. I just wanted to be done.

"No. That doesn't make sense. You're my spirit guide . . . or whatever," he insisted.

"Yep, one that you don't listen to." I wiped under my eyes and shifted on the bed to face him again.

He struggled to pull himself into an awkward half-sitting position. "Okay, I might have been wrong about that. I didn't throw your papers away."

"It doesn't matter, Will. I can't stay," I said wearily. That was the conclusion I'd reached while waiting for him to wake up. "I've only got a few hours left here, less if I'm here and Gus shows up again, and I've got some stuff to do."

"Things you put off doing until you had no choice." His

shoulders slumped and he sagged back onto the bed.

"Exactly." I nodded. "You were right about that. And"—I hesitated—"you were right about my mom."

He looked up, surprised. "Alona," he said, his voice gentle, not pitying. There was a difference, and I could recognize it now.

I waved away his words and the sudden stinging in my eyes. "Shut up, I don't want to talk about it now." I took a deep breath. "But I wanted you to know you were right. And . . . yes, some of those things I wrote down from Grandpa Brewster and the rest, they probably aren't what's holding them here. But"—I leaned closer making sure I had his attention—"some of them are, and you can do something for those people. Hiding doesn't help anyone, including you. You need to know that."

He looked away. "What about you? You're my spirit guide. You're supposed to stay here for as long as I need you."

I smiled. "You don't need me. If you did, I wouldn't be disappearing, right?"

"We don't know that."

The sound of voices in the hall grew louder. "Someone's coming. I better go." I took a deep breath, steeling myself to push off his bed and actually leave. Finally leave.

He caught my arm before I could get down. His hand rested warmly against my skin, not passing through or sinking in. He pulled me toward him, his pale blue eyes bright with emotion, and I let him. His mouth, so warm and soft, brushed over mine, once, twice . . . and lingered. I snuggled closer to his heat, bracing my free hand against the pillow. He let go of my wrist to thread his fingers through my hair and tilt my head. Suddenly, I was being kissed, really kissed, and I leaned into him, tasting him as he tasted me.

The loud clatter of something hitting the floor in the hallway broke us apart.

"Maybe you should have done that earlier," I said, trying to catch my breath and feeling deliciously warm for the first time in days. "When I was alive."

He smiled, his cheeks flushed. "When you were alive, you would have hit me."

"Yeah. True." I slid off his bed and walked around to the other side.

"Let me come with you," he said quietly. "I can help."

I shook my head. "What then? When I'm gone and they find you've escaped? What kind of measures do you think they'll take next time?"

He didn't say anything. I folded his free wrist back into the restraint, wrapping the fabric as loosely as possible, and he let me. I was right, and he knew it.

I smiled at him, his image suddenly blurry with tears. "You want one last piece of guidance, not that you'll listen?"

"Alona—" His voice broke.

"Tell your mother the truth. Your dad had his reasons for keeping this secret, okay, fine. But that didn't work out so well for him. You don't owe anything to him, you aren't obligated to do what he did just because you share the same gift."

"And if she doesn't believe me?"

I tapped the restraint around his wrist. "Kind of hard for her to make things worse, right?"

"Stay. We'll figure something out."

"Please don't make this any harder, okay?" I forced a choked laugh. "I'm scared enough as it is."

"Alona, please. Just wait!" He struggled against the restraints.

I straightened my shoulders and gave him my biggest, see-it-from-across-the-football-field smile. "Can't. Time's up." I touched his cheek but pulled away before he could try to grab me. "I'll come back to you if I can. If not . . . see you on the other side someday, maybe." Then I walked through the door and down the hallway before he could change my mind.

## ❧ 16 ❧

# Will

I pulled hard enough against the restraints to shake the bed, and succeeded only in rubbing my wrists raw. Okay, so Alona had a point about the consequences of breaking out of here, but did she have to tie me up again to prove it?

"Having a little trouble?" A little girl, probably about ten or eleven when she died, with blond pigtails and pink striped pajamas rolled her heavy wheelchair through the partially closed door.

I ignored her.

"Oh, come on," she said. "I know you can hear me."

She wheeled herself closer, but I turned away, facing the ceiling, and concentrated on twisting my wrist inside the binding. The right restraint, the one Alona had undone, was looser than the other.

"I saw that blond chippie with the foul mouth leaving your room. So, I know you can talk to us," the little girl continued.

*Chippie?* She almost caught me with that one, nearly got me to turn my head and look at her. Alona and I had, after all, been shouting pretty loudly there for a while. But even if this girl had heard something, there's no way she could be sure it was us. "Us." Now that was a funny term to be applying to me and her highness, Alona Dare. But kissing her . . . no matter how long I live (or don't live), I will never forget her mouth, warm and soft, moving under mine, the heated silk of her hair wrapping around my fingers and that small, pleased, almost inaudible, sigh she gave.

"I have to get out of here," I muttered. Even as I lay there, Alona could be disappearing into nothingness.

"I can help you," the little girl volunteered instantly. "I just need you to do me a favor. It's real easy."

I barely resisted rolling my eyes.

"I know you can do it, too. I heard some of the others talking about you. If you help me," she gave a shrug of her thin shoulders, "maybe I can help you."

In avoiding her gaze, I ended up staring at my jeans lying over the back of the visitor's chair with all my other clothes. I'd picked up all the notes Alona had thrown down in frustration and put them in my pocket. Not that I'd had a chance to tell her that. In the last few minutes of seventh hour, just before the fire alarm had rung, I'd even written part of Grandpa Brewster's letter. It had started more as a gesture, to show Alona I was listening (and that it wouldn't really change Grandpa's situation), but when I got going, it just seemed like the right thing to do. Maybe she had a point. It was time to stop running. But how? How would anyone believe me now?

"Come on, please?" the little girl wheedled, rolling her wheelchair closer to my bed.

Out in the hallway, I heard my mother's voice, getting closer.

"—was completely inappropriate, and you expect me to trust you after that?" she asked.

"Julia, I swear to you, I never let my writing interfere with the treatment of your son."

Miller. Alona was right.

"Don't call me Julia," she said with more command in her tone than I'd heard since before my dad died.

"Okay, okay," Dr. Miller said in this annoyingly fake soothing voice. Didn't this jerkoff know how to do anything right?

"We need to find out what's wrong with him. Locking him away is not the answer," she said.

"Don't think of it that way, Julia. With the right medications and intensive therapy . . ." Miller paused. "You'd still be able to visit him on Sundays."

Oh, hell, no. I tugged harder at the restraints, succeeding only in losing another layer of skin.

"Okay, suit yourself. I guess you don't want out of here bad enough." The ghost girl started to roll her chair backward.

"Getting out isn't the problem," I said wearily. "Staying out is. And she's not a . . . chippie."

"Ha, I knew it!" She squealed in delight.

I raised an eyebrow.

"That you could hear me, I mean," she said.

"Honey, who are you talking to?" My mother pushed open the door to my room with a frown.

I hesitated, a million familiar lies tumbling to the tip of my tongue. *It was the radio. I was talking to myself. I was singing. . . . rehearsing lines for a play . . . quoting my favorite line from* Ghostbusters. Lie after lie after lie. I could have given her any of them, but the words just wouldn't come.

"I don't know," I said finally. I looked to the little girl. "What's your name?"

Miller's eyes nearly bulged from his head, such was his joy. My mother just seemed . . . resigned, and a little scared.

"Honey, it's me," my mother said. "Dr. Miller came by for a visit, too."

I ignored them and kept my gaze steady on the girl.

She shrugged finally. "Your funeral. My name is Sara, Sara Marie Hollingsford."

I nodded. "Nice to meet you, Sara Marie Hollingsford."

My mother sucked in a breath. "No."

Miller approached. "He's having another episode. Now, Will—"

"You stay away," I told him. "Mom, I'm fine. I've always been fine. I really can see and talk to"—there was no easy way to soften the next part—"the dead."

She shook her head. "Not again, William." Her voice broke.

"Yes, again, the whole time. I just stopped trying to convince you because it seemed easier to let you believe what you wanted. That's what Dad did and what he told me to do."

She blanched. "Your father knew?"

"He was what I am. Grandma Killian, too, I think." I'd never met her because she'd died before I was born and evidently had not stuck around. From what my father had said, though, on the rare occasions I could convince him to talk about it, he'd inherited his "gift" from his mother.

A strange look crossed my mother's face. "Bridget?"

"What?" I asked, trying not to sound too eager.

She shook her head as if trying to talk herself out of something, but the words escaped anyway. "She told me once that my grandmother had left the necklace for me, not Charlotte. I had no idea what she was talking about. She'd only met my grandmother once, at our wedding. Then when Char got married a few years later, she wore the pearls that were my grandma's favorite."

Not surprising, Aunt Charlotte, who lived in California, and my mother had grown up the bitterest of rivals from the stories I'd heard.

"Don't tell me you're starting to believe this." Miller sighed. "Julia, your husband committed suicide because of a deep depression and repeated schizophrenic episodes. Schizophrenia has a genetic component, which can be passed down to offspring."

"So does this . . . gift, curse, whatever," I shot back at him. Then I turned my full attention to my mother. "Dad killed himself because he was hiding."

She took a step back. We never talked about what happened to my dad, ever. It was almost like she feared saying the words would make it happen again.

"The pressure to behave normally, to ignore dozens and dozens of voices around him, all the time . . . it just got to him, I think. But I'm done hiding." The ferocity of that declaration startled even me, but it was genuine.

"I've heard enough of this. We'll discuss this tomorrow after your tests are complete." Miller started for the door.

"You want proof," I said.

He stopped and turned around with a tight smile. "I suppose my great-aunt Mildred is waiting there for a message."

*Mildred?* "Uh, no, it's just me and Sara for the moment. Unlike the movies or TV, I can only talk to whoever's here, and she doesn't have a message for either of you." I looked to Sara for confirmation and she nodded. "But I'm wondering if she'd be willing to play a little game."

She shrugged. "Why not?"

"Okay, Dr. Miller over there." I gestured to him with my chin—I could have asked them to release the restraints, but I didn't want them to think this was a trick to help me escape. "He's going to step out into the hallway, close the door, and write a word on his prescription pad. The only rules are that it has to be clearly written, and the pad stays where he can see what he's written at all times."

"This is ridiculous," he muttered, but he went into the hall and pulled the door shut behind him. He was probably already writing it up as a new chapter in his book.

Sara followed. A second later, she said, "He's holding it too high."

"You'll need to lower it a little," I called to Miller. "Sara's in a wheelchair."

My mother gave a soft gasp.

"Um, I don't know this word." Sara sounded uncertain.

Shit, I hadn't thought about that. Maybe I should have gone the number route instead. "Can you spell it?"

"A-N-A-B-O-L-I-C."

"Anabolic," I called out.

No response.

"What's he doing?" I asked.

"He looks kind of mad. Wait, he's writing another word."

"Mom," I whispered. "Do you believe me? That's all that matters."

She hesitated, brushing a strand of hair off her weary face, and only then did I realize she was still in her diner uniform. Someone must have called her at work. The number was in my wallet. "William, I want more than anything for you to be well, but—"

"Um, *vest-ig-all*?" Sara tried.

I frowned. "Spell this one, too."

She did.

"Vestigial," I shouted out. Thank God for the SAT vocab section.

"He's writing another one and . . . I'm not saying that!" I laughed.

My mother looked at me sharply.

I shook my head. "He wrote some kind of swearword. Will you spell it, Sara?"

"No!" she said.

"Please?"

"First four letters spell 'bull,'" she said huffily.

"I do believe the good doctor is questioning my authenticity. It's *not* bullshit, Dr. Miller. I promise you that."

"Now he's just scribbling a bunch of letters. *X, Y, Q* . . ."

I repeated them after her, and the door burst open again, Miller with his pad in hand, looking wild-eyed. Sara rolled in after him. "How are you doing that? You've got spies in the hall," he accused.

"You're right," I said. "Her name is Sara, and she died in . . ." I looked at her.

"1942," she supplied.

"1942," I finished.

Miller's mouth worked, but no sound came out.

My mother plucked the top sheet off his pad and glanced at it. She paled, and her mouth tightened.

I held my breath.

Then she told Miller, "Make your name with someone else's son. We're done here." She frowned at me. "William, stay put, I'm going to get you checked out of here. Don't think you're off the hook, though, young man. You have a lot of explaining to do."

I'd never been so happy to have my mother angry with me. "Okay."

She turned on her heel and marched off down the hall. Miller trailed after her. "But, Julia . . ."

"Thanks," I said to Sara. "What can I help you with?"

"My brother gave me his St. Michael medal when I went into the hospital. It's still in my file. They took it off when they did X-rays. I want him to have it back."

I nodded. "I think I can do that." Getting into the file room might be tricky, but I'd have help. "I have to do something else first, and then I'll be back."

She cocked her head to one side and gave me an evaluating look. "You're going after the blonde."

I nodded.

She shook her head. "Good luck with that. She seems like a pain."

It was only after Sara rolled through the door that I realized everyone had left me still in restraints. Damnit, I could have been up getting dressed. I had no idea how much time Alona might have left.

"Sara?" I called. "Mom? Hello?"

Fortunately, the door to **my room** opened again right away.

"Oh, good," I said. "I thought you might have been too far away to—"

It took my brain just those extra few seconds to process what I was seeing—someone, not my mother, backing into the room with a wheelchair. An already occupied, modern wheelchair, its passenger slumped to the side at an odd and unnatural angle.

"Will!" Joonie cried, her voice all high-pitched and kind of crazy sounding. She spun the chair around to face me, and Lily, her eyes as dull and empty as they'd been for the last eight months, stared blankly in my general direction. A Ouija board rested in her lap. "We're so glad you're awake."

## ❧ 17 ❧

# Alona

It took me forty-five minutes, twelve cars, and one tow truck to get home, using a convoluted system of sliding into one vehicle and riding until they veered off my desired course. Then I'd jump out—or better yet, wait until they reached a red light—and try to find another car going in the right direction.

There had to be a better way for spirits to travel, but I was not going to be around to find it. The strange pressure I'd felt in Killian's hospital room was only getting stronger.

I walked the last three blocks home, watching grown-ups pull into their driveways after a long day of work, kids playing one last game of tag before being called into dinner. Summer, my favorite time of year, was coming. Mornings to sleep in late and still get out of the house before my mother was awake. The whole day free to do whatever and go wherever I wanted. The ability to spend almost every night over at Misty's house without anyone suspecting it was because, more than anything, I didn't want to go home.

When I looked at my house, I saw it differently. I don't remember much from the first twelve or thirteen years of relative happiness, mostly because now it felt like everything had just been building toward these last few years of misery.

That's where my mother knelt on the driveway and begged my father not to leave. There's where he drove over the then-carefully sculpted flower beds, nearly taking out a concrete birdbath, to keep from hitting her, not that it stopped him from leaving. That boarded-up window on the second story, that's right next to the shower where she "slipped" on wet tile, fell, and broke the window, slicing open her arm. When I found her, the shower was bone dry. Mother, however, was not. She reeked more of alcohol than blood, and considering the massive amounts of the latter on the floor, that was really saying something. And the garage door . . . don't even get me started on that. How hard is it to remember to look behind you to make sure the door's open before you start to back the car out?

Just walking up to the house, I could feel a familiar tension making my jaw ache and my shoulders tight. She'd never hit me, no matter how drunk she'd gotten. Oh, no, not Cheryl Dare. Instead, she'd just suffocated me with her neediness. Cherie was a victim of an adulterous and inattentive husband. None of this was her fault.

The saddest and most pathetic part of all of it is she did it all for my dad. Like, if she showed him how vulnerable and messed up she was without him, he'd *have* to come back. Where is the logic in that? I'd have pretended that I didn't need him, that I'd never needed him. Actually, it wouldn't have been pretending. I would never let anyone turn me upside down and inside out the way she let my dad.

That was the problem with my mother. She was beautiful, and she didn't know how to be anything else. Not like me, she was nothing like me. I got her looks, but Dad's brains. When he chose it, he could be a very cold and calculating son of a bitch. The only thing my dad did, whenever word of Mom's problems and escapades eventually reached him (some of the neighbors were still friends with him and the new wife), was call me.

Everyone wanted to know what I was doing that day, the day I died. What made me cross the street without looking? What took me from college-bound cheerleader to black-and-white memorial material for the yearbook?

God, I wish it was something cool. Interesting, at the very least. The truth is, it was just another day.

My cell phone rang right before I slammed my gym locker shut. If my dad had waited another couple seconds to call, or if I'd ignored the ringing, my life would have changed dramatically. He was scheduled to meet with my mom at Eickleberg and Feinstein's at 7:30 a.m., before he went to work. They were discussing changes to alimony, child support, and how to handle my college tuition. It had already been decided, mostly by my father, that I would be attending school within easy driving distance, obviously. Someone had to stick around and keep tabs on my mother. Hence, my graduation present, the Eos.

Anyway, it was now 7:00, and my father wanted to know, could I please go make sure *she* was up and on her way?

I could have explained I was already at school. Details are so not my dad's thing, so he probably didn't remember my schedule or, more specifically, that I'd signed up for zero-hour gym. But I didn't bother. I knew he wouldn't call the house or go over there, just as I knew that my mother was probably at home waiting for him to do just that. If she missed this meeting, Gigi, the new wife, wouldn't hesitate to pressure my dad to scale back his payments to us even further. She wanted kids. He said they couldn't afford it.

It should have been a simple thing, something I've done dozens of times before. Make up an excuse, slip out of school or cheerleading practice or a party to go home, clean up whatever mess my mother had made in the hopes of attracting my father's attention, and send her back to bed or the hospital or whatever, depending. Then go back to my normal life, pretending nothing was wrong.

But on this day, a cool and beautiful first morning in May, something inside me snapped. *She ruins everything.*

*I hate her.* That's what I was thinking when I stepped off that curb on Henderson. If karma came in bus-size servings, some people would probably say I got what I deserved for thinking that. After all, logically speaking, all of it was as much my father's fault as it was hers. He was the one who'd cheated and left, the one who used me as a shield against her. But she was the only one with the power to stop it, to pull herself back into something vaguely resembling a parent instead of a giant black hole of neediness. She just refused to do it.

Now, standing outside my house, her house alone as of Monday morning, I felt a familiar surge of resentment. I'd died, and she was *still* controlling my life, holding me hostage as my "unresolved issue" as Killian liked to put it.

I swallowed back my frustration, lifted my chin, and stepped onto the porch. I would forgive her for being her: flawed, imperfect, human. I could do that, right? Looking down at my feet, now flickering in and out of existence again, I guessed I'd have to.

*Just get in, say you're sorry and you forgive her, and then get out.* If I hurried, maybe I could make it back to Killian. I was worried about him trapped in that hospital with no one to help him. Plus, if I was leaving, really leaving for good, I didn't want to be alone. He'd kissed me. Maybe he would wait with me while it happened. I coached myself across the threshold of the front door into the foyer . . . and stopped. Something was different.

I turned in a circle, looking into the living room, down

the hall to the kitchen, into the now-empty and dusty room that had once been my dad's study. It took me a second to realize what was wrong. All the blinds were up, the curtains drawn back. The last blaze of light at sunset poured in through naked windows, landing on the polished floor in long rectangles. Never in the last few years had she even allowed me to open the blinds, let alone opened them herself. All-day hangovers were a bitch, one that she usually medicated against. Keeping the house dim was a required precautionary measure. At times, it had been like living with a vodka-saturated vampire.

But now . . . I turned again in a slow circle, an uncomfortable feeling of uncertainty in the pit of my stomach. It was almost like walking into the wrong house.

Then, from the kitchen in back, I heard the familiar clank of bottles, and relaxed.

"I know it's difficult, but you're doing the right thing," said a soothing female voice that drifted out from the kitchen.

That was *not* my mother. I frowned and walked to the kitchen.

At the table, my mother sat with her back to the doorway, and across from her was a black woman I'd never seen before. Her hair was cropped close to her head, emphasizing the lines of her face and her beautiful dangly hammered-silver earrings. They were too big for my tastes, but she pulled them off. Her skin was gorgeous, though lines by her eyes suggested she was older than she looked, maybe even my mother's age.

As I watched, she reached over to squeeze my mom's hand. Balled-up tissues were strewn across the tabletop, scattered between two coffee cups. My mother's ever-present tumbler was nowhere to be seen. What *was* this?

I stepped farther in the room and caught the sharp scent of alcohol. Empty vodka bottles, probably the very ones I'd manipulated yesterday, now stood lined up on the counter, like good little soldiers. In the sink, my mother's emergency backup supplies—gin, tequila, and rum—gurgled out of their tipped-upside-down bottles and down the drain, forming a potent brew. The cabinet under the sink, where she'd hidden her extra stash of bottles, stood open, and I could see nothing in there now but cleaning supplies.

A horrible suspicion formed in the back of my mind, and I turned to face my mother. She looked twenty years older with no makeup to hide the dark circles under her eyes. When she picked up her coffee cup, her hand shook so much, the coffee, still steaming, sloshed over the edge. Neither she nor her visitor seemed to notice, or they were ignoring it.

My mother cleared her throat. "I want to thank you for coming over. I wasn't sure I could . . ." She gestured weakly in the general direction of the sink.

The other woman smiled, revealing bright white teeth with a tiny gap in the front. "Cherie, that's what sponsors are for, to help you through."

*No drink in her hand, alcohol bottles emptying into the sink, and . . . a sponsor?*

"Holy shit," I said. "I die and *now* you quit drinking?"

A burst of fury, white and pure, exploded soundlessly behind my eyes. I felt like I couldn't breathe, hatred boiling up into my lungs. "Now you decide to be a grown-up?"

My mother shook her head. "It's my fault, Angela. The . . . accident." Her voice broke and she grabbed for a discarded tissue.

"You're damn right!" I shouted.

"How?" Angela asked. "Were you driving the bus? Did you force your daughter out into the road?"

"No, but . . ." She hesitated.

"Might as well have." I spun away from them and raked my arm through the bottles on the counter, intending to smash them all to the floor. Just one tipped over . . . and it didn't even crack. My mother and Angela looked up, but neither of them seemed alarmed or even very startled.

*Dammit.* I reached out to try again and realized my arm was gone from the elbow down. Not flickering, not faded, but gone. *No, no, no.*

I stormed to my mother's side. "What is the matter with you?" I demanded, a fine tremor of rage running through my body. "I was coming here to forgive you. And what, you've decided that you wasted enough time, wasted MY LIFE, and now it's time to pull things back together? Fuck you."

After that, my disappearing began in earnest. I could feel all that negative energy Killian had gone on about building inside me, dying to be released. In seconds, both arms and legs were gone, and I could feel that cold line, the one that divided "not here" and "here," creeping up my body.

"I feel like she must hate me," my mother whispered.

"You're right!" I yelled, before my mouth could disappear.

"No." Angela shook her head. "I'm sure, wherever she is, she knows you loved her and she forgives you for the mistakes you made."

"Shut up, Angela. You don't know me." At least, that's what I would have said, if I could've. The room had grown misty and vague. I could no longer see much beyond my mother and Angela, and even they were beginning to blur around the edges. So, this was it. I wouldn't make it back to Will, then. My eyes burned with tears.

My mother gave a tight smile. "You don't know Alona." Her smile faded. "The worst part is, even if she did forgive me, I don't deserve it."

I froze, what little was left of me.

"Cherie—" Angela began.

"No, listen. That morning, Monday morning, I was supposed to meet Russ at the lawyer's office. But I waited, I deliberately did not get up, did not get dressed, because I thought Russ would come. I just wanted to talk . . ." She broke off into a sob. "I never dreamed he would pull her out of school."

"Did you tell her you're sorry?" Angela asked quietly.

She shook her head. "It's too late. She's—"

"It's never too late."

She hesitated, then looked down at her hands folded on the table with the tissue clutched in between them. "Alona, my baby . . ." Her throat worked but no sound emerged. She swallowed hard and took a deep breath. "I am so, so sorry. I didn't mean for this to happen. I just wanted everything to be the way it used to be, and I . . . I messed up. Now, it can't even be the way it was with just you and me." Her gaze traveled around the room, and for a second, it landed on me. Her eyes are the same shade of green as mine. It was like staring into some twisted mirror and seeing what I would have looked like in twenty years . . . under the weight of grief and guilt. "I am so sorry."

I wanted to keep fighting, keep shouting, but looking at her, something tight inside me eased. My anger just slipped away, like a heavy weight I couldn't be bothered to hold on to. Through a hazy glow, I saw Angela reach over and give my mother a tight one-armed hug.

"It's going to be okay," she said.

Delicious warmth spread across my skin. Huh, maybe Angela was right. It felt like I was floating in the most perfect pool on the most perfect summer day. Something about that . . . I frowned. It seemed familiar, as if I'd experienced it before or heard someone talking about it. . . .

I looked up slowly, feeling almost drugged with this sudden sense of peace, and noticed the golden hue of the light surrounding me. My happily sluggish brain put the pieces together. This was it, finally! The light had come for me, and it was just as Will had described it. Will!

"Wait." I forced myself to focus long enough to push the words out. "Wait, I can't just leave him. He needs . . ."

The light intensified, absorbing everything, including whatever thought I'd been trying to convey, into a big, white, happy glow of nothingness.

## ❦ 18 ❦

# Will

"Joonie, what are you doing?" I fought to keep my voice steady.

"You know, it took me a while to figure this out." She pushed Lily's chair farther in and then turned and closed the door. "I always knew you were different. I just figured it was plain old crazy, like your dad and everything." She sounded way too cheerful, eerily so. "Then that night, the first night they let us visit Lily in the hospital, you remember?" She continued without waiting for an answer. "Your mom had left, and you fell asleep in the chair. I decided to try the Ouija board. I thought maybe I could talk to her that way, you know, tell her to wake up." She narrowed her eyes at me. "But something else happened instead, didn't it?"

*Gus.* That was the first time I'd seen it.

"I called to her and she came, didn't she?" she asked. "You saw her."

Alarm bells rang in my head. Maybe Alona had been right about Joonie after all. "J," I said as gently as possible, "I'm glad you came to visit, but my mom's working on getting me discharged so—"

"Oh, no." She shook her head. "Can't have that. Not yet." She darted around Lily's wheelchair to grab one of the visitor chairs. She dragged it across the room and angled it under the door handle, wedging the door shut. "That's better."

She turned to face me again with a scary smile. "You can see them, can't you? Ghosts, spirits, whatever. That's why you're always trying not to hear things, why you've always got your head down, so you don't react to them."

Oh, not good. I tried to redirect her attention. "Joonie, what are you doing with Lily? Is she supposed to be out of her room?" She seemed to be doing okay from what I could tell. She didn't need a respirator to breathe, but I wasn't sure how long she could be away from her IV. It was hard to see her this way, her eyes dull, face slack. She was empty.

Joonie waved her hand dismissively. "Her body is fine. They left her all by herself in the basement to wait for an MRI."

That explained how Joonie had gotten Lily here, though not why she'd brought her to my room.

"You know, I tried doing this the easy way," she said

reproachfully. She pushed Lily's chair closer, her eyes bright and her cheeks pink like she had a fever. "I tried to get you to come to the hospital. And yesterday, in the cafeteria, I know she was there with you."

"No." I shook my head. "She wasn't."

She frowned at me. "Nobody goes down into the first tier to pretend to make a call, Will."

"It wasn't her," I insisted. "She's not here."

But Joonie continued like she hadn't heard me. "I told her to talk to you, to ask you to help. We just need you to do a little favor, Will. That's all."

"What do you want?" The nurse's call button was well out of my reach in these restraints, and I guessed that shouting for help probably wouldn't get me very far, not with whatever evaluation Miller had on file for me.

"It's easy. I want you help me put Lily's soul back into her body."

I stared at her. Apparently, the part of regular Joonie was being played by *Twilight Zone* Joonie tonight. "Are you crazy? I can't—"

She shook her head fiercely. "Don't tell me you can't do it. Don't lie!" Her face turned a violent red. "You've been lying this whole time."

How long could it possibly take to discharge one patient? My mom would be back here any minute, right? She'd notice the door was stuck and call someone for help. The safest thing to do was probably just keep pretending this was normal. Sure. "What are you talking about?"

She tilted her head back with a harsh laugh. "Oh, like you don't know."

"Um, actually . . ." I shrugged, or did the best I could with my current restrictions.

"Fine. You want to make me say it. All right." She nodded and just kept nodding, like her head was loose on its axis. "I found Lily, she was my friend first."

"Okay," I said slowly. "So far, I'm with you."

"But she preferred you," she snapped.

Baffled, I tried to follow her line of thinking. "Nothing ever happened between Lily and me. You know that. We were just friends, all of us."

"No." She shook her head. "Not *just* friends, not all of us." She looked at me, as if willing me to understand.

Suddenly, it clicked. The way Lily's presence used to make Joonie light up. How angry and hurt she'd been after their big fight last summer. How completely devastated she'd been after the accident, even though they hadn't even spoken in months. Alona's hints about Joonie having a crush.

"Oh, Joon. I didn't know. I didn't know you and Lily were . . ." I trailed off awkwardly. Sometimes my gift, my curse, whatever you want to call it forced me to live mostly in another world, trying not to see, hear, or feel certain things. Evidently I'd done my share of not seeing in this world, too.

"We weren't," she said wearily.

"Then I don't understand." Maybe it was just me and my repeated head injuries, but I still couldn't figure it out.

265

Joonie came around the side of the wheelchair to lean against my bed and stare at Lily. I resisted the urge to scoot my lower body, at least, away from her. She was freaking me out a little.

"I kissed her once," she said. "Did you know that?"

Obviously not.

"Last summer." She smiled at the memory.

"Before the fight." About boys. That's what Joonie had said. They'd fought about boys. I closed my eyes at my own stupidity. Sure, they'd fought about boys, as in, Lily liked them and Joonie didn't.

"What happened?" I asked, though now I could sort of guess.

"She ended it, fast. I thought she was going to run, but she didn't. She just kind of looked at me and said, 'I wondered.' Then she proceeded to take my hand and tell me that while she cared about me very much, she didn't feel *that* way." Joonie rolled her eyes, and tears slipped down her cheeks, making dark streaks on her face. "Probably the nicest way anyone could have ever told me no, but I . . ." Her voice trembled.

"You panicked."

She nodded.

That I understood. Keeping a secret for so long, it starts to feel like a vital part of you. You get so used to living with it that way, the idea of being exposed feels life-threatening.

"I . . . I said all kinds of awful things to her. Accused

her of being a tease, leading me on, which she hadn't. I told her to stay away from me and you, or . . . or I'd tell everyone she kissed me, that she'd forced me."

For Lily, one who aspired to be included, dreamed of walking amongst the first-tier elite, Joonie's threat would have been enough.

She looked at me, her eyes pleading for understanding. "I was just so scared. It's hard enough at home already, and if people at school found out, word would spread, and you know someone would eventually tell my dad."

Her father hated her dyed hair, torn clothes, and piercings. I was afraid to think of what he'd do if he found out her alternative choices extended beyond her look. He was more of an Old Testament kind of preacher.

"That night was my fault," Joonie said. "If I hadn't pushed her away . . ."

I shook my head. "No, J, listen. She tried to call me that night."

"She did?" She sounded surprised.

"She didn't leave a message, but she tried. I had my headphones on, so I didn't hear it ring. She still counted us as her friends, enough to call when she needed someone. I didn't tell you because I knew you blamed yourself for the fight. I was afraid you'd think that her calling me meant she felt like she couldn't call you. I didn't want you thinking you were somehow responsible. It's not your fault. She called. She . . ." I broke off when Joonie started to laugh, a harsh and horrible sound, full of anguish and sharp edges.

"Look at you, so earnest and innocent." She smiled bitterly. "She called me, too, Will. Twice. I talked to her."

I stared at her, the world as I knew it shifting and falling around me. "What?"

"Ben Rogers used her and threw her away, just like he always does, and her little teen-princess pals didn't want anything to do with her anymore." Joonie shook her head in disgust. "So she called me and I . . . I told her she got what she deserved." Her voice broke, and her shoulders shook in a silent sob.

I shook my head in stunned disbelief. "And the second time she called?" I forced myself to ask.

"I hung up on her."

"Joonie," I breathed.

"I figure that was right about when she started crying so hard she couldn't see and lost control over her car," she said flatly.

"Oh, my God."

She knelt down next to Lily. "So you see why we have to do this. I need to take it back. I need to undo it."

"Joonie." I pulled against the restraints, trying to sit up. "You can't. She's gone. Really and truly gone."

She sighed. "I thought you might say that." She reached for the Ouija board resting across Lily's legs. The second her hands touched the planchette, shadows flickered and swirled to life in the corner of the room behind her. Gloomy Gus. *Crap*. I'd never seen a ghost respond so promptly. It was . . . weird.

"I know you're lying," she said, her tone devoid of any emotion. "I've seen what happens to you when I call to her on the other side. She's angry with me for what I said and with you for helping me."

"She's not angry. It's not her. It's . . ." In truth, I didn't know what it was. This close, with Joonie right here in front of me, I could see a thin wisp of smoke leading from Joonie to the growing monstrosity that was Gus. Like a leash or . . . a pipeline.

I froze. *Energy is just energy until it finds me.* That's what I'd told Alona. If Joonie, in her efforts to communicate with Lily, was sending out massive amounts of negative energy— all that guilt, grief, and shame flowing from her, oozing from her every cell—what was to say my presence wouldn't cause it to manifest in the same way as a ghost? The door—or rather the call, to use the analogy I started with Alona—went both ways. It was usually energy from the dead side using me to take form, but why couldn't intense energy, focused through a Ouija board, from the living side do the same thing? That would explain Gus's lack of personality (other than angry) and why I'd never seen a ghost like it before. It wasn't a ghost at all.

"I'll call her," Joonie said. "You just help me get her back where she belongs."

How was I supposed to do that? Even if we could somehow reach Lily, which we couldn't, it wasn't like stuffing an unwieldy pillow back in its case. There has to be a connection between body and soul. But wisely, for once in my life, I kept my mouth shut. "Okay, I can help you. I need my hands, though." To get the hell out of here.

She cocked her head to one side and gave me an evaluating look. "No. I don't think so."

"You want me to help, I need my hands."

She frowned, and Gus expanded, spreading out from his corner with tendrils headed straight for me. "No, you'll only try to run."

Really? Was there any sane person who wouldn't at this point? I shook my head. "No, I won't. I want to help you."

"I don't believe you," she said fiercely. Her fingers on the planchette turned white with the force of the pressure she applied, and Gus oozed forward.

I flinched and turned away.

Joonie sucked in a breath and looked around the room. "She's here, already?"

"It's not her, Joonie. Please, I promise you." If Gus came crashing down on me and I couldn't run . . .

Across the room, the door handle suddenly rattled back and forth. "Will?" My mother called. "What's going on in there?"

I took one look at Joonie's eyes, warning me without words to stay quiet, and shouted, "Mom, get help."

After that, things happened kind of fast.

Gus surged forward. It crested above me like some kind of horrible wave and then flung itself down on me. I screamed, and it poured down my throat, filling my airway and sealing off my lungs.

"William!" My mother beat against the door frantically.

I couldn't breathe, and the sheer coldness of Gus penetrated to my very core. Fighting back took more energy than I had, and everything, including my weak flailing in self-defense, had dropped into slow motion. Except for me dying; that was happening fast enough.

A bright flash of light appeared suddenly in the center of Gus and burst outward, tearing it to shreds. The horrible pressure on my chest and throat eased, and I sucked in air by the lungful, coughing and sputtering all the while.

"Can't leave you alone for a second, can I?" an all-too-familiar voice asked.

I blinked my watering eyes, clearing my vision sufficiently enough to see Alona standing next to my bed. She looked . . . amazing. More beautiful and somehow more real. Like I'd only been seeing a projection of her true self before. Her hair was shinier, her eyes brighter. In short, she looked like a vision. So much so that I began to wonder if I hadn't already started the great transition.

"Dead?" I croaked.

She snorted. "Not hardly. This time, anyway."

At that point, Joonie seemed to notice a difference in that I was breathing again and not struggling to live.

Gus began gathering the shreds and wisps of itself, building again.

"Oh, for heaven's sake." Alona reached over the arm of Lily's wheelchair and started pushing the planchette around the Ouija board. I couldn't see what letters she picked, but

Joonie, quite helpful in her messed-up and out-of-it state, called them out loud.

"S-T-O-P. U-R-F-O-R-G-I-V-E-N."

Then, as a final touch, Alona slipped her hand inside Lily's and moved it to touch Joonie's on the board. I gaped at the sight. She'd said something about it before, but I'd never imagined . . .

Joonie looked back and forth between Lily's hand and her still, empty face, and then she began to weep.

Alona, with a little difficulty, managed to pull herself free from Lily's hand, looking as disconcerted by it as I felt. Then she smiled at me. "Told you you needed me."

"Yeah," I said, my voice cracking. "Does this mean you're back for good? I could use a little spiritual guidance."

She bit her lip with a frown. "I don't know. I'm not even sure how I . . ." Her eyes widened, and a glow, so bright I had to squint, enveloped her. She stretched her hand out toward me, and I reached for it . . . but caught only air.

"Alona!" The light surrounding her intensified until I could no longer see any part of her. Then it vanished, with an audible pop, taking her with it.

When the janitor and the security guard finally forced the door open a few minutes later, that's how they found us. Joonie sobbing on the floor, holding Lily's hand, and me still tied to the bed, my eyes watering. I wasn't crying. No, not at all. It was just the light. Or something in my eye. Yeah, that's it.

# ❧ EPILOGUE ❧

# Will Killian

Twenty-six days had passed since I'd last seen Alona Dare. In that time, my mother had permanently jettisoned Dr. Miller, and we'd realized neither of us was in a big hurry for a replacement. I worked from Alona's notes and kept the ghosts . . . spirits . . . at bay by helping them out as best as I could. I sent Sara's brother his medal with a fake letter from the hospital, explaining it had been found during routine file reorganization. I'm proud to say that Grandpa Brewster did, in fact, move on into the golden light shortly after I sent anonymous letters to his son and grandson.

Other than that, I did my homework, passed my finals, and, at my mother's insistence, sent in applications for late admission to a variety of schools. In true parental spirit, she'd bounced back from my revelation about seeing the dead quickly enough to point out that if I wasn't hiding anymore, I didn't need to leave town, and could therefore attend classes at a university—as was the original plan for me. Yeah, she kind of had a point.

We celebrated my eighteenth birthday on May 30, just my mom and me. She was getting used to the idea of what I am, but that almost made it harder for her to accept what my dad did instead of just telling her the truth. She was working on it, though.

Joonie was doing okay. In trying to explain the whole mess of what happened at the hospital without outing me (which also probably would have made her look a little less than stable, anyway), she ended up inadvertently outing herself. Or maybe not so inadvertently. She seemed relieved. I understood the feeling. When she was released from the hospital, though, after all kinds of psych tests, evaluations, and counseling, her parents refused to let her come home. She ended up living in this sort of halfway house/group home. It was all right. I went to see her there every couple of weeks. A therapist, a nice woman named Joan Stafford, made house calls there on a regular basis, and Joonie said that helped. She'd missed too much school to graduate with our class, but with a few summer classes, she'd get her diploma. Once she turned eighteen in August, she was moving to New York to live with her middle sister, Elise, who, it turned out, had had her own reasons for attending Wellesley.

Graduation day, June 1, dawned bright and suffocatingly

hot for so early in the summer. They set up the stage in the middle of the football field, causing me to voluntarily set foot on the playing field for the first time in four years. I kept expecting to get tackled. When Principal Brewster called Alona's name and her mother stepped up to accept the diploma on her behalf, I couldn't help but look around. No sign of Alona, though, not even when Principal Brewster revealed a sketch of the memorial plaque with her name that would be attached to the new bench in the Circle. It was our senior gift to the school, suggested anonymously by yours truly and funded by donations that Misty Evans had relentlessly pursued. Alona had wanted to be remembered in the style she was accustomed to, and now she would be.

I waited, shifting uncomfortably on my plastic chair and sweating under the polyester gown and the dress shirt my mother had insisted on, until my name was called.

"William James Killian." Principal Brewster looked like he'd sucked down an entire lemon-tree orchard to get a look that sour. I loved it.

I left my chair, walked up the aisle, and ascended the steps. Behind the stage, Liesel, Eric, Jay, and a few others cheered wildly as I shook the superintendent's hand and then Brewster's. He handed me my diploma but kept my other hand captive in a crushing grip.

"I don't know how you managed this, but I know something just isn't right with you, boy."

"Yes, sir," I agreed cheerfully. "But I beat you and that's all that matters to me." I yanked my hand out of his grasp, switched my tassel to the other side of my cap right there in front of him, just to taunt him a little, and bounded down the stage and back to my seat, feeling lighter than I had in years.

"Glad to see you learned your lesson about playing well with others," Alona said dryly in my ear. Her familiar light and flowery scent drifted over my shoulder.

I jolted and started to turn.

"No, no, don't turn around," she said impatiently. "You're almost out of here. Don't make a scene by talking to someone who isn't there."

"Where have you been?" I whispered, pretending to look through my program.

"You saw the light. You know where I've been."

"But since then?" I muttered.

"I had some things to take care of."

"Like what?"

"You'll see." She sounded positively gleeful. "Just keep watching. Things are about to get very interesting."

"Are you back for good?"

She made a frustrated noise. "Just watch. Ask questions later."

So, I watched. At first I didn't even know what I was looking for. Then Principal Brewster called for Ben Rogers. My hands clenched into fists. For the last three weeks, I'd had to let him walk around, smirking like the ass that he was, because I couldn't touch him. Not until after graduation. Well, graduation would be over in the next twenty minutes, and then I'd do my best to pound his face into the . . .

The first ripple of giggles from the audience as Ben walked up the side aisle tipped me off that something was up. The giggles turned into a roar of laughter and then hooting and hollering. Only when Ben drew even with my row could I see the source of the hoopla. A paper sign had been taped to the back of his gown, right at his shoulder blades. In big block letters, it read, I HAVE A TINY PENIS. WANT 2 SEE?

I laughed. "Awesome."

Ben, completely bewildered, but accepting the added attention as his due, simply thrust his fist up in the air in a gesture of triumph as he climbed onto the stage. Yeah.

Behind me, Alona smothered a laugh. "What an ass."

"I couldn't agree more," I said.

Next to me, Jillian Karson gave me a look and shifted her chair farther away. Whatever.

"Meet me after," Alona said.

"Where?" I asked, prompting another glare from Jillian.

"You know where."

By the time I could risk a casual glance behind me, she was gone.


After the ceremony, I made my way over to the bleachers and my mother. "I'm proud of you," she said.

"Thanks."

She hesitated. "Your dad . . . he's proud of you, too, I'm

sure, even if he can't tell you that himself."

I'd confessed to her my original suspicions about dad being Gloomy Gus a while ago and she'd tsked at me for thinking that my father would ever haunt me. She was right, of course. One way or another, my dad was gone and, I hoped, happy now in a way he couldn't have been in life.

"Thanks, Ma." I gave her a hug. "I need to go check on something. I'll meet you back at the car?"

She nodded, and Sam, my mom's boss at the diner and the only other person I'd invited to graduation, took her arm to help her down from the bleachers. I didn't think she needed the help, but I suspected she liked it. And Sam, too. That was cool. He was a good guy.

I left the two of them behind and headed toward the main entrance of the school. On the way, I passed Ben Rogers, holding the sign that had been stuck to his back. "But it isn't," he insisted to anyone who would listen. Unfortunately, no one seemed to believe him.

As I approached the Circle, I could see Alona sitting on her bench, her long legs stretched out in the sun.

"So what happened to being nice?" I asked when I reached her.

She squinted up at me. "What, the thing with Ben?"

I snorted. "Yeah, 'the thing with Ben.'"

She shrugged. "Not my idea. It was Leanne's. I heard about it when I visited Misty."

"Misty?" I asked.

Her gaze barely flickered from mine. "She was my best

friend forever, and she kept my secrets. I'm not going to let Chris get in the way of that."

"Oh." Quite a different song than she'd been singing before about their relationship, but maybe the round-trip visit into the golden light changed that . . . and her.

She shrugged. "Besides, Chris slobbers a little when he kisses. Ick."

That startled a laugh out of me. No, same Alona.

"Anyway"—she looked at me with some exasperation— "when I was visiting Misty, I learned something interesting. Apparently, Leanne and Ben hooked up freshman year, and she never got over him dumping her. That's why they refused to talk to each other."

"She waited four years to get even?"

Alona grinned. "Never piss off the girl who sits behind you at graduation, especially if it's Leanne Whitaker. That girl can hold a grudge like nobody's business."

We sat there in silence for a moment. "It was nice, though, for Lily, I mean," I said.

"For all of them," Alona corrected. "But, yeah, for Lily."

"So," I ventured, "you're back."

"Yep."

"That's a little unusual, I think."

"Hmm."

I swallowed back my irritation. "You're going to make me ask again, aren't you?"

She gave me an innocent look. "Ask what?"

"Are you staying . . . or just passing through?" I

asked through gritted teeth.

"Why? Does it matter to you?"

A thousand smart-ass replies leaped to mind, but she would be expecting that. So, I went for the truth. "Yeah, it does."

Her eyes widened and the faintest hint of pink spread across her face.

I grinned. Had I just embarrassed Alona Dare, *the* Alona Dare?

She sniffed. "Someone has to keep you out of trouble. Might as well be someone who knows the stupid crap you get yourself into all the time. And . . ." she traced the grain of the wood on the bench with her fingertip, "there may also be a small issue of me still learning to consider others before myself."

"I was never in trouble except when . . ." I paused as her last sentence sank in. "Ha! You got held back because *you* don't play well with others," I crowed. "Told you it was about being nice."

"Whatever." She rolled her eyes. "Being a poor winner isn't nice, either," she pointed out, but she got up and came to sit beside me.

We sat in comfortable silence for a long moment.

"Thank you for my bench," she said almost shyly.

"How did you know it was me?"

"Oh, please. As soon as I heard Misty talking about it, I knew it was you. Who else would have come up with that quote?"

When it was finished, beneath her name and dates, the plaque would read, "Beauty is truth, truth beauty,—that is all/Ye know on earth, and all ye need to know."—John Keats, "Ode on a Grecian Urn."

I shrugged, unaccountably pleased.

She edged a little closer. "So . . . thanks." She leaned in and before I realized it, she kissed me. Her mouth tasted warm and sweet, and when her hand touched my chest for balance, every cell in my body stood at attention.

She broke it off first, pulling away from me and touching the corners of her mouth as if to make sure her lip gloss was still in place. It was, by far, the sexiest thing I'd ever seen.

I cleared my throat. "If that's for a bench, what happens if I suggest a whole dining room set?"

She laughed and slid away from me. "In your dreams, Killian." She tucked her legs up under herself and gave me what I recognized now as her "getting serious" look. "Okay, so college. Let's talk dorm room decor. I'm thinking we really need to go beyond the whole milk crates and dark, moldy-smelling comforter—"

I groaned. "I think this is a little outside your responsibilities as a spirit guide."

She shot me an offended look. "I have to stay there, too, you know."

I considered her words and all the various pleasant and unpleasant ramifications. "Well . . . that ought to make things interesting," I said weakly.

She grinned. "No point in living otherwise."

# ❧ ACKNOWLEDGMENTS ❧

My thanks to my fabulous agent, Laura Bradford, for taking me on. To my editor, Christian Trimmer, who is ten kinds of awesome and made this book better than it ever could have been without him, and everyone at Hyperion. To Ed and Debbie Brown and Stacy Greenberg for help when I needed it most. To my supportive family, especially my parents, Steve and Judy Barnes. To my husband, Greg, for understanding what this means to me. And to my sister, Susan, who inspired me to write this story.

DON'T MISS THE NEXT
GHOST AND THE GOTH NOVEL

Queen OF THE Dead

## ❧ 1 ❧

# Will

On television, ghost-talkers run antique stores, solve crimes, or stand on a stage in a nice suit giving the teary-eyed audience a toothy, yet sympathetic grin.

I, however, was entering my second hour of hiding in a prickly tangle of brush with an increasingly cranky spirit guide, all for a ghost who might not even show up.

The Gibley Mansion in Decatur's historic district had been falling apart for years. But it was officially scheduled to be torn down tomorrow morning, which meant tonight was Mrs. Ruiz's last chance to make peace with the place where she'd served as a housekeeper for most of her life. So, we were waiting (and waiting and waiting) for her on the east side of the house, in the former rose garden, where she'd keeled over twenty-some years ago while digging a hole for a new bush.

Unfortunately, ghosts don't always do what you expect.

"Can we go now?" Alona nudged me, sounding annoyed. "I have to pee."

Case in point.

I just looked at her. Since she hadn't had anything to eat or drink in well over a month, I seriously doubted that was a genuine concern. Besides which, I hadn't ever heard of any ghosts visiting a bathroom unless, of course, they'd died there. (No, I've never met Elvis, but it's an educated guess.)

Alona tried again. "I'm cold?"

That was at least possible, especially given what she was wearing. Alona Dare, former Homecoming Queen, varsity cheerleading co-captain, fashionista, and mean girl supreme of Groundsboro High, had died in her gym clothes—short red shorts and a cheap white shirt. If you don't believe in karma, that alone should give you cause to reconsider.

But given that it was an early Monday evening on what had been a blazing hot June day, and I could still feel the heat rising from the ground beneath us, she was probably more comfortable than I was in jeans and the long-sleeve T-shirt I'd worn to protect myself from rampant thorns.

"Fine." She dragged out the word on an impatient sigh. "I'm dead and I'm bored. How much longer do we have to wait?"

"She'll be here," I whispered. "Soon." I tried to sound more certain of this than I actually was.

"Why are you whispering?" she asked with a frown.

"Because, unlike you, *I* can still be arrested," I pointed out.

Apparently fearing that the mansion might be a target for last-minute vandalism or pranks, the city had boarded up all the windows, hung about nine hundred NO TRESPASSING signs, placed caution tape around the entire perimeter, and hired security guards to make regular patrols. We'd slipped onto the property when the guards had changed shifts.

Alona waved my words away. "Dopey couldn't catch his own ass if it was on the seat next to him."

She might be right about that. In fact, I was kind of banking on it. Dopey, as Alona had dubbed the security guard on duty, was currently dozing behind the wheel of his rent-a-cop car, which was parked in the driveway about twenty yards away. Loud snores emerged from the open car windows. I just hoped he would keep on snoring until after our business with Mrs. Ruiz was done, assuming she even showed up. Sometimes ghosts, when faced with final resolution of their earthly issues, panicked.

"Did you, by any chance, think to find out what time she died?" Alona asked with just enough sarcasm to suggest she already knew the answer.

"No." Which I could see now had been an oversight. But Mrs. Ruiz had caught me off guard by approaching me at the grocery store. It had been challenging enough to find out what she wanted without freaking out the entire produce aisle, including my mom.

"I would have," she muttered.

"You were unavailable for consultation," I said through gritted teeth.

For somebody who was dead, Alona had an active social life. She was forever dropping in to spy on living family and friends, despite my warnings against that, and attempting to socialize with other ghosts.

The latter, I suspected, had not been going so well. Most ghosts moved on to the light too quickly to concern themselves with making friends while in this in-between place, what I called Middleground. The ones who remained tended to be a little too obsessed with whatever was keeping them here—an injustice, unrequited love, finding their murderer, etc.—to be good company for very long. Trust me, I know—from years of overhearing them.

But I also thought it might be because Alona did not really make friends easily. In life, she'd collected followers. There was a big difference between the two, as she'd found out after she'd died a couple of months ago and had to hear all her former "friends" talking about her.

There were a few ghosts who hung around her—like the sorority girl from Milliken who'd drowned in a hazing accident and now walked around with lake weed threaded through her hair and left wet footprints everywhere. Sometimes I wondered if they thought being friends with Alona would earn them a higher place on the running list of spirits we were trying to help attain closure. Sometimes I think Alona wondered about that, too.

But she kept trying, which I had to give her credit for, even though that meant she was gone sometimes when I needed her, like at the grocery store with Mrs. Ruiz. If I didn't know better, I would have suspected she staged her absences deliberately to remind me how much I was dependent on her help to keep the ghosts at bay.

Alona had gotten bounced from the big white light about a month ago, and helping other ghosts who were stuck in-between earned her the karma points, for lack of a better term, to allow her to regain entry someday. At least that was the theory. I got the impression that Alona's sources in the white light hadn't been all that specific. She refused to talk much—at all, really—about her time there. As she told me once, it wasn't like she'd been greeted at the gates by some big guy in white robes and Jesus-type sandals. It was more a feeling than anything else.

Alona shifted impatiently. "Why do we need Mrs. Ruiz anyway? Can't we just go in and get the thing, whatever it is, and bring it to her?"

I shook my head. "She didn't say what or where it was." Mrs. Ruiz's ability to make peace with her past was evidently tied to some object that was still hidden inside the house. "So, unless you want to search under every floorboard and in all the walls—"

She sighed. "Okay, okay."

But she wasn't done yet. I could sense the wheels turning in her mind. Even though we'd gone to school together for years, I'd only known Alona—as in actually having spoken to her—since she'd died. But that was long enough to know she didn't give up that easily.

She stood abruptly.

"What are you doing?" I hissed.

She looked down at me, unconcerned. "What? If we're staying, I need to stretch. We've been sitting here for hours. And Dopey couldn't see me even if his eyes were open, which"—she glanced in the direction of the security guard's car—"they're not."

She reached behind herself and caught her ankle and pulled her leg toward her back, bending forward slightly. Her long blond hair slipped forward over her shoulder, and a wave of her light flowery scent washed over me.

I looked away. Alona Dare had the best legs I'd ever seen. Long and toned with smooth skin that made you ache to touch them to see if they felt as good as they looked. I'd had fantasies about her and those legs since the sixth grade. And she knew it.

I shifted uncomfortably and kept my gaze locked firmly on a nearby tangle of leaves. "If that security guard sees the branches moving, he's going to come running over here," I warned. Thanks to my "gift," if that's what you wanted to call it, Alona—and all other ghosts—had physicality around me, the same as she would have if she were alive. Dopey might not be able to see her, but he'd definitely notice bushes moving in a way that didn't look wind-generated.

"He'd have to be awake first," she said back, mimicking my warning tone. Out of the corner of my eye, I saw her switch legs and stretch the other one, giving a small sigh of pleasure.

I swallowed hard. I guess stretching still felt good even when you were a ghost. I know it looked good.

"There. Much better." She sat down next to me again, closer than before. Her shoulder pressed into me, and her leg rested against mine.

Thirty seconds ago, I'd been concerned about nothing other than finding Mrs. Ruiz and getting in and out of the house undetected. Now all I could think about were those two points of contact between us, connecting in a white-hot line of awareness.

I turned to see her watching, so close, so very close to me.

"What?" she asked.

I cleared my throat. "You have a . . ." I reached out and pulled a bit of leaf from her hair. The blond strands slipped like silk through my fingers. I'd touched her hair before, wrapped my hands in it when kissing her, as a matter of fact, and I wanted nothing more than do it again right now.

"Thanks." Her mouth curved in a knowing smile, and I was lost, even though I knew better.

I leaned closer, drawn to her mouth like it was pulling me in with some mysterious gravity of its own, half expecting her to push me away.

But she didn't. Her mouth was warm and soft under mine.

I sat up straighter without breaking the kiss and slid my

hand to the back of her neck, pulling her closer and slipping my fingers into her hair again.

She moved with me willingly and made that same sound of pleasure I'd heard from her before. I could feel her softness pressing against my chest. Oh, God. She just felt so good.

I pulled back for a second and watched her eyes open slowly. She looked as dazed as I felt, but with a touch of self-satisfaction. She'd planned this, of course.

"So is this when you try to talk me into leaving again?" I asked, breathless. I was all too aware that Alona knew my weak spots and wasn't afraid to use them against me. Not that I minded at this exact moment.

She didn't try to deny it. She leaned in and kissed the edge of my mouth. "Maybe I'm not so bored now."

Good enough.

She rose up on her knees and balanced herself with her hands on my shoulders before laying a series of tiny kisses along my cheek. Her breath was warm, and her eyelashes fluttered against my skin like small caresses. Her scent filled me, overwhelmed me with the desire to shut out everything but her. This girl who equally drove me crazy and made me care about her more than I should. She was the only one who understood. The only one who could help make what I was more bearable, even if she occasionally tortured me in the process.

I slid my hand down her back to her hip, where the edge of her shirt met her shorts. And she let me. More than that, she moved closer, her mouth suddenly hungry on mine. My hand slipped under the hem, and I stroked the bare, warm skin of her stomach with my thumb.

She pulled back sharply, her hand catching mine and holding it in place. "Wait."

I shook my head, trying to think while my body was screaming at me to keep going. "Sorry, I just—"

"No." She squeezed my hand. "I hear something."

*I don't care!* I wanted to shout, but I swallowed the words.

She let go of my hand and cautiously pushed herself up to her feet to look out and over the tangle of brush that protected us from view of anyone walking by.

"Is it Dopey?" I whispered, taking advantage of her momentary distraction to try to adjust the front of my pants. If I had to run now, I'd be in big trouble.

"No." Her voice held a strange note. "Not him."

"Well, then what—"

She turned to face me, and I realized what I'd heard in her voice was suppressed laughter. The very same thing danced over her expression.

"It's Mrs. Ruiz," she said. "I think." She sounded almost gleeful.

Ah, now it made sense. Because Alona had been off doing whatever when Mrs. Ruiz had approached me, this was her first glimpse of the . . . woman.

"Don't," I told her. "We're here to help."

I stood up, carefully, and peered out to see for myself.

Alona was right. Directly across from us, Mrs. Ruiz

had finally materialized, her garden spade in hand. She was looking around like she was searching for just the right location to dig the hole that would kill her.

"Are you sure it's *Mrs.* Ruiz?" Alona whispered in my ear, clearly delighted.

Okay, so Mrs. Ruiz was not a small woman or particularly . . . feminine. She was beefy with broad shoulders that belonged on a coal miner. The shapeless but heavily patterned housedress she wore didn't help matters, making her look that much more like a man in drag. The not-so-faint outline of a mustache on her upper lip was a little . . . off-putting as well. But still, she needed our help.

"Stop," I said to Alona. Then I eased out from behind the tangle of branches, keeping an eye on Dopey, who, thankfully, continued to snore throatily. Alona followed.

Mrs. Ruiz saw us coming and gave me a curt nod of acknowledgment. She frowned at Alona, which had the unfortunate effect of drawing her two eyebrows into one big one. I could almost feel Alona shaking with the need to spout something spiteful but funny.

"Some people aren't as obsessed with appearances as you are," I said quietly over my shoulder to Alona.

"Yeah, well, I wouldn't be obsessed with my appearance if I were her, either," Alona said, not as quietly as I would have liked.

"This way," Mrs. Ruiz said when we were close enough. She gave Alona another dark look and then slung her spade over her shoulder and started toward the house, ignoring

Dopey and his car like they weren't even there.

"Cut it out," I said to Alona under my breath once we'd passed the security guard and Mrs. Ruiz was far enough ahead on the worn walkway to the front door.

"Oh, come on," she said. "Even you can't blame me for this one."

"I mean it."

She stayed quiet for a second. Then she looked thoughtful. "Ten bucks she's got a tattoo of an anchor somewhere on her body."

"Alona!" I whispered as loudly as I dared.

"What, you've seen it?"

I glared at her.

"She has a 'stache that would put a porn star to shame—hello, it's called waxing?—and you're lecturing me about—"

I pointed to her feet, which were beginning to flicker in and out of existence, as though a faulty movie projector were involved.

She sighed. "Damn."

As a being of mostly energy, she was dependent on keeping the energy flowing by remaining positive, i.e., nice. Which annoyed her to no end, unfortunately. Made for some highly entertaining moments on my end, though.

"She looks very strong and was probably very . . . capable at her job," Alona said carefully. I could see she was dying to make some further remark, like how it was hard to keep a good man down. Or, how handy it was that she could carry the cows around while she milked them, or whatever. "You suck the fun out of everything," she said to me.

It wasn't my rule, just a rule of existence here, but I knew she hated being reminded of it. "Everything?" I asked, taking in her rumpled hair and the way her lips still looked puffier than usual, thanks to our kissing session.

Her cheeks turned pink, but she rolled her eyes and stalked past me to where Mrs. Ruiz was waiting on the front porch.

Nice. I was taking that as a compliment.